Also by Amber Garza

When I Was You
Where I Left Her

Look for Amber Garza's next novel
Then She Disappeared
available soon from MIRA.

A MOTHER WOULD KNOW

AMBER GARZA

mira

Recycling programs for this product may not exist in your area.

ISBN-13: 978-0-7783-8648-3

A Mother Would Know

Mira
22 Adelaide St. West, 41st Floor
Toronto, Ontario M5H 4E3, Canada
BookClubbish.com

Printed in U.S.A.

For Eli, the best son a mom could hope for.

A
MOTHER
WOULD
KNOW

"We all have a Monster within; the difference is in degree, not in kind."

—Douglas Preston

1

When he comes to the door, I don't answer immediately. Instead, I stare through the peephole, studying him. It's only a matter of time before I'll forget him altogether. He'll stand before me, appearing much like he does now, and I'll look back at him blankly, the same way my mom used to eye me, no recognition at all.

His dark hair is bushy, unkempt, as if he hasn't had a decent haircut in a while. His mouth is obscured by a thick beard.

He glances around, no idea he's being watched. When he knocks again, I draw back from the peephole and turn the knob. Swinging the door open, I push my lips up into a wobbly smile. Our eyes meet. At first, he doesn't react. His face remains stoic. Or maybe I can't see the smile through his mess of a beard.

He takes a step forward. "Mom."

"Hudson." I bury my face in his shoulder. He smells like wood, pine needles, faintly of cloves. It's foreign, a reminder of how many years he's been away from home. Yet somewhere, hiding beneath that unfamiliar scent and all that hair, is my little boy. The one I'd read bedtime stories to and sat on the ground for hours playing Hot Wheels with. The one who'd cried on my shoulder and tucked his chubby little hand into mine when crossing the street. I hug him too long. His arms loosen and float away from my body, but mine are still looped around him.

Reluctantly, I release my hold. Leaning against the door frame, I peer over his shoulder and down the large sweeping staircase spanning the front porch, to the car parked along the curb. An older Honda Civic, the gray paint faded and chipped.

"You can go ahead and bring your stuff in," I say.

"For sure." Reaching down, he snatches up the duffel bag sitting by his feet. Slinging it over his shoulder, he walks forward.

I raise a brow. "Is that all you have?"

He nods, and I don't know why I'm surprised. The past few years he's lived a vagabond existence, crashing at friends' or girlfriends' houses, sometimes renting rooms from strangers. Kendra has often expressed disdain for his lifestyle, saying there's no way she would ever be able to do it. And she's right. She couldn't. She needs security. But I admire Hudson's courage, his ability to take risks.

Hudson moved out the day he turned eighteen, as if he couldn't wait another minute to be away from us. But he'd pulled away from me long before that.

As an infant, Hudson was only happy in my arms. In his toddler years, he remained glued to my side. Even in early elementary school, he followed me around, his sticky hands always reaching for mine. But around the time Hudson turned nine, things started to take off for my band, Flight of Hearts.

I was gone a lot, and in that time, Hudson grew more attached to his dad. I couldn't blame him—just hoped that one day he would understand why I missed his eighth-grade graduation, his junior prom. Ambition comes at a cost, especially, unfairly, to working mothers. But since Darren died five years ago, Hudson and I have rarely spoken, and he's only been home a handful of times. It's like the mutual connection between us was severed. Or maybe my inability to stay settled at home affected Hudson in its own way.

I've never stopped missing my little boy, though. The one who would sit close to me on the couch, one hand on my arm, as if preventing my escape.

And now he's here.

I need him, and he's come running.

"Well, sure, he probably has nowhere else to go," Kendra had said to me a few days ago, a hint of bitterness in her tone.

I usher Hudson inside, my hand lifting, itching to rest on his back. But I fight the urge, leaving it to hover a few inches away.

"I'm not a baby, Mom," I remember him saying repeatedly as a sullen, metal-mouthed teenager.

He's in his mid-twenties now, and I have no idea how I'm supposed to act. With Kendra, I don't have the same problem. She's been an adult since she was five. Bossy. Independent. Responsible. Hudson took a little longer to mature.

"I got your old room ready." It's weird to think about Hudson being back in his former bedroom. The one he grew up in. So much has changed.

"My old room?" His spine straightens, his head cocking to the side.

"Yeah, is that a problem?" I have no idea where else I'd put him. Kendra's old room? Darren's former study?

"No, of course not." He runs a hand through his hair, and I catch the edge of a tattoo circling his upper right arm.

I can't make out what it is, though. "I just…it's just…been a while, I guess."

When he makes his way up the stairs, my instinct is to trail after him, but I stop myself. Wrapping my arms around my body, I lean against the wall, watching his back as he climbs the steps.

Hudson has never been a big talker. His sister is. I used to joke that she sucked up all the words in our house, leaving none available for the rest of us. Still, his silence today is unnerving.

When I hear the click of his bedroom door, I sigh. Pushing off the wall, I walk toward the kitchen to make some tea. The floorboards creak beneath my slippers. The clock on the wall ticks. Bowie barks from the backyard. Other than that, it's deathly quiet like always.

A woman and her dog all alone in this big Victorian house.

The first time I saw this house, it beckoned to me. A whisper. An outstretched arm. The curl of a finger, bony but elegant. Its pull was hypnotic.

I stood at the curb, staring up at the imposing staircase, the shuttered windows, the pointed roof. It reminded me of my grandma. Not because she had a house like this, but because she was strong, tall in stature and had a presence that overshadowed everyone around her. That was this house.

The surrounding homes were lower—at street level with only a few steps leading up to a small porch. This one sat high above them, more than a dozen steps leading up to a large wraparound porch. None of the other homes had the personality this one did.

"Can you imagine the stories this house holds?" I whispered under my breath, the words coming out in white puffs that disintegrated in the air like cigarette smoke. Without a word,

Darren put his arm around me, steadying me as we made our way up to the front door, the cold January air enveloping us. We'd left the kids with a sitter, since Kendra was only seven, and Hudson five.

Jan, our real estate agent, had a hard time getting the lock to work. And with each passing second, Darren's uneasiness showed in the way he held his jaw, the way his hold on me tightened.

As if I couldn't pick up on the subtle clues, he finally let out a frustrated grunt. It was obvious he already hated the house. Not that I was surprised. He'd made it clear to me that he wanted a newer home. Granite countertops, crown molding and updated appliances. But when we'd toured the ones he liked, I felt stifled. Uncomfortable. A fish flopping in the sand.

I wanted a house with history. A heartbeat. A voice. From what Jan had told us, this house had gone through multiple owners in the ten years before we'd bought it and then had been vacant for months. It was in obvious need of some TLC. The paint was chipped in spots, and in one of the rooms there was an odd wallpaper, red with black circles that almost looked like floating heads.

"A fixer-upper," Darren had called it.

"Charming," I'd countered, causing Jan to smile.

Despite all the issues, the house gave me a sense of comfort. Familiarity. Inside its walls, I became a fish that had finally found the water and breathed deeply through its gills.

Plus, I'd always wanted to live in midtown, and this was the perfect time. I'd just joined a new band called Flight of Hearts, and we'd hopefully be playing a lot at clubs and bars in this area.

It wasn't until after we'd moved in that I found the newspaper articles about six-year-old Grace Newton's mysterious death inside this home over fifty years ago. She'd died of a brain bleed, caused by a fall down the stairs.

It was ruled an accident, but many neighbors and family friends suspected it had been anything but. According to some of the newspaper articles I'd read, there were reports of bruising on Grace's skin for months before her death. And even the coroner had said she had contusions and cuts that were old; healing. Not from the fall.

Many people in this neighborhood believe that Grace haunts this house. Roams the halls. Plays in the attic. Traipses around the backyard.

When we first started hearing the rumors, Darren said they were ridiculous. But I'm prone to think they're true. From the moment we moved in, I could feel her. A breath at the back of my neck. A charge in the air. A presence in the room. And sometimes when I took pictures of the kids in Hudson's room, orbs appeared on the photos after I had them developed. Seriously. It's why I suspect Hudson's room had once been Grace's.

The AC kicks on above my head, startling me. I hug myself tighter.

It's eerie to think about the similarities between Hudson and Grace. Both were the younger of two siblings. They might have shared a room. I've seen pictures of Grace: dark hair and chocolate brown eyes—same as Hudson's. They had the same delightful smile, and a matching dimple on the left cheek. But most startling of all: both of their lives were irrevocably changed by an untimely, suspicious death.

Eeny, meeny, miny, moe…
Catch a tiger by the toe…

Mom took us to the zoo this week. My favorite part was the tigers. One of them kept pressing his face against the glass. It made me giggle. I wished I could reach inside and pet him.

"No, trust me, you don't want to do that," Mom assured me with a little cluck of her tongue.

"Why not?" I asked, peering up at her, eyes wide. "He looks just like Dexter, and I love petting Dexter."

"Dexter?" Mom raised her eyebrows.

"Cliff's cat." Cliff was our neighbor. His cat sometimes made his way over to our lawn.

"Oh. Right. Well, Dexter is a cat," Mom said. "This is a tiger."

I stared through the glass, standing so close the tip of my nose brushed it. The tiger slunk past, walking slowly and stretching out his front paws the same way Dexter did. My right sock slipped down my calf, and for a second it felt like a bug. I reached down to scratch it, then tugged the sock back up. "He's cute."

"Just because something's cute doesn't mean it isn't dangerous," Mom said. "He's a natural-born predator."

Andie pushed off the enclosure, backing away from the

tiger cage, frowning. "I don't wanna look at the tigers any-more. They scare me," she said, looking up at Mom with tears in her eyes, her lower lip trembling. She pressed her knees to-gether, the lace from her knee-high socks rustling like leaves in the wind.

"Aww, it's okay, sweetie." Mom put her arm around my sis-ter, and they started to walk away.

Reluctantly, I followed. When we got around the corner, my sister pointed to the monkeys and squealed. "Let's go there!"

I frowned. We'd already seen the monkeys twice today. Why couldn't we stay at the tigers?

Andie turned to me and stuck out her tongue. As I glared back, Mom's words floated through my mind: *"Just because something's cute doesn't mean it isn't dangerous."*

2

As I make dinner later, the calendar on the wall taunts me, reminding me why I asked Hudson to come. Every square written in. Filled with things I'm afraid I'll forget. Neon-colored Post-it Notes are stuck all over the fridge, reminders of where I left my keys, my purse, what time to take my medication.

My life hasn't always been like this.

It started with small things. A word on the tip of my tongue and then, poof, gone. Never to be remembered again. Keys lost, then found hours later in a place I hadn't recalled leaving them. Misplacing basic household items. Putting them away where they clearly didn't belong. A couple of times I'd forgotten to put food out for Bowie.

But the last straw was a month ago.

Kendra called me around six o'clock at night, frantic, out of breath. "Are you almost here?" she asked.

Sitting on the couch, legs tucked up under my body, a glass of wine in hand, I said, "Am I supposed to be?"

"Are you serious, Mom?" she huffed. "You're supposed to watch Mason tonight."

"I am?" After setting my wine on the end table, I slid off the couch, hurried into the kitchen.

"Yes, I have class, and Theo is working late," she said impatiently, as if we'd already been through this. But I had no recollection of it.

I stood in front of the calendar tacked to the wall. Kendra harped on me about using the one in my phone, but I preferred the old method. I liked seeing it sprawled out in front of me in a tangible way. Kendra had to be wrong. Maybe she'd forgotten to ask me. When I looked at the day in question, my mouth dried out. *Mason, 5:30 p.m.*, I'd written.

"Oh, my god." My hand flew to my face. "I'm so sorry. I'll be right over." I was grateful I'd only just poured my first glass of wine.

"No." A heavy breath floated through the phone. "I'm already late for class, anyway. It's not even worth it at this point."

After saying goodbye, I hung up, dread filling me. This was far from over. Kendra would add this to the growing list of disappointments that she'd throw at me whenever she needed to make a point or get a dig in.

It's safe to say, she's not my mini-me. We're completely opposite. I don't mind it. I'm proud of the woman Kendra has become. A good wife, and a great mom to a sweet baby boy. Not to mention that she does all this while juggling the demands of nursing school, preparing for a career in caring for others.

Even though I could never live her life, it doesn't mean I can't appreciate it. Kendra has a much harder time with our differences. She's never understood me.

I remember feeling that way about my own mom. Incidentally, I think Kendra is a lot like she was. If only Kendra could've gotten to know her better before her mind went. My mother was diagnosed with early-onset Alzheimer's when I was in my thirties, she in her fifties.

I'll never forget the first time she forgot who I was. I knew about her disease, but so far she'd forgotten items, where she was, how she'd gotten there, where she'd left things, what she'd been doing when she walked into a room. People, she still recognized. The few important ones, at least. I'd gone to my parents' house for a visit, holding a bouquet of spring flowers—violet and pink hues—my mom's favorites. I'd said, "Hello," and handed them to her, then leaned down to kiss her cold cheek. But she'd pulled back, stared up at me, lips stretching out and eyes widening into an expression akin to terror. "I'm sorry, who are you?"

"It's Valerie, Mom," I said firmly. "Your daughter."

My explanation only seemed to confuse her further.

It was like a plunge into icy waters that stole my breath. Took the wind out of me.

The disease transformed my smart, capable mom into a confused child. Nothing could stop it. And that's the reason I refuse to see a doctor, despite all of Kendra's pressuring. I know what I have, and I know what it will do to me. There's no magic pill or cure.

Turning away from the calendar, I peek inside the oven to check on the lasagna. Heat blows over my face, bringing with it the scent of cheese and tomato sauce. Lasagna had been Hudson's favorite when he was younger. I hope it still is.

He's been in his room all day. I can hear the television blaring through the wall, and I kind of wish I hadn't put one in there for him.

I wanted to spend the afternoon catching up. For the past few days, I've been anxious for Hudson to be here. To finally have another body in the house. Noise. Commotion. Excitement.

After Darren passed away, the hardest part for me was the silence. I'd wake up in the morning, expecting to smell coffee in the air, hear him puttering around downstairs. Even though it's been five years, I'm still not used to the silence. Ultimately, it's the reason I got Bowie. My friendly chocolate Lab has been the best companion the past few years. He's kept me sane.

I never thought I was the type of woman who needed companionship. My independent nature is something I pride myself on.

But the perpetual quiet, especially at night, ushered in unwanted memories.

The ambulance, the stretcher, the unmoving body covered with a blanket.

For some reason, having Bowie's warm body beside me stills the images. Quiets the voices.

Over at the hutch, I pull out a couple of the fancy plates with the flowers dotting the edges that I'd inherited from my grandma. It's been a while since I used them. I place them on the dining table, then think better of it. The table seats eight. We historically only use it for large family meals or company. It will feel too imposing for just Hudson and me.

After snatching the plates off the table, I go back into the kitchen and set them down in the breakfast nook. *Much better.*

After pulling the lasagna out of the oven, I open a bottle of wine and place it in the center. I arrange some bread on a platter. Toss a salad. Once everything's ready, I hurry upstairs and down the hall to Hudson's room. It takes several knocks before he opens the door.

"Dinner's ready," I say, thinking how that simple phrase was one I'd taken for granted for so long. Maybe even resented. The daily expectation of motherhood; of domesticity. But today the phrase tastes sweet in my mouth like creamy cheesecake.

"Cool." Hudson nods, his hair unkempt, an indentation from the pillow sliced across his cheek. That's the boy I remember—eyes red, a yawn on his lips. In this moment, the lost years cease to exist as if we've traveled back in time.

If that were possible, I would do it differently. Repair the damage. And I'd start with the day Flight of Hearts' first album released.

It was a moment I'd been looking forward to for years, one I'd anticipated would be the best day of my life. I'd been singing with Flight of Hearts since Hudson was five, Kendra seven, but for many years it was my side gig—a way to make money on evenings and weekends. It had been hard to get backing for our jazz fusion sound. Mac, the guitarist who leaned more toward rock, had started the band with his childhood friend Kevin, who played both keyboard and saxophone. Kevin introduced Mac to his friend Tony, a drummer. Rick, who played bass, joined around the same time as me. We both answered an ad and auditioned. It was when I joined as lead vocalist that we came up with our unique sound. Mac thought I had a Joni Mitchell vibe. And since I played keyboard, we could utilize more of Kevin's saxophone.

The more we played, the more we gained a fan base. Eventually, we started booking gigs all over town, and then finally got our first big break, touring with Yellow Vinyl. It was after that tour that we recorded our first album.

Our album's release party was being held at the Full Moon Tavern, my friend Suzanne's place and the home of our very first real gig. Darren was stuck at the office and had called to say he'd be a little late to the party. He worked for the state and had recently been promoted to management. I wasn't mad about it, though. It would give me some alone time with the guys in the band without having to worry about including Darren.

I wore a red slinky dress, leopard-print pumps, my hair in an updo. Ashley, the teenage girl who frequently babysat for us, was running late as usual. Standing at the front window, staring out, I bounced my leg up and down with impatience. It was my big night, and I didn't want to miss any of it. The rest of the guys were probably already at the Tavern having their first drink.

Groaning in frustration, I abandoned my post and hurried

up the stairs. Kendra was in her room, lying on the top of her bed, math book open, punching numbers into a calculator and scribbling onto her notebook. She was different than I was at her age. Always so responsible.

Leaning against her door frame, I stared at her a minute.

Her head bounced up, her eyebrows rising. "What?"

"Ashley's not here yet, and I'm running late."

"Then go." Kendra went back to her homework as if already bored with this conversation.

I hesitated a moment, praying for a knock at the door. Darren would kill me if I left the kids alone. But he might not even have to know. Ashley would undoubtedly show up any minute. Probably right after I left. And although Kendra was only eleven, she was more mature than any other eleven-year-old I knew. Besides, she watched Hudson all the time during the day when I was busy plunking away on the piano, writing songs or practicing. Lost in my own world.

Mind made up, I shoved off the wall. "I'm gonna head out. When Ashley gets here, let her know that I left money on the counter if you guys wanna order a pizza."

"Okay," she said without lifting her head again.

When I reached Hudson's door, it was closed. "Hudson." I rapped on it, and it swung open within seconds. A sheen of sweat clung to Hudson's skin, his cheeks red. Behind him, action figures lined his floor.

"Shouldn't you be doing homework?" I asked.

"I finished," he said.

I didn't know if this was true. Darren would probably demand to have a look in his backpack, but I didn't have time for that right now.

So instead, I put my arms out. "Give me a hug. I'm taking off."

Hudson paused, his gaze flickering to the doorway. "Ashley's here?"

"No, not yet, but she will be."

"And you're gonna leave us?" His voice got higher, making him sound much younger than nine.

I mussed his hair with my palm. "Ashley will be here any minute."

"Then why don't you wait?"

"I would, but I'm running behind."

Hudson wrapped his arms around my waist as if trying to lock me in place. I pried his fingers off. "Alright, that's enough. I love you, but I really have to go."

"Wait," he called before I reached the stairs.

"What?" The word came out forcibly, much harsher than I'd meant.

He looked down, his fingers playing with the bottom of his shirt. "Nothing," he mumbled.

I sighed, feeling bad about my outburst, but this was my big night. *My* party. Was it so bad that I wanted to get to it? Hudson wasn't as independent as his sister. Sometimes he was scared of the dark, and I knew he didn't like it when Darren and I were gone at nighttime. It was a phase we'd all gone through as children. He'd be fine.

"I'll see you later. Okay, buddy?" Without waiting for a response, I hurried down the stairs and out the front door.

When I got to the Full Moon Tavern, Suzanne had our album playing loudly through the speakers. And Jerry, Suzanne's husband and bartender, had an appletini—my favorite drink at the time—waiting for me. I was on my second one when Darren finally showed up.

Enjoying the celebration, I never even thought to check the flip phone buried at the bottom of my purse. If I had, I would've gotten the message from Ashley, explaining that she'd been in a car accident on the way to my house and wasn't going to make it. And, even more importantly, the frantic call from Hudson saying he was scared and begging me to come home.

When Darren's mobile phone rang, he did answer, but it wasn't the kids. It was the police. There'd been a break-in at our house. While I'd been drinking and partying, not giving one thought to my children, they'd been at home, terrified and without supervision, hiding from an intruder.

When we got home, Kendra was in the front room, answering the police's questions, adultlike and stoic. But Hudson was upstairs, hiding under his bed, shaking like a leaf caught in a windstorm. Not much had been stolen—some of my jewelry and a few electronics. The police could only lift partial prints, and none matched with any in the system. Insurance covered the damage, and everything eventually got fixed and replaced.

But Hudson became much more anxious. Worried and nervous. Afraid to ever be alone. Jumping at every little sound. He was never the same after that night.

Neither was our relationship.

"I made lasagna," I say now as we walk together down the hallway. The walls are lined with family portraits. Darren's and my wedding photos. Hudson and Kendra as babies all the way up to young adults. Pictures with the four of us wearing matching sweaters or similar colors.

In my favorite one, we are standing in the middle of a beautiful field in white shirts and dark denim jeans. I remember Kendra having a bad attitude that day because she wasn't happy with how her hair turned out, and Hudson was teasing her about it. I had snapped at them right before the picture was taken. You'd never know it, though, by our large smiles, and the way we were all leaning in close to one another.

The perfect family.

3

"Lasagna used to be your favorite," I ramble as we clomp down the stairs. "I hope you still like it."

"Yeah." He shrugs, not an ounce of emotion on his face. "Lasagna's good."

At the bottom of the stairs, I hear the sound of Bowie's dog tag rattling and his sharp paws clicking on the hardwood floors. I turn. He's trotting in our direction, ears flopping.

"Hey, sweet boy." I reach down to pet his head. His fur is coarse and smells faintly like grass. "You remember Bowie. Right, Hudson?"

"Yeah," Hudson says, making no attempt to interact.

Bowie heads over to him, wagging his tail, but Hudson moves back, fisting his hands at his sides, almost as if he's scared.

It all comes back to me then. The barbecue at the neighbors' when the kids were young, the summer after we'd moved in. Peter and Karen Grainger, two doors down, had a pool the kids had spent all day in. In the evening they'd finally dried off and were having Popsicles, the edges of their mouths painted in red-and-blue stickiness. I was sipping a beer, laughing with my neighbor and former best friend Leslie, grazing on chips and dip, when I heard it. The deep growl. The loud bark. By the time I looked over, the Graingers' dog had a little boy's face in between his teeth. Hudson was only feet away, watching in horror.

"C'mon, boy." I usher Bowie away.

When Bowie saunters off, I glance back up at my son. "Um…" I clear my throat. It's weird how nervous I am. I have no idea what to say or how to behave. It has nothing to do with my memory issues. I recall everything about Hudson. It's the normal discomfort of having an adult son. One I hardly know anymore. In the past five years, we've rarely spoken. Maybe once a quarter, and only when Hudson needed something. I have his cell number, but often when I call it, it's turned off—I assume from lack of payment. When he called a month ago to tell me that his girlfriend had broken up with him and kicked him out, he mentioned that it might be a while before he could contact me again. Desperate, I'd offered to pay his phone bill for the next several months. With my mental state diminishing, I didn't want to risk not being able to reach him. I'm so glad I did that, or he might not be here tonight.

As we approach the table, I realize that I don't even know if he drinks wine. I pick up the bottle, anyway. Offer him some.

"Sure," he replies.

It's not exactly enthusiastic, but I'm relieved he doesn't say no. There's nothing else to drink in the house. Darren liked hard liquor—whiskey or gin—and also indulged in the occasional beer, but I usually stick to wine, and I don't do it regularly.

I used to drink almost daily, and I preferred cocktails, but when Darren was diagnosed with liver cancer, a result of years of alcoholism, I gave it up. Only recently, I've indulged again. It helps me relax.

Ice shifts in the ice maker. The refrigerator hums. I pour us both a glass of the dark purple liquid, filling it way past the halfway mark. I feel like we could both use it. I hope it will cut the awkwardness.

When I sink down into my chair, it creaks beneath me. Hudson plops down across from me and takes a gulp. He almost sucks down half the glass in one fell swoop, reminding me of when he was young. He could chug an entire glass of orange juice in mere seconds and eat a sandwich in just a few bites.

I lean back, drawing the glass to my lips. The acidic tang lingers on my tongue.

"You didn't have to do all of this," Hudson says. "I could've picked something up."

His statement stings, but I know it isn't meant to. If Kendra had said it, it would've been a dig, a reminder of all the meals I didn't cook them growing up. But I'm certain Hudson's only trying to be helpful. "No, it's fine. I wanted to make dinner," I say, and then add with a wink, "while I still remember how." After the words leave my mouth, I worry that it was an inappropriate joke. In bad taste.

But then Hudson laughs for the first time since arriving. I laugh, too, and it feels nice. I can't remember the last time I truly laughed. It's why I was looking forward to having Hudson back. He's always been the funny one. The silly one, who likes to joke and tease.

Between bites of lasagna and sips of wine, I try to think of something to say. A dozen questions pop into my mind all at once like the finale of a fireworks show.

What happened between you and your ex?

What have you been up to since?
What kind of work have you been doing?
Do you have any job prospects now?
What are your plans?

But I can't bring myself to ask them. I don't know much about his ex, other than that her name is Natasha. Or is it Natalia? Natalie? Well, I guess I don't even know that. But I'd tried to get him to tell me more about their breakup when I'd called to ask him to stay here, and he'd clammed up immediately. Jobs seem to be a sore subject as well. Our first night together shouldn't be spent on uncomfortable conversations. Plus, I don't want him to feel pressured or interrogated.

So we eat in silence.

Hudson finishes before me. I'm still a little hungry, but I abandon my plate and replenish both of our wineglasses before inviting him to join me in the family room.

"I can help you clean up," he says, eyeing the plates, silverware and serving platters.

I wave away his suggestion. "I'll get it later," I tell him, heading toward the family room.

The beauty of living alone is doing things in my own timeframe. Darren hated messiness. He couldn't ignore dirty dishes in the sink, a table that needed clearing. It had to be done immediately. But it doesn't bother me.

The family room has always been my favorite. Many a morning, I've sat in the window seat, sipping coffee and watching the sun rise. I'd redecorated over the last few years with vintage and antique pieces, my favorite being the rolled-arm blue velvet sofa that I found at an estate sale here in midtown about a year ago.

Darren would have hated it.

"What's all this?" Hudson asks, moving toward the baby grand piano in the corner. His fingers light on the box and file folders littering the top, disturbing the dust that's constantly accumulating.

"Oh." I follow him, set my wineglass down and pick up a file folder. "It's just stuff about the house."

"What kinda stuff?" Hudson grabs a few papers out of the box.

"The history."

"These are all articles about Grace Newton's death," he says.

"Yeah, I wanted to see if I could learn anything new about it."

"And did you?"

"I mean, not really. Just that the police had originally suspected the dad, and eventually the mom. There were even people who thought maybe it was one of her older siblings. But, you know, eventually it was ruled accidental."

His forehead becomes a mess of squiggly lines. "Why're you so interested in this?"

I get the same kind of questions from Kendra.

"It's creepy enough that you chose to live in this house. Why do you fixate on its morbid history?" She's said a version of this repeatedly over the years.

I shrug. "It's my home. I'm curious about its history. Besides, I've been living alone in this house with Grace for the past five years. Shouldn't I know about her?" Making light of it, I wink.

Hudson doesn't laugh. His concerned expression deepens.

I nudge him good-naturedly on the shoulder. "Oh, come on. I'm kidding." I open the file folder in my hand. "Look, I've been able to trace the genealogy back to the original owners of the home. I'd always thought it was Grace's parents. But it wasn't. It was her grandparents, who built the home in 1910. Then it was passed down to Grace's parents and eventually Grace's siblings. Isn't that cool?"

"I guess." Hudson drops the articles back into the box, and then, wandering over to the couch, he takes a sip of his wine.

I frown as I close the file folder, his dismissiveness making me feel stupid. "Well, I find it interesting."

"Yeah, no, I think it is," he says, even though his tone betrays that he doesn't. "I was just surprised. I thought maybe the box was filled with, like, new music you were writing or something."

"Oh." I carry my glass to the couch, joining Hudson. "No, I don't have any new music."

"You're not doing music at all anymore?"

"No, not right now."

"Why not?"

I close my mouth, run my tongue along my top teeth a minute, thinking of how to answer. I have no idea how much Hudson knows. Kids understand a lot more than we think. And he was a teenager when Flight of Hearts broke up. But he was also dealing with his own crisis—*Heather*—and on the heels of that, his dad got sick.

What he doesn't know won't hurt him.

So I give him the pat answer: "It's just not the right time."

Hudson lets out a bitter sound, kind of between a snort and humph. "Seems like this is finally the right time."

I'm dumbfounded. "Really?"

"Yeah, I mean, you have nothing else going on."

I run my fingertips along the stem of my wineglass, my flesh catching on a minuscule chip in the glass. A tiny bubble of blood appears. I wipe it away. "That's not true. You have no idea what I've got going on. You haven't been around."

"Neither were you when we were growing up."

"That's not fair." I expect this kind of pushback from Kendra, but I'm a little surprised that it's coming from Hudson.

"I was working. And it's not like you were alone. Your dad was with you."

"Yeah," he huffs. "Dad."

"Don't speak ill of the dead," my mother always said.

It's not like I don't know what he's referring to, but I'm in no mood to get into a conversation with Hudson right now about his father. The one we are already having is uncomfortable enough. It's not like it's the first time I've been berated for the time I spent away from my family. The insults used to come from the other moms.

"She's never around," they'd whisper, loud enough for me to hear when I'd pass them at the school or in the grocery store.

"That poor Darren does everything for those kids."

It wasn't true. But so what if it was? Darren was their dad. Was it so terrible for him to do things for his own children? He's the one who wanted to be a father so badly in the first place.

I've taken the abuse all these years, but now I'm tired of it.

"I shouldn't have to make excuses for pursuing my dream," I snap. "You'd understand if you'd ever had one."

The sides of his mouth twitch. One eyebrow cocks, the vein in his forehead pulsing.

"I'm sorry," I say, wishing I could shove the words back inside.

"You always go too far, Valerie," Darren used to say, frowning. *"Aim right for the jugular."*

My statement doesn't even ring true. Hudson had had a dream once. For many years, actually, he'd wanted to become a professional baseball player. Worked hard at it, too, and he was pretty good. Darren cautioned him to come up with something more realistic, but I'd admonished Darren for his negativity. My parents had been that way about my dream to become a professional singer, too. Many Christmases, I asked for voice or piano lessons, but never got them.

I did save my own money from Christmases and birthdays in order to buy myself a keyboard when I was ten, though. After that, I taught myself how to play the chords. Finally, in high school, I got a job at a local pizza place and made enough to pay for lessons on my own. My parents always told me it was a silly dream. They thought I should focus on more practical goals. To my dad that meant going to college or "beauty school" (his words, not mine). To my mom, that meant marrying a rich man. Neither of their ideas appealed to me in the least, and I had hoped to one day prove them both wrong. Show them that my dream wasn't silly. That music was a viable career. But by the time Flight of Hearts' first album was made, Mom's mind was gone. Dad was still alive, but he never acknowledged my success. I think he went to his grave thinking I'd chosen the wrong path in life.

I'd had no intention of squashing my son's dream. I did everything in my power to support it—paying for lessons, driving him to practices and dropping him off at the batting cages. Unfortunately, Hudson's life came crashing down after that horrible incident in high school, and he gave up on his dream. Pretty much gave up on everything.

It wasn't his fault, and now I feel like an ass for what I said.

Hudson stands. "I think I'm gonna go to bed."

"No. Wait." I stand, too, glancing at the red liquid remaining in his glass. "At least finish your wine."

"Fine." He knocks it back. "I'll put my glass in the sink," he says, hurrying from the room.

Sighing, I sink back down on the couch to finish my own glass. By the time it's empty, the house is quiet, save for Bowie's snoring, the occasional tick of the clock, the moaning of the floorboards beneath my feet. There's no way to walk stealthily in this house. Every step creaks and cracks like an old lady's bones. I'll admit, I found it annoying when the kids were younger, when the noises would wake them just as I'd gotten them to sleep.

Now it gives me comfort. A familiar symphony of sorts. A soundtrack to my life.

Though the soundtrack has had its darker notes. I'd noticed a peculiar hook and eye latch on the outside of Hudson's door the day we'd walked through with Jan but hadn't wanted to mention it to Darren then. I took it down the day we moved in. But I never got it out of my head. Why was it there?

Who had been locked inside?

And, more importantly, why?

In the early days of living here, I often dreamed of a child trapped, knocking and screaming from inside her bedroom. Sometimes I even believed I heard her, hollering in my nightmares.

But it wasn't until after the kids moved out and Darren was gone—when I had become determined to redecorate the way I wanted—that I noticed the other oddities. The words carved in the walls of the attic, childlike scribble that I could barely make out, but I swore one said HELP and another, EVIL. There were also scratches inside the door of one of the children's closets as if someone had been locked inside and tried to claw their way out.

That's when my obsession with finding out the history of this house had truly taken shape.

I carry my wineglass into the kitchen, rinse it in the sink. Then I clear the table, putting the lasagna in a container, but tossing the remainder of the salad and hardened bread. I leave the dishes soaking in the sink to get to tomorrow. After drying my hands, I check the lock on the side door, bolting it.

As I head over to the light switch, I catch movement in the window across the street.

A dark figure stands on the other side of the glass, staring up toward my window.

Leslie.

Surely, she sees me, but she makes no attempt to move or conceal herself. She remains stock-still, her body facing me, backlit by a glowing lamp. I stare back. A challenge.

She stands even taller. A warning.

Shivering, I swiftly close the blinds, blocking her view. Even after the slats click into place, I can still see her, the image burning in my mind—the outline of her shoulder-length hair and trim frame. I clutch the counter and take a deep breath.

I wait a few seconds, and then, with my heart pounding, I peek through the blinds. She's gone. Curtains cover the window where she stood.

Below it, luscious flowers bloom, lining the entire porch and front yard. Leslie has always had a green thumb. When she first moved in fifteen years ago, I'd watched her as she revived the front yard, planting and pruning. After about a week of Darren pestering me to welcome her to the neighborhood, I strolled across the street with the purple iris I'd bought her—a welcome gift.

Little did I know that five years later, I'd stand in this very spot, watching her tear apart that same iris, scattering the bright petals all over her grass in a rage.

If he hollers let him go...
Eeny, meeny, miny, moe...

I looked down at my burned hand—the angry red welt and swollen skin—and winced. The pain was intense, despite all the ointment Mom had slathered on it. It throbbed like a steady heartbeat. I'd been lying in bed for hours. It hurt so bad I couldn't sleep.

I knew it wasn't an accident.

There was no way to prove it, though.

It all happened earlier this evening when my sister and I were helping with dinner. We were having tuna casserole. When the egg noodles were done, Andie asked me to hold the colander in the sink while she poured the pasta in. I didn't want to hold it, and I told her so, but she insisted.

"If it falls over, the noodles will go down the drain. Is that what you want? Don't be such a baby," she snapped.

I shook my head and reluctantly walked toward her, staring down at the checkered linoleum under my feet. When I reached the sink, I tucked my fingers around the edge of the colander.

When the scalding water hit my skin, I squealed and leaped back.

"Whoopsie," Andie said with a little shrug of her shoulders.

I stared back at her, cradling my hand as it turned an angry red.

Dad came rushing in.

"It was an accident," Andie was saying. "I didn't mean to."

"Of course you didn't," Dad replied, inspecting my hand as tears filled my eyes. "Let's run this under some cold water, okay?"

As Dad flicked on the faucet in the opposite sink, I couldn't help but notice the smirk on my sister's face.

4

In the morning, Hudson is gone.

The bedroom door is open, the room empty. My heart catches. I step inside. It's decorated much differently than when Hudson was younger. The walls used to be covered in baseball posters and shelves bearing all of his trophies. He had an A's comforter, bold green, bright yellow. Now the comforter is gray, charcoal pillows on top. The paintings on the walls are ones I've collected over the years from antique fairs and thrifting. They're abstract, colorful. I wonder what Hudson thinks of it.

My mind jolts back to our argument the night before.

"You'd understand if you'd ever had one."

Why had I made it personal? Said something so vile and untrue? If only I'd kept my big mouth shut.

Behind the bed, I catch the edge of a strap. I follow it to the duffel bag it's attached to. My insides uncoil. Thank god, he didn't leave.

I feel silly for even entertaining the thought. Where would he go?

~~I was doing him a favor, even if I told Kendra it was the~~ other way around.

"I just worry about you living alone," she said a few days after I'd flaked out on babysitting. Then her eyes widened as if having an epiphany. "Hey, maybe you should come stay with us."

I shook my head vehemently before she even got the entire sentence out. "No way."

She frowned.

"Sorry," I muttered, realizing that came out harsher than I meant it to. "But I'm not some old, decrepit lady, Kendra. I'm in my fifties."

Kendra sighed. "It's not about your age, Mom, and you know it."

"I'm not leaving my house, and besides, I don't want to be an imposition."

"You need someone looking out for you."

"I'm fine," I told her.

"I just wish someone could come stay with you. You know I would if I could." Shaking her head, she added, "God forbid Hudson would ever step up and help out."

"He might if I ask him," I said.

"Yeah, right." She snorted.

I'd never told Kendra about Hudson's girlfriend kicking him out. As far as I know, Kendra and Hudson only talk a handful of times a year—birthdays and holidays. She couldn't know that Hudson would have been homeless if I hadn't asked him to come home.

After leaving his room, I head back to mine. Sunlight filters in through the open windows, the air around me already warming. Usually, I wake up before the sunrise. But last night I had a hard time sleeping. I'd tossed and turned, Leslie's figure in the window rattling me. I had a series of fragmented dreams. Leslie crying, mascara raking down her cheeks. Pointing fingers. Hurling accusations. Hands caked in mud, leaves stuck to her palms, dirt under her nails.

I prefer going on walks early in the morning, when the sky is still dark and the air is cool. The neighborhood is peaceful at that hour. No watchful eyes. No whispered chatter. Just the scent of damp grass and crisp air, and the sounds of birds chirping, an occasional dog barking or car driving by in the distance, sprinklers ticking on.

By now the neighbors are most likely out in full force. But I urge myself to change into walking clothes and tennis shoes. I've been reading articles on the correlation between physical and mental health, and I'm convinced the morning walks are helping to keep my memory sharp. Besides, Bowie will go berserk if I don't take him out.

He comes running the minute I grab the leash off the hook near the door. I laugh while securing it.

When I step outside, Bowie swiftly runs down the front stairs, tugging on my arm. I stop, pulling the leash taut, noticing Hudson's car sitting at the curb. I glance back up at the house, wondering where he went without his car. But then Bowie moves forward, and I clamber after him.

I'm relieved to find Leslie's front yard empty, no car in the driveway. Usually, by now, she's sitting on her front porch drinking coffee. Sometimes alone, but often with a group of other neighborhood ladies—Beth, the neighbor to the left of Leslie, Shelly from a few doors down, and Tessa, whose house is next door to mine. I know all three of them from back when Leslie and I hung out. Once upon a time they were my friends, too, but clearly their loyalty had always been to Leslie. Lately, I've noticed a few women I've never met. One lady I recognize as the new owner of the Winterses' former home. I'm not sure where the other women came from. Shelly and the new ladies all work, though, so often they can't stay long. Beth is a retired teacher, so she has all the time in the world. Leslie never worked when she was married, but after she and James split up, she got some type of administrative job. I think at an insurance firm. I haven't seen her leave for work for over a year, so maybe she's retired, too. My shoulders relax as Bowie and I hurry past. A few houses down, a kid runs around outside, action figures stuffed in his chubby hands; a man waters his grass. But they are newer. People I haven't taken the time to meet. Barely lifting my head, I wave, offering a curt smile. I'm not interested in making conversation.

I learned my lesson about becoming friends with neighbors years ago.

I think back to my first conversation with Leslie, fifteen years earlier when I'd brought her the iris. Grateful, she'd invited me in for tea.

I remember it was mint, fragrant and strong. No cream.

"Where's the rest of your family?" I asked, glancing around. The furniture was sparse, walls still bare, boxes littering the floor.

"Oh, my husband, James, and my daughter, Heather, are at the store right now. They should be home soon."

"You just have the one daughter, then?"

Leslie nodded. "You?"

"Two. A girl and a boy. Kendra is twelve, and Hudson's ten."

"Heather's ten, too."

"We should get the two of them together sometime, then," I suggested, and in that moment it seemed perfect.

A friend for Hudson and a friend for me.

For a while, it had been.

Bowie stops walking, and I know what's about to happen. I crinkle my nose. Definitely my least favorite part of these walks. After I clean up his mess, we continue on.

One of the things I've always loved about this street is that no two homes are alike. All of them were built in the early 1900s and have gone through many remodels since. Take, for instance, the house next door to Leslie's. The one on the right that belongs to the Ramos family. That house had always been the smallest on the street, single-story, not much bigger than my first apartment with Darren, I'd guess. But five years ago, they'd added a modern second level to the home, complete with a balcony and large picture windows. Now Leslie's is the smallest, and the one in most need of repair with its chipping ivory paint and hideous dark brown trim.

We turn right at the next intersection. If we went left, we'd hit the main street, which would take us to restaurants and shops. Instead, we're met with more homes. Trees drape over the road, meeting in the middle like hands stretching out, their fingertips grazing. Bowie sniffs in the dirt, barks at a shaking bush. A lizard or bird inside, perhaps.

I yank on the leash, guiding him down the sidewalk. A couple of bikes whiz past, leaving a breeze in their wake. Drawing a few strands of hair back from my cheek, I hurry forward, trying to keep up with Bowie. Sweat gathers along my shoulder blades, slides down my spine. It's much warmer than our usual walks, and I wish again that I'd gotten up earlier. Every September I'm reminded of how late fall arrives here in Sacramento.

We make our way down the sidewalk, flanked by Victorian and colonial homes, large sweeping staircases and wraparound porches. We're entering an even nicer neighborhood than ours. To my left is one of my favorite homes in this area with its rounded windows and curved chimney, resembling a fairy-tale cottage.

We make a full loop of the block and head for home.

After rounding the corner onto our street, I spot Leslie on the sidewalk in front of her house, talking with a man who appears to have been on a jog. He's wearing short shorts, and a T-shirt that's damp with sweat, tennis shoes on his feet.

Then he turns his head, and I realize it's Hudson.

I pick my pace up to a jog.

"…doing back here?" Her tone is venomous, voice rising. I see Beth peek out her front window. No surprise there. I bet other neighbors are getting an eyeful, too.

I don't hear Hudson's response, but it's clear he gives her one, because there's a slight pause before she practically shouts, "No one wants you here."

I'm so winded when I reach them that my breath is shallow, my heart racing. I swallow down the burn in my throat and lungs and force words out. "I do. I want him here."

Leslie's head snaps in my direction.

I gulp in air and continue, "He's my son. He's always welcome here."

"Not after what he did to Heather," Leslie says.

"I never hurt Heather," Hudson says softly, trying to catch Leslie's eyes, but she won't look at him. She keeps her eyes on me.

"I know what you did," she says, unmoved.

I grab my son's arm with my free hand, guiding him away. "Come on, let's get outta here."

She's been spewing these allegations for years.

Enough is enough.

"You have to believe me," Hudson says over his shoulder as I yank him away. "I promise I never hurt her."

"Let it go," I say firmly, knowing there's no getting through to her. She's too entrenched in her own beliefs at this point. Her hatred toward us runs too deep.

"I don't believe you," she hollers after us. "And I'm going to make sure this entire neighborhood knows what you're capable of, what kind of monster you are."

Hudson's muscles tighten beneath my grip.

"Ignore her," I say through gritted teeth as we make our way up the front steps. "It's all words. She can't actually hurt you. Let's get inside, and I'll make breakfast."

"For sure," he says, wiping his sweaty forehead with the back of his hand.

"Were you running?" I ask as I unlock the front door.

I didn't know my son was a runner. He hadn't been when he was younger.

"Yeah, it's somethin' I took up a few years ago."

As he steps inside the house behind me, the toe of his shoe hits one of the succulent pots lining the porch. "You have a lot of these."

"It's kind of a hobby."

"Buying plants?" His brow furrows.

"No. I arrange them." I've always been a creative person. Music used to be my outlet, but when I stopped that, I had to find things to fill that void. For a while I took a dance class at the rec center with my best friend, Suzanne. Recently, I started taking an art class there. I tried to get Suzanne to join that with me as well, but she couldn't make the time work for her schedule. And about a year ago, I discovered I had a knack for creating succulent planters. I've never had a green thumb, but succulents are easier to keep alive.

When we get inside, I unhook Bowie from his leash. "So, I was thinking maybe we could grab dinner out tonight. Maybe Suzie Burger?" It had been a favorite of his for years.

"Actually, I'm gonna go out with my buddies tonight."

Wiping his forehead with the back of his hand, he makes his way to the kitchen.

I follow. "Which buddies?" It seems pretty fast for him to have already made new friends.

"Browning, Griff and the Beast." He pulls a water out of the fridge, unscrews the top.

It takes a minute to register. Jared Browning, Mark Griffin and Adam Stetson. His friends from growing up, their old nicknames acquired out on the baseball field. He'd become friends with them in junior high.

"I kinda assumed they'd all moved out of the area," I muse aloud.

"Nah." He takes a sip.

Some of it saturates his beard, and suddenly I'm mesmerized by it. How hot must it be to run with that thing on his face? I know it's a style nowadays. I'm not that out of touch. I see guys all over town with bushy beards wearing skinny jeans, long T-shirts, and thick black-rimmed glasses. According to Suzanne, their fellow millennials call them hipsters. Even Kendra's husband, Theo, has one, although he keeps it shorn close, nicely trimmed. I wish Hudson did that, at least, so I could see his face.

"Browning lives close by, actually. He only stayed with his parents in Oregon for like a year before moving back. Too much rain, he said. Stetson and Griffin live like a half hour away."

I lean against the counter. "What are you boys gonna do?"

He shrugs. "Dunno. Maybe hit up a bar or club or something. Browning said he might have a lead on a job for me, too."

"What kind of job?"

"Not sure." After tossing the empty water bottle in the

recycle bin, he moves past me, his hand lighting on my shoulder momentarily. "Gonna hit the shower."

Hudson talking about going out with his buddies gives me a sense of déjà vu.

"Mom." A quick intake of breath. A crackle in the phone connection. "I need you to come quick. Something bad happened."

"How bad?" I sat up in bed, heart pounding. In the bed beside me, Darren rolled over and turned on the lamp on his nightstand. The light blinded me.

"Really bad." His voice shook, and he sounded more like a child than a teenage boy. "I'm scared, Mom. I think I might be in big trouble. I really need you."

I thought back to the night of the release party. How I'd left him alone, and then not answered when he called later, panicked and scared. It had to mean something that he'd called me tonight, not asked for Darren. This was my moment to make things right.

"Okay, calm down. Tell me where you are."

A low growl reaches my ears, causing the memory to fade. My neck prickles. Hudson freezes.

"Bowie!" My dog's hackles are up, his teeth bared. It's a rare sight. Usually, he's so friendly. "Stop it. It's just Hudson. You know Hudson." But my words aren't helping. Bowie barks. Growls again. Hudson takes a step back. Heat spills across my chest as I lunge forward. Standing between them, I place my hand on Bowie's fur and gently pet him. "It's okay, boy." I feel his body relax.

Hudson watches warily as he moves around us. Once he leaves the room, I stare down at Bowie, narrowing my eyes.

The only other times he'd acted like this was when he thought I was in danger.

5

Over the next few days, Hudson and I fall into a routine. I wake up early for my morning walk, and upon returning often find Hudson leaving for his run. He spends most of the day in his room, only emerging for meals or to go out with his buddies.

It's not exactly what I'd envisioned when I invited him to come stay. There are a million little projects around the house I'd love for him to get started on—a door hinge that's broken, a floodlight in the backyard that's been out for months, rain gutters that need cleaning out, a few window screens that need replacing—but I don't have the heart to ask. My mom always nagged at me about everything. She had no problem putting together lists of chores and projects, and then constantly interrogating me about where I was at with them. I swore I'd never be like her, and so far I've been good at sticking to that. I certainly don't plan to break my streak now that my son is an adult.

But I do wish Hudson would do something—anything—productive. Even if it's for himself. The last time the subject of a job came up was before the first time he went out with his friends. He's gone out every night since, but the subject has yet to be revisited.

I feel like tonight is the night.

"Have you been applying for any jobs?" I ask him, picking up a crispy French fry and dipping it in ketchup. We finally got our Suzie Burger fix, and now we're sitting at the kitchen table across from each other with crumpled bags, ketchup packets and napkins littering the table between us. All day long lately, I hear the TV muffled through the wall of his room, but it's possible to apply for jobs on our phones now, so perhaps that's what he's doing. I hope it is.

He shrugs, hamburger fisted in his hand, liquid dripping down his wrist. "I mean, I've looked, but nothing sounds good."

"What kind of work *would* sound good?" I know Hudson worked at a lumberyard at one point. And I think he's had a couple of retail jobs. I vaguely recall a brief stint at Home Depot. But other than that, I have no idea what kind of jobs he's been doing the last few years.

I also have no clue what he wants to do with this life. Baseball was his one passion. After he gave that up, I don't know if he found another one.

He chews. Swallows. Wipes his face with a napkin. "I don't know. I'm good with my hands. That's why I'm hoping that job with Browning's uncle works out."

"Oh, yeah. What's happening with that?"

"Browning's working on it."

That doesn't sound too promising.

"What kind of work is it?" I ask.

"He manages a mine."

"A mine? They have those out here?"

"Yeah, this one is near Vista Falls."

That's only like thirty minutes away, so not bad. "Is it underground?" I shiver at the thought.

"No, Mom." He grins in an amused way. "It's not a coal mine. They mine clay, mostly. It's aboveground. Outside."

I nod, feeling a little comfort at that.

In the meantime, though, it would be nice if he could help me out around here. As much as I hate the idea of giving him a list of projects, it might actually be helpful. For me and for him. He clearly has no direction. A lot of the time you learn what you're good at by doing. Practicing. It wasn't until I took voice and piano lessons that I got the confidence to start performing in earnest.

Prior to that, I'd always thought I wanted to be a singer in theory. Fantasizing about it while dancing around my room with my hairbrush in hand, boom box blaring behind me. I'd gone to a few open call Music Circus auditions, but never got a role. But the connections I made in lessons helped me book a few gigs, playing at weddings and parties. The more I performed, the more I loved it. And the better I got.

Perhaps Hudson needs that same motivation.

The ringing of a phone cuts through my thoughts.

"Oh." Hudson hurriedly wipes his fingers on his napkin again before shoving his hand down into his jeans pocket. The ringing increases in volume as he tugs it out, bringing it to his ear. "Hey, dude, what's up?" Scooping up his wrappers, he bunches them in his free hand and carries them to the garbage can. He laughs heartily. "Cool. Sounds legit." After tossing in his trash, he draws the phone from his ear. "Sorry," he whispers to me. "Thanks for dinner."

I nod in response.

"Yeah. Of course I'm in," he says into the phone as he swaggers out of the kitchen.

I stop him before he can fully walk away. "Hey, Hudson."

When he turns in the doorway, eyebrows raised slightly, holding the phone away from his ear, I say, "Kendra and Theo are coming for dinner Friday night. They really want to see you, so don't make plans, okay?"

"Okay." It's not quite the enthusiastic response I was hoping for. Then again, I'm not really surprised.

From the day Darren and I found out I was pregnant with Kendra, we argued about having more children. I'd been happy being an only child, but Darren had hated it, always dreaming of having a sibling, preferably a brother he could hang out with.

Eventually, he got his way, and we gave Kendra a sibling. Not that it made her happy at all. The two of them fought incessantly while they were growing up. It would be so nice if they could become close now.

I finish off the last bite of my burger, then stand and collect the remaining wrappers. The sun is starting to go down outside, the sky becoming hazy, bright pink around the edges.

Leslie's windows are bright and open. I catch her silhouette in the kitchen, standing over the counter, pouring something, it appears. Tea, probably. It's always been her drink of choice. Back when we were friends, her idea of a fun evening was to sip tea on the couch and watch TV. I think it's part of why I liked her so much. We balanced each other out. She grounded me. With her, I could unwind, let my hair down. I didn't need to be on—the life of the party. Likewise, she could explore a more edgy side of herself on the evenings when I coerced her into a girl's night out.

Darren thought she was the ideal woman. I know because

he used to throw her lifestyle in my face when we fought about how much I went out at night.

"Leslie's always home with her family in the evenings," he'd say like that was a life to be envied.

It's not like he had any right to get on me about how I chose to live my life, anyway. He might have been home with the kids, but lord knows he wasn't sitting on the couch drinking tea like Leslie.

He hid his drinking problem from all of us for a while. But I often smelled alcohol on his breath when I came in late from a gig to find him asleep in our bed, faceup, snoring loudly. It didn't worry me, though. I assumed he'd had just a drink or two. I would never begrudge him that. I liked to drink as much as the next person. I knew Darren enjoyed drinking when I married him. We always drank on our dates—cocktails before dinner, wine during, port after. When we planned our reception, Darren was way more interested in the wine list than the food choices. But I never thought it was concerning. My parents also enjoyed drinks in the evening and frequently had cocktails or wine with dinner.

But when I began regularly finding empty whiskey bottles hidden in the garbage can outside, I realized Darren had a problem.

The severity of it hit me one night when a gig got canceled at the last minute. I headed home, thinking Darren and the kids would be glad to see me. Excited, even. I stopped on the way home, picking up a carton of Rocky Road, which was Darren's favorite. I was certain it was something Leslie would've done. She always had James's and Heather's favorites in her fridge. And for once, I wanted to be that kind of wife. The one who doted on her husband. Had his favorite ice cream in the freezer.

I bounded up the front steps, grocery bag in hand.

"Hey, guys, I'm home!" I called from the door.

To the right, the television blared. When I turned, Darren hopped up off the couch as if he'd been caught red-handed doing something seedy. My gaze snapped up to the TV thinking maybe he'd been watching porn or something. I heard movement upstairs, so I figured at least one of the kids was up there. But a rerun of *I Love Lucy* played, not exactly something to be embarrassed about.

"Hey, what are you doing home?" he asked. That was not the welcome I'd been hoping for.

"Gig got canceled." I stepped in further, taking in his flushed face and glassy eyes. My chest pinched as I held up the grocery bag. "I brought home Rocky Road."

"Thanks, babe," he said, which was uncharacteristic in so many ways. He rarely called me "babe."

Peering over his shoulder I spotted the bottle of Macallan on the coffee table, an empty glass beside it, amber-colored liquid coating the bottom. I frowned.

"Where are the kids?" I asked.

"Oh." He ran a hand down his face. "Upstairs doing homework." His words came out a little too slow, slightly slurred.

"Have they had dinner?"

"Yeah, they wanted mac and cheese. Kendra made it." He beamed with pride the same way he always did when he spoke of Kendra. Often, he told me about all the ways she'd helped out when I was gone. I'd assumed she liked helping her dad. They'd always been so close. But now I wondered if she did it out of necessity.

The thought made me feel slightly ill—and angry. I couldn't help but think bitterly about all the times he'd gotten on my case about going out with the guys after shows and getting a ride home—on occasion—drunk. How often he'd compared me to Leslie and the other women in the neighborhood as if he wished I could be more like them. How dared he expect me to be some Stepford wife when he was at home getting shit-faced by six o'clock?

All that time I'd assuaged my guilt about leaving my kids with the fact that they had an attentive, loving dad at home. Many women I knew raised their kids alone, their husbands always gone. And those kids turned out fine. Why did it matter if it was the man or the woman home, as long as one parent was? But that night, as I stared at my husband's red, sweaty face and unfocused eyes, I wondered if maybe I'd been wrong all along.

Maybe we were both absent parents.

I awaken in the dark to Bowie barking sharply. The floorboards creak. I sit up in bed, covers falling around my waist.

Grace?

I listen for the familiar sounds. The ones I've always assumed were her. Soft footfalls of a child. Rhythmic bouncing like that of a large ball. The plastic bouncy kind Darren used to buy for the kids from those big crates at the grocery store.

These footfalls are loud, though. Clunky.

An adult.

A man?

I glance at the clock. Two in the morning. *Hudson?* Getting out of bed, I follow the noise. When I first heard it, it seemed to be coming from the hallway, but now it sounds like it's downstairs.

The house is pitch-black. I turn on the hall light, pale yellow flooding the space. I blink as my eyes adjust, then look around to see if Bowie is following. He's nowhere to be seen.

Some watchdog.

At the bottom of the stairs, my soles hit the hardwood floor. "Hudson?" I call out.

Nothing. Creeping forward, I suppress a shiver.

I peer to my left into the kitchen. Moonlight spills inside, casting a bluish glow. It's empty. Turning to the right, I enter the family room. The light from upstairs drifts down here, and I can make out the shape of the couch and recliner, the piano beyond that.

I take a few more steps, and that's when I see Hudson, curled up in a fetal position on the couch. Why is he down here and not in his bed?

He's wearing nothing but his boxers, and he's shivering.

I reach for the blanket draped over the edge of the couch and gently lay it over him. He doesn't move. As I stare at him, I wonder if he's been sleepwalking. It's something he'd done sporadically as a child.

Once he'd gone outside and thrown a ball right through the window. Another time he'd tossed a cup of water all over his sister as she slept. She swore up and down he'd done it on purpose and only used sleepwalking as an excuse, but I believed him.

The other times, it had been like this. He'd walk into a room and either stand there, stock-still, mouth open, or curl up in a fetal position, breathing deeply. Once I found him nestled amid the shoes on the floor of my closet when I went to grab my robe off the door.

With him asleep, I feel bold. Reaching out, I place a gentle hand on his head and whisper good-night, the way I used to when he was a boy.

6

Kendra arrives an hour earlier than I'm expecting. She appears stressed, her hair a little disheveled, her face damp from sweat. She's weighted down on both sides—an oversized diaper bag on one shoulder, the car seat hanging from her right hand. Mason is sound asleep inside, his long eyelashes resting against his porcelain cheeks. As she sets him down, I marvel at how serene he is despite all of my daughter's nervous energy.

"Everything okay?" I ask.

"Yeah." She drops the diaper bag, and it lands with a thud. "It's just been a long day. Mason's been whiny. I think he's teething."

"Well, he looks peaceful now." I smile down at my grandson.

"Thank god." She blows out a breath. "He finally fell asleep on the way here."

"Where's Theo?" I glance through the front window.

"He called an hour ago to say he's working late tonight. That's why I headed over early. I needed a break."

Cupping my daughter's elbow, I smile. I haven't always been the person she runs to when in need. It feels good to be useful lately. Perhaps all it took was her becoming a mom to finally understand me better. "Come on, I'll get you a glass of wine, and you can relax."

She freezes. "You know I don't drink, Mom."

"Oh, that's right." Up until about a year and a half ago, Kendra would have the occasional drink. But when she and Theo decided to have a baby, they made a no-drinking agreement. I'd thought at first it was just going to be through the pregnancy. When she decided not to nurse, I assumed she'd have the occasional drink then. But now I get the feeling it may be indefinite. "Sorry. I forgot."

She looks over at the counter, where a half-empty wine bottle is open, flanked by two full bottles.

"I see Hudson is rubbing off on you," she says in her all-too-familiar disappointed tone.

"Oh, come on. We've just been enjoying ourselves." I wave away her comment, refusing to feel ashamed. Just because she's made the decision not to drink doesn't mean the rest of us have to follow suit. "No harm in that." I open the fridge. "I do have some iced tea made."

"That sounds good." She leans over, propping her elbows up on the counter.

I pour her a glass, the ice crackling as the tea hits it. "Sugar?"

"No, thanks." She shakes her head.

I take in her long, flowy top. She doesn't say much about it, but I know she's bothered by the extra baby weight. Mason is only six months old. These things take time. But I remember what it was like after my babies were born. The change in my body was hard for me. That's why I keep my thoughts to myself and slide the glass in her direction.

She picks it up and takes a sip.

I hear the front door pop open. "Mom, there's a stray baby in the entryway," Hudson calls out jokingly. "I'm hoping you know who it belongs to." He appears in the doorway of the kitchen, grocery bag in hand.

Smiling, Kendra turns. "That would be your nephew."

"He's gotten so big." Hudson sets the bag down on the counter.

"That's what happens with babies when you never see them. They grow." Even though Kendra's tone is trying for light, I detect the irritation underneath, and my muscles tighten.

Hudson must not pick up on it, though. He reaches out to give his sister a side-armed hug. My body uncoils as Kendra returns it.

"Mom, they were out of that coconut drink you like, but they had the lemon one," Hudson says while putting the groceries away. He rips open a big bag of sunflower seeds and pops a few in his mouth before stuffing it in the pantry.

Kendra's brows rise in a mixture of surprise and appreciation.

"That's fine," I say. "Thanks."

Hearing Bowie's paws on the floor, I hurry into the hallway. I don't want him bothering Mason. I call him to my side and stroke his fur. Mason is thankfully still asleep in his carrier, his little neck bent downward, the straps cutting into his soft skin. *That can't be safe.* As I guide Bowie toward the back door, I mull over what to do about Mason. Do I move him so his neck is upright and run the risk of waking him up or do I mention something to Kendra? I've learned the hard way that Kendra doesn't want or need my parental advice. I have to tread carefully with her.

I open the back door so Bowie can head outside. When I return to the kitchen, I pull the bag of marinated chicken out of the fridge. Without looking at Kendra, I say in a nonchalant tone, "The playpen is still set up in the office from the last time you were over." I thought I'd taken it down, but earlier today when I went to set it up, I found it already put together.

Kendra turns, peeking down the hallway. "Okay, yeah, I'll take you up on that. Looks like he's still out." She pushes off the counter, muttering under her breath, "Thank god for small favors."

While she heads out of the room, I reach into the fridge and pull out a few cheeses and a container of grapes. I had planned to have dinner ready when Kendra got here, but since she's so early, I figure I should put out some snacks.

"Want me to start the grill?" Hudson asks while I arrange the cheeses on a platter.

"Yeah, that'd be great."

I set a cluster of grapes next to the cheeses and add crackers around the sides. The scent of charcoal wafts in from an open window. I hear Kendra's footsteps in the hall. For a moment, it's as if no time has passed. Closing my eyes, I imagine Darren beside me, pouring whiskey into a small glass. I'm struck with an odd, immediate sadness. One that hits me from time to time.

Hudson re-enters the room, setting the lighter down on the counter. I scoot the cheese platter closer to him. He snatches up a grape just as Kendra walks in, heaving an audible sigh of relief.

"Got Mason down successfully?" I ask with only a twinge of disappointment. Kendra clearly needs a break, but my arms are itching to hold him.

She nods, her hand jutting out to grab a cracker. After taking a bite, she glances at her brother.

"What have you been up to since you've been back, Hudson?" she asks.

He shrugs, chewing on a piece of cheese.

Kendra's eyes narrow. "You been lookin' for work?"

His eyes shift toward me as he swallows.

"Maybe the interrogation can wait until after dinner," I say, and flash her a smile. I'd like to keep the evening light and fun.

Kendra frowns. "I was just making conversation."

"I think he has a lead on a job. Isn't that right, Hudson?"

He nods, wiping crumbs from his beard. "Not just a lead. It finally panned out. I start Monday."

This is the first I'm hearing of it. Why hadn't he told me earlier? "Oh, wow. Congratulations. This is the one with Browning's uncle?"

He nods.

"Browning?" Kendra's head cocks to the side.

As I dump the chicken out onto a platter, the juice from the marinade spatters my arm. I grab a towel and sweep it over my skin.

"Yeah, we've been hanging out a little," he says, answering her unspoken question.

Kendra lets out a harsh, grating laugh. "So that's what you've been doing since you've been back. Partying with your old friends?"

My spine straightens like a dog with its hackles up. "Kendra, he just told you he got a job. And he's been doing a lot around here. He's really been helping."

"Good," Kendra says, and to her credit, it sounds like she means it. Snapping her fingers, she pushes off the counter. "Oh, I almost forgot. I have your vitamins." She hurries into the hallway. "I also brought you some probiotics." When she returns, she holds two large pill bottles. "I've done a ton of research lately on the correlation between memory and gut health."

"Her memory actually seems pretty sharp." Hudson pops in another grape.

Kendra's head snaps in his direction, her eyes flashing. "Oh, yes, well, you would know. You've been back—what—a week?" She presses her palm to her chest. "I couldn't possibly know what I'm talking about. I've only been here every day for the past few years while you've been off doing god knows what."

Hudson huffs. "Here we go."

"What's that supposed to mean?"

"Okay. That's enough," I cut in. "Hudson's right. I've been fine this week." Smiling, I snatch the bottles out of Kendra's hands. "But I'll take the vitamins. Maybe that's what's been helping." I'm not sure this is true. For a while, I'd been taking them religiously, but I'd still felt off-kilter, my mind fuzzy. I've been more sporadic in taking them lately. Kendra's lips curl upward slightly, so I know I've appeased her. "I'm just glad you're both here. It's been so long since we've all been together."

They look at each other and smile, clearly a truce for me, but I'll take it.

"Hudson, why don't you put the chicken on the grill," I say, pointing to the dish on the counter.

Nodding, he moves around us. The scent of the grill mixed with clean air and grass wafts in when he opens the back door and heads out with the chicken.

"You don't always have to be so hard on him, you know." Going into the fridge, I slide open the middle drawer and grab a bag of salad.

"I just worry about you, Mom," she says. "He's here to take care of you, and I was making sure he's doing that."

I shake my head, laughing. "You act like I'm a hundred years old."

"Trust me, no one thinks you're a hundred."

"Okay. Eighty." I wink.

"When you're eighty, you'll probably still look better than me." Kendra's palm slides down her belly.

She often says self-deprecating things, but this feels different. Charged. She's always been built more like her dad. Got his metabolism, too. She's curvier than I am, with olive skin, large bright eyes, full lips, curly dark hair. I open my mouth to tell her how beautiful she is when a baby's cry pierces the air. Kendra's eyebrows rise, her body tensing.

"I can go grab him if you want."

She waves away my suggestion with a flick of her wrist. "Nah. That's okay. I got it." But as she leaves the room, there is a heaviness in her walk, a tightness in her muscles.

Kendra has never known when to accept help. Martyring herself is what she's good at.

While she's gone, I busy myself tossing the salad. Smoke from the grill caresses the back window, thick and gray. Once the salad is tossed, I fill a pitcher with iced water and set it down on the counter near the sink.

Babbling over my shoulder cuts into my thoughts, and I spin around.

Kendra walks in, Mason facing forward in her arms. His legs dangle under his onesie. His eyes are bright, his cheeks pink, and a pacifier plugs his mouth.

"There's my little man," I coo. Thrusting out my arms, I say, "C'mere. Come see Grandma." I never thought I'd be okay with being "Grandma." When Kendra was pregnant with Mason, she'd asked if I wanted to be Mimi, Gigi or even Glamma. But at the end of the day, I like being just plain old Grandma.

Wonders never cease.

I can't help but notice the way Kendra's expression changes into one of relief as I draw him into my arms. He smells like diaper wipes and faintly of baby powder. The top of his head is soft and silky as I run my nose over his peach fuzz.

The back door swings open. Hudson walks in, carrying a platter of chicken. Smoke rises up behind him like an exhaust pipe. Light gray tendrils float in before he can close the door with his free hand.

"It's aliiive," Hudson croons about the baby like an actor in a horror movie.

Bouncing Mason up and down, I say, "Silly Uncle."

After Hudson places the platter down on the counter, he saunters over to his nephew and tickles under his chin. Mason squirms in delight.

"He's cute. Clearly he takes after his uncle," Hudson says with a wink.

Kendra smirks, one eyebrow raised. "Is that so?"

I'd forgotten how much I missed this. The bantering. Teasing.

Knocking at the front door interrupts us, and I feel a little annoyed. I know it's Theo, and I have nothing against him, but now that he's here, the dynamic will change. He's more like Kendra. Intellectual, bordering on arrogant. Pensive and a little quiet. Not that I expected Kendra to marry someone fun-loving like Hudson, but it would've been nice. Maybe even loosen her up a bit.

"Sorry I'm late," Theo says, checking the watch wrapped around his wrist as he enters. He wears slacks and a collared shirt, his hair gelled to the side. He's good-looking, I'll give him that. Polite, too, I think as he leans over to peck me on the cheek, thanking me for having him over.

Mason is happy to see him, kicking and smiling the minute Theo says hello. I hand the baby over to his dad.

"Dinner's ready," I say.

"Well, I got here just in time, then." Theo smiles, showing off a row of insanely white teeth.

He and Hudson catch up as Kendra and I set the table. Dinner is uneventful. Theo talks a lot about work, taking up most of the conversation with things I couldn't care less about. The world of finance isn't something I find fascinating. The bored look on Hudson's face as he shovels food into his mouth shows me he feels the same way. But at least he and Kendra aren't arguing.

Thank god for small favors.

Kendra interjects a few times to share how nursing school's going. And Mason babbles from his high chair occasionally, forcing us all to pay attention to him. When he does this, I wonder if he's as tired of the conversation as the rest of us.

After dinner, Hudson offers to clean up while I put on a pot of coffee and get out dessert.

"I'll take this little man, then." Theo tosses his napkin down, walks over to the high chair and pulls Mason out.

"You have to wipe him off first," Kendra says, her tone severe.

"He's fine," Theo says between gritted teeth.

"He's gonna get food all over your shirt."

"I don't care," Theo says, smiling at Mason and drawing him close.

"Oh, really? *You* don't care about how you look. That would be a first."

Hudson throws me a *yikes* expression as he balances a stack of plates on his arm and deliberately walks into the kitchen. I trail behind him as Kendra says, "Stop bouncing him, Theo. He just ate."

"Are they always like that?" Hudson asks, turning on the kitchen faucet.

"Um…not always. But you know how Kendra is."

"Yeah, I do." Hudson chuckles, snatching up a rag.

Kendra and Theo's bickering continues in the other room as Hudson finishes up the dishes and the coffee percolates.

"What do you think about having…" I blink. My mind is nothing but a dark, black space. Completely blank. The word is on the tip of my tongue. One I use all the time. I'm staring at it on the counter, and yet I can't for the life of me remember the word… *Oh, god. I am turning into my mom.* I swallow hard, my mouth drying out.

"Yes?" One side of Hudson's mouth curls upward in an amused way.

He's not worried, and I get that. When the kids were younger, I did this kind of thing all the time. But that was different. Back then I was struck with inspiration, a song lyric leaping into my mind at inopportune moments, causing me to lose my train of thought.

"Umm…" I reach for a word I can remember. "Coffee and…" I point at the platter on the counter, at the thing I can't say.

"Dessert?" Hudson helps me out, and only then do I see a slight frown, a deepening of the creases in his forehead.

To ease his worry, I let out a light laugh. "Yes, sorry, I got distracted."

"Eavesdropping on their argument?" He smiles knowingly, his head bobbing toward the dining room, where Kendra and Theo are speaking heatedly in hushed tones.

I don't answer, but I know he takes it as a yes by the smirk he flashes me. I smile back, allowing him to think that.

"Anyway, should we take this all out to the front porch?" I ask Hudson, thinking of evenings a decade or more ago, kids eating ice cream on the steps while Darren and I sat on the porch swing. I'm determined not to let my momentary brain lapse get the best of me.

"That sounds cool," he says in his normal, chill tone. Sometimes I wonder what it would take to excite him at this age.

I fix a tray with a carafe of coffee, my fancy china cups and two slices of pie. I know Theo and Kendra won't have any of the dessert. They're always on some diet or another. Then I carry the tray out to the front porch and set it down on the wicker table next to the porch swing. The air is cool, smelling of roses and damp grass. Above me the porch light clicks on as the sun lowers. Birds chirp in the distance. Somewhere on the street I hear a cat meowing.

When everyone else joins me, I take Mason into my arms and sit with him on the porch swing. Pushing with my toe, we swing back and forth, and he lets out a squeal. Hudson digs into a piece of pie, but Kendra sticks to coffee. Theo comes out with his wineglass replenished, and I'm a little surprised. He'd had a glass at dinner as well. Apparently their no-drinking agreement has become one-sided. Kendra eyes him, raising a brow as if to let him know she notices, too.

"Do you see that bird, Mase?" I point to a hummingbird, hovering over the bird feeder hanging from the porch awning. Its feathers are red with shiny blue accents. Mason coos and smiles, his arms lifting as if to grab it.

Hudson finishes his piece of pie, discarding the plate on a table nearby.

"I've never understood how you can eat so many sweets and stay thin," Kendra says, her bottom lip protruding like she's about to pout. "Remember our trip to Disneyland when you were like eight, and you literally had a dozen churros a day?"

"Not a dozen." Hudson shakes his head. "But a lot."

Kendra laughs.

"A dozen churros? That's nasty, man." Theo wrinkles his nose in disgust.

I often wonder if he was ever a child, or if he was born an adult.

"Nasty? Have you never had a churro? They're delicious," Hudson counters.

"They're good, but not dozen a day good," Kendra says.

"Wasn't that also the trip where you tossed my Mickey Mouse ears out of the car window on our drive home?" Hudson asks his sister.

"Only 'cause you kept hitting me in the head with them."

Hudson laughs. "Oh. Right. Well, I'm sure you deserved it."

At this, Theo laughs, too.

"Is that girl waving at us?" Kendra sits forward, squinting.

I scoot forward, too, looking in that direction. A pretty young woman is jogging, white earbud cords hanging from her ears. She slows her pace, waving up at the porch.

"I don't know her," Kendra adds. "Do you?" I think she means me, but it's Theo who answers.

"Oh, yeah. Molly, hi." Theo moves down the front steps.

The young woman tugs the cords from her ears and stops running. She saunters forward to meet Theo, walking up the first few steps.

"I didn't know you lived around here," Theo says.

"Yeah, I rent a place right around the corner. Can't miss it. It's the smallest one on the street and has a giant flag sticker on the mailbox," she says. I can picture it. I pass by it every morning on my walk with Bowie. The woman points upward. "Is this your house?"

"No, my mother-in-law's." He indicates me and then says, "Molly and I work together. Molly, this is my beautiful wife,

Kendra, my son, Mason, my mother-in-law, Valerie, and brother-in-law, Hudson."

Kendra's hello is a little lackluster, not that I blame her. I never liked it when I met gorgeous women who worked with Darren. I can't help but notice Hudson's smile has grown infinitely larger now that Molly's here.

After she returns to her jog, Hudson slaps Theo on the back. "Man, she is hot."

"Nice." Kendra rolls her eyes.

"Dude, hook me up," Hudson adds.

"Really?" Theo raises his brows, then shrugs. "Okay, I'll see what I can do."

7

"Mom? Mom?" Hudson's voice is echoey as if he's speaking in a large, empty cathedral, the words bouncing back in an eternal loop.

It's warm and bright here—not a cathedral, I think dreamily, but a big, empty stage, blazing under the wash of the spotlights. I hate to leave it, but his words keep yanking at me.

"Mom." This time his tone is more insistent.

I jolt at a firm hand on my shoulder. Reality comes into view, light floating in through the window and painting the floor.

"Are you okay?" Hudson's teeth look like they're about to pierce his bottom lip. His pinched eyes and gathered forehead make him appear much older than he is.

"What time is it?" I ask groggily, hoisting myself up to a seated position. Squinting, I peer out the living room window, at the sun high in the sky.

"Three-thirty," Hudson answers.

"In the afternoon?" On the table in front of me is a half-drunk cup of coffee, an empty glass.

"Yeah. I had my first day at the mine today, and I just got home."

Oh, that's right. He'd already been gone when I woke up this morning.

I'm wearing my walking clothes, shoes still on my feet. Have I been lying here since my walk? Pinching the bridge of my nose, I desperately search for the day I've clearly lost.

Theo's face materializes in my mind, and I'm momentarily confused as to why. But then I remember: he stopped by yesterday evening. I'd been surprised by his arrival and for a few panicky seconds thought I'd forgotten about watching Mason again.

But then he'd said, "I'm taking Hudson out. Guy's night, you know?"

I did vaguely recall them making plans for Sunday night on Friday when everyone was over.

Theo called up the stairs for Hudson, checked his wristwatch, pulled out his phone. When Hudson swaggered into the room wearing cologne, a wrinkle-free shirt, his nicest pair of jeans, his hair styled, I briefly wondered if this outing had anything to do with the pretty blonde girl Theo had introduced us to.

The rest of the night is a bit of a blur. I think I had a glass or two of wine, and watched some TV. *The Crown*, maybe?

But what about today?

Leaning forward, I finger the mug on the table. A few sips of coffee are left at the bottom, the scent of vanilla cream still lingering. With my shoes still on, my toes feel a little sweaty in my socks.

But what did I do after I went for my walk and had coffee?

I return my attention to Hudson, who has now given up

his post hunched over me and is perched on the other end of the couch. His wary expression has yet to vanish, though.

"How was your first day?" I ask, feeling bad that I haven't yet.

"Good."

"You weren't too tired after your guy's night?"

He shakes his head. "We didn't stay out too late. We both had work this morning."

"I was a little surprised you two went out," I say honestly.

"Me, too. It was his idea. I almost said no, but thought, what the heck. He's my brother-in-law. I should give him a chance, you know?" A slow smile creeps across his face. "And you know what? That guy isn't half bad."

"Really?" This is even more shocking to me. "Did he drink?"

Hudson hesitates, then says, "Yeah, but don't tell Kendra."

"Don't worry. I'm not getting involved in this." I rub my fingers over my temples to suppress my raging headache. I hear the dog door swinging open from the kitchen, and Bowie's paws on the floor. He bounds into the room and heads straight to me. I lower my tired arm, resting my hand on his head.

Hudson's smile slips. "Are you sick?"

"Yeah, maybe." I press the back of my hand to my own forehead, the way I used to do for my children when they were young. My skin does feel hot. Honestly, I feel relieved. A virus, I can handle. Losing the entire day to Alzheimer's is something I cannot. Not yet.

Not now.

Reaching up, I touch my greasy hair and cringe. "I need to take a shower."

"Why don't I help you upstairs?" Hudson stands, reaching for my arm.

I gratefully accept his help, allowing him to guide me upward. As we walk up the stairs, I rest my head against his shoulder. Bowie passes us and disappears into my room before we reach the fourth step. My mouth is dry, my tongue sticky. I swallow hard. Once inside my room, I shake Hudson off. I'm desperate to change out of my walking clothes. They still feel damp as they cling to my skin in an uncomfortable way.

"I'll be fine," I say to him. "Thanks."

"You sure?"

I nod.

"Okay." He starts to back out of the room, but then stops. "Let me know if you need anything."

"I will."

While I'm in the shower, a wave of nausea rolls over me, and I have to lean against the wall, breathing deeply in and out until it subsides. When it finally does, I wash my hair and body swiftly and then turn off the water. Shivering, I wrap myself in a towel. Moisture fills my mouth as the nausea returns.

Dropping to my knees, I hunch over the toilet bowl. Nothing comes out, though. Maybe I just need to eat something. Peeling myself off the floor, I go into my room and put on a pair of fuzzy jammies.

Bowie leaps onto my bed, already curling up at the bottom as if anticipating I'll be in it soon.

Too weary to go downstairs, I lie in my bed, propping the pillows up under my head. I know I should eat something— it's well past lunch and I can't remember eating anything this morning. Then I text Hudson, asking if he could bring me a bowl of soup.

For sure, he texts back.

Within fifteen minutes, he enters with a bowl of soup on a TV tray. I force myself to eat half of it before he returns to retrieve the bowl.

I read for a little bit before falling back into a deep sleep.

My dreams are disjointed, a jumble of memories that don't fit together.

Heather sitting in my living room looking exactly like she did the last time I saw her, drinking tea with her mom. But Leslie's not the age she was back then. At first it's hard to tell. She's worn her hair in the same style for fifteen years. A short, bleached bob. She's always worn one side tucked behind her ear, too. It's her clothes that show her age—the elastic pants and floral top, indicative of the way she dresses now...

I join them, my own cup of tea in hand, just as Kendra walks in holding Mason. We all sit together chatting like nothing is amiss.

Several times in the night, I awaken from stomach pain and nausea. When I do, I find proof of Hudson's presence. A cup of fresh water on the nightstand, a plate of crackers and one time miraculously still-fizzy Sprite in a glass. It gets me through the night.

And in the morning, I feel a little better.

On my way to the kitchen, I pass the living room, noticing that Hudson has cleaned up my mess from yesterday. The cups have been picked up, the blanket folded on the edge of the couch, the pillows fluffed.

The kitchen is bright and airy. Even though I feel a lot better, my stomach is still a little iffy, so I decide to stick with a piece of toast. I pop a slice of bread into the toaster before filling the coffeepot.

Leslie is outside talking with Beth and Shelly. She's wearing the same kind of elastic-waisted pants and floral top that she'd had on in my dream as if she'd stepped right out of it and onto her front porch. It causes a chill to brush up my back. Staring at them, I think about how different our lives could have turned out. In my dream, we'd been having tea together with our daughters. It's what I'd envisioned for our future back when we were friends. For seven years, I saw Heather almost daily. She was as familiar to me as my own children. Her laugh, her smile, her mannerisms—I knew them like the back of my hand. Now they haunt my dreams.

"Mom?" Hudson's voice startles me. I'd assumed he'd already left for work. But then I glance at the clock. It's early. Way earlier than I usually wake up.

I whirl around, feeling like a child caught with her hand in the cookie jar. Forcing a shaky smile, I'm glad he can't read my thoughts. Then he'd know that I was thinking about the one thing we never talk about—Heather—and what we did.

On Wednesday morning I find Hudson's car still parked in the driveway, even after I return from walking Bowie. He should be gone by now.

Worried he's slept through his work alarm, I rap on his bedroom door. "Hudson?"

No response.

I try again, knocking louder this time.

Through the door, I hear rustling, a muffled moan. I step back, hand suspended in the air. Is someone in there with him?

Biting my lip, I whirl away from the door, having no desire to walk in on him and a girl. I'd done my share of that when he was younger.

That's actually how I'd found out his and Heather's relationship had changed. She practically lived at our house back then. Hudson and Heather had become fast friends within a month of her family moving into the neighborhood. She was the only other child on the street who was Hudson's age. I wasn't sure whether their being a boy and a girl would matter at that point, whether they'd have already grown awkward or self-conscious around the opposite sex—but I needn't have worried.

Daily, they were running back and forth between our two houses. They spent hours on Hudson's Nintendo, elbowing each other over *Mario Kart*, taking turns coaching one another through *Zelda*. The summer they were twelve, they made movie after movie on Leslie's digital camera, mostly slapstick murder mysteries in which Heather played a detective and Hudson every other character including the victims. Hudson loved baseball and, with the right needling, could usually coax Heather into throwing a ball around the backyard, unless her friend Katie O'Connell was over—it used to irritate Hudson to no end when she'd show up and Heather chose "girl time."

One afternoon when the kids were fifteen, Leslie called and asked me to send Heather home to help with dinner. I knew they were upstairs in Hudson's room—I could hear music filtering down through the floor—and I didn't even consider knocking before barging inside.

Their mouths were fused, their hands locked around each other's bodies.

Immediately, they shoved off of one another, looking stricken. Heather didn't even need to be told that her mother had called—she'd just grabbed her backpack and fled, mumbling, "Bye, Valerie."

"Are you really that shocked?" Mac had asked me when I told him at our band's practice later, and I guess I wasn't. "Their hormones are raging. Their brains are under scaffolding."

"Thanks for that analogy," I'd responded sourly, but I knew he was right.

Now, hesitating at Hudson's door, I hear him call out in a weak tone, "Mom?"

I push the door open, and he rolls over in his bed, his bloodshot eyes connecting with mine. His face is sweaty and pale.

"Oh, god, it got you, too, huh?" Cringing, I back away, keeping my distance.

"Seems like it," he mumbles. "Thanks a lot."

I laugh lightly. "Well, the good news is it's only a twenty-four-hour bug. You should be better by tomorrow. I know I felt terrible on Monday, but by Tuesday morning I was right as rain." Oh, god, did I really just use that phrase? My mom used to say that.

He groans.

"Can I get you anything?"

He shakes his head.

"Did you call into work?"

He nods, eyes closed.

"Okay, get some rest."

He grunts in response as I close the door.

The hallway is quiet, the clock ticking downstairs.

Hickory, dickory, dock,
The mouse ran up the clock...

Something was inside the wall. It scratched late at night when I lay in my bed, long after being tucked in. The first night I heard it, I got down on my hands and knees and crawled under my bed, trying to figure out what it was. For a few panicked seconds, I got stuck there, the rust-colored carpet choking me, but I never did find it.

Afterward, I ran into my parents' room, and headed straight for their bed.

I padded across the carpet to reach them. Dad faced the wall, arm tucked under his pillow. I almost giggled. We slept the same. Mom was closest to me, her face staring up at the ceiling, her arms down by her sides. She looked like the pictures I'd seen of mummies in their tombs. I reached out and poked her shoulder.

She jolted, gasped.

"Oh, my god. You scared me to death," she said.

I wished I could hide then. Slip into a cubby in the shelving built into the wall behind my parents' bed. Or better yet, disappear like the Invisible Woman.

"I'm scared," I said, admitting I wasn't a superhero at all.

"Of what?" she asked, sitting up.

"There's something in my wall. I can hear it scratching."

Mom sighed. "There is nothing in your wall. You're just imagining it."

"But there is," I insisted, tugging on her arm. "Come see."

"I'm too tired for this." Drawing her arm out of my grasp, she ran a hand down her face, pushed back her hair. "You need to go back to bed. You're fine."

I glanced at Dad, wishing I'd woken him instead.

"I mean it. Go to bed." Mom was already lying back down. There was no changing her mind.

Reluctantly, I slunk into the hallway, huffing and puffing the whole way. But Mom was not swayed. I could hear her even breathing as if she'd already fallen asleep again.

"It's a mouse."

I squealed and jumped, Andie's voice startling me. She stood in front of me, long nightgown skimming her bare feet.

"What?" I held my palm to my heart and breathed deeply.

"The scratching in the wall. It's a mouse. Trapped."

"Trapped?" I felt cold all of a sudden, little bumps rising on my skin until my arms looked like chicken legs before they're cooked.

She shrugged. "But don't worry. It'll die soon."

"It will?"

"Yeah," she said, like I was stupid. "But that's a good thing, right? Then you won't have to hear the noise anymore."

I nodded, but my stomach felt all yucky like that time I got the flu.

"Besides, it's the mouse's fault for going in there."

Every night since then, I'd been unable to sleep. Clutching the edge of my covers, I lay in bed on my side and listened to the scratching. I stared at the wall, picturing the mouse stuck inside the small space, unable to get out. I wondered if the scratching was for my benefit. Could the mouse hear me? Was it hoping I'd try to rescue it? Mom would kill me if I tried to cut a hole in the wall. How would I go about doing that, anyway? I remembered that few panicked seconds when I thought I was stuck under the bed, and then I felt sick thinking of how many days the poor mouse had been in there. When I couldn't take it anymore, I'd cover my ears with my hands.

"It's the mouse's fault for going in there."

My sister's words floated through my mind. Was that what she really thought? That the mouse was getting what it deserved.

Should one wrong move seal our fate?

8

Tap. Tap. Tap.

The sound is soft at first, barely audible, fusing with the show I'm watching. Then it increases. I grab the remote, click the volume down. The television goes blank. Darkness envelops me. I blink. Must have pushed the wrong button. I'm always confusing them lately. As my eyes adjust, objects come into view. The shape of my feet under the throw blanket, tenting it at the edges. Beyond that, a dark figure. My skin prickles. A young girl stands by the couch, holding a large ball in the crook of her arm.

"Grace," I whisper, running my fingers along the blanket to steady myself. In the corner, Bowie sleeps peacefully. I wish he was over here with me.

Tap. Tap. Tap.

Wait. That's not right. She's not bouncing the ball. She's standing stock-still.

I twist around in the dark. The tapping is coming from

upstairs. When I look back to where Grace had been stand-ing, my shoulders sag. There is no girl. Only the recliner, my jacket draped over the side.

The tapping continues.

My bare feet are ice against the hardwood floors. While the cool air and breeze felt great this morning at breakfast, it had gotten colder as the day progressed. By ten o'clock the temps had dropped down into the sixties, as if we'd bypassed the rest of summer and were heading into fall. My wardrobe hasn't got-ten the memo yet. I still have on my summertime pajamas, pants and a T-shirt, but lightweight, unlike my winter flannel ones.

I hurry up the stairs. Hudson's door is open, but I know he's not home. He went out with friends tonight. Just like he has the last few nights. I'd been right. The bug he got from me only lasted twenty-four hours. He was good as new by Thursday. It's Saturday now, and he's hardly been home in the last several days.

I step forward, peek inside. As expected, the room is empty.

The tapping has stopped.

What had it been?

I stand still in the middle of the hallway, holding my breath, straining to hear. The only sounds are Bowie's deep breath-ing from downstairs, the wind outside, the house settling. No tapping.

Turning, I take a step toward my room, and hear it again. This time it's more like knocking.

Palms moistening, I hurry back down the stairs. Bowie's head lifts from his bed in the corner when I enter the family room. Snapping my fingers, I urge him to my side. The noise is coming from somewhere past the kitchen. I inch my way across the floor, squinting. The back porch is dimly lit, cast-ing an eerie blue glow.

A loud slamming noise comes from the backyard. I flinch.

Bowie barks, darting out the dog door.

My pulse quickens as I unlock the back door and turn the knob. A gust of cool air sprays me in the face, stealing my breath momentarily. It's even cooler now, the wind fierce—a summer storm. My hair whips around my face as if I'm holding a hairdryer to it. I sputter, calling out for Bowie. His barking rings out from the far side of the yard.

Batting my hair out of my eyes, I follow his voice.

The side gate swings back and forth, whacking the fence repeatedly.

Ah, the knocking.

I force the gate closed and lock it, wondering why it was open in the first place. The wind couldn't have knocked the lock loose. I rack my brain. Had I left it unlocked at any point?

I can't remember.

Her eyes are wide. Blank. Her jaw slackens, a little drool clinging to her lips. "Who are you? What do you want?" She speaks in a jarring, angry tone.

"It's me, Mom. Valerie." I reach out to touch her bony fingers, but she swats them away.

It was Hudson who had taken out the trash last. Maybe he'd left it unlocked and I only just now noticed because of the wind. *Yes, that has to be it.*

Satisfied, I beckon Bowie. My teeth are chattering by the time I reach the back door. A few days ago, I'd been lamenting the heat. Now I'm shivering and hugging myself, fantasizing about a warm bath.

When we reach the top of the stairs, Bowie growls, throwing his back end up like he's preparing to attack. Heat snakes up my spine. Sitting directly in front of my bedroom door is a bouncy ball. I step forward, reach out and scoop it up. It's bubblegum pink and smells like cheap plastic. But it's real. Not a figment of my imagination.

I look up and down the hallway. It's eerily quiet.
Where did it come from?

Before I finally fell asleep last night, I left the ball next to
my bed. This morning, it's not there. I search for it but find
nothing. Had I dreamed it? Or am I officially losing my mind?
The sky is overcast, gray clouds lining it, but the wind has
died down. It looks like it might rain later, so I hurriedly put
on a pair of joggers, a long-sleeved shirt and tennis shoes. I
love early morning walks before a storm when the air feels
crisp and fresh.

Bowie trails after me as I leave my room. When I get to
Hudson's, his door is slightly ajar. I'd heard him get in around
3:00 a.m. Had he taken the ball? It seems unlikely, but I can't
stop myself. I have to check. At this point, I can't be certain
it was even real, but I'm desperate to prove to myself it was.

The door creaks as I press it open with my palm. Behind
me, Bowie races down the stairs, clearly ready for his walk.
Inside, Hudson is asleep, faceup, arm bent under his head.

There's no ball in sight. Standing on my tiptoes, I try to see
the other side of his bed, but I'm not tall enough, so I walk
quietly, making sure to check every inch of his floor. Hudson
is shirtless, and with the way he's holding his arm, I finally get
a good look at his tattoo. There's a word circling his bicep, but
it's in a different language, so I can't decipher it.

My breath catches in my throat. Underneath the tattoo is
a pear-sized, deep purple bruise. Squinting, I move closer to
him, noticing a fresh scratch on his face, the skin around it
raised and pink, the line disappearing into his beard. Was he
in a fight?

He stirs, rolling in my direction, his arm sliding off the pillow and falling to his side.

I hold my breath. Not wishing to get caught standing over

my grown son's bed, I back slowly away. I don't make it far before his hand clamps around my wrist. I suppress a shocked squeal.

"No," he says, his voice muffled, sleepy. "Don't go."

I look back at him. His hold tightens, but his eyes are still closed, his breathing deep.

"It's okay," I say, prying his fingers from my arm. Once free, I tiptoe away from the bed.

"I didn't mean to," he whispers when I reach the doorway. I freeze.

"I'm sorry," he says so quietly, I wonder if he's said the words at all or if I imagined them.

As I reach for the handle of his door to tug it closed, his cell phone lights up. I can't help but lean over and peek. It's a Facebook notification. Someone commenting on a post. It irks me. Hudson has never accepted a friend request from me. The only reason I joined Facebook was to stalk my children, mostly Hudson, since Kendra only posts medical articles. I've asked Hudson why many times, and his response is always that he rarely uses his Facebook account. I believe him because I know he doesn't often have use of a computer or phone. It appears that maybe he's active now.

However, that's not what catches my attention.

It's the text above it.

The one that says: Bro, stop hitting me up or I'm gonna block you.

The name of the texter is listed only as Blondie.

Another bark rings out.

Hudson's body reacts, twitching as if startled. I click his door closed and hurry down the stairs. Bowie is right where I suspected, a ball of nervous energy in front of the door. His tail whacks me in the leg as I hook his leash onto his collar.

The minute I open the front door, he tears down the steps. It takes all my strength not to topple down them.

The neighborhood is quiet this morning. No cars driving down the street. No people outside. I find myself wishing for a simpler time when I didn't have to worry about Hudson being out all hours of the night, coming home with bruising and scratches or getting cryptic messages from girls named Blondie. Where could that scratch have come from? Was he so drunk that he fell? And what kind of fall would result in a scratch on the face? Maybe it happened during a run—he scraped it on a tree branch or something—although, if that were the case, I probably would've noticed it yesterday. And it did seem awfully fresh.

Up ahead, commotion catches my attention. Police cars. Officers roaming about. Yellow crime tape running the perimeter of a yard to my right.

My stomach drops. I know that house. It's the one with the patriotic sticker on the mailbox, one of Bowie's favorite sniffs, now an anchor for fluttering police tape. It's the same house Theo's coworker had said she lived in.

A couple stands nearby in their pajamas, eyes wide as they take in the scene from the yard of the house next door. I yank on Bowie's leash, slowing him down.

"What's going on?" I ask the couple.

"They found a body," the woman says, her gray bob swinging as she shakes her head.

My mouth dries out. "Whose body?"

"The woman who lived there," the man says impatiently, like the answer should be obvious.

I search my brain for her name. "Molly?" I croak.

The woman beside him nods, confirming my suspicion. "Apparently, her friend came to pick her up for some fitness class and found her."

"Oh, my god." My hand flies to my mouth, acid rising up in my throat. "How did she die?"

"No idea." The man shakes his head.

"I saw her with some guy yesterday, though," the woman says. "Some young guy with a big beard."

My stomach knots. *Hudson.*

"I'm sure she talks to lots of people. Best to leave the investigation up to the police," I say quickly. It might not have even been foul play, I think, and then shudder that my mind went there so fast. It could've been an accident. An undiagnosed heart condition. An illness. Suicide. These things happen.

No one knows that better than me.

"It's true," the man interjects, his frown changing ever so slightly, transforming his look of concern into one of judgment. "Lots of guys in and out of there." His tone, a mixture of jealousy and disgust, is one I'm familiar with.

It's the same one people used to use when talking about me.

"She's gone a lot. Playing at clubs at all hours."

"Must be interesting being in a band with all guys. I'm not sure my husband could deal with that."

It makes me feel bad for my earlier statement. Who cares if she talked to a lot of guys? I never should've added to the gossip. Years ago, after my friendship with Leslie ended, I swore to myself I'd never again get sucked into unhealthy conversations behind people's backs. It wasn't fair, and it never ended well.

Without another word, I tug on Bowie's leash, guiding him back the way we came.

When I reach my house, I notice Leslie sitting on her front porch, cup of tea in hand.

I slow down but my heart is racing, my breath shallow. She's the last person I want to see right now. Her intense stare burns a hole in my head.

Swallowing, I turn away from her and make my way up to the front door.

Hudson is still asleep, his door closed the way I left it. The sound of his deep breathing, along with the occasional snore, follow me into my bedroom. I think about the text, the bruising and the scratch.

He hadn't gotten in until 3:00 a.m.

"I'm scared, Mom. I think I might be in big trouble."

What time had Molly died?

Shaking my head, I force the thoughts away. He'd gone out with his friends last night. Not with a girl. He'd met Molly one time, with the rest of us. Unless the young man the woman was referring to really was Hudson. Then again, she was older. Forgetful like me.

Why am I even thinking like this? I blame Leslie. All that stalking and staring is getting to me.

What happened to Molly is a tragedy, yes, but Hudson wasn't involved. It's nothing like what happened with Heather.

9

"Wanna go get dinner? I'm starving," I say Sunday evening when I find Hudson in the kitchen grabbing a bottle of water out of the fridge. He'd slept most of the day. Even after he'd woken up, he mostly stayed in his room. I heard the TV going.

I'd worked on some of my succulent planters outside, played with Bowie and then showered. My hair is damp at the edges.

"Yeah, me, too," Hudson says, unscrewing the top of the bottle. "Let me just go change real quick."

He's still wearing his flannel pajama bottoms under his T-shirt, and as he lifts the bottle to his lips, the bruise on his arm is fully visible. Under the harsh kitchen light, the scratch on his face looks even worse than before.

"What happened?" I ask, blocking his path and pointing to his arm.

"Oh." He rolls his eyes. "Just got into it with some guy at the bar last night."

"You got into a fight?" I'm taken aback by how nonchalant he's being about this.

He shrugs like it's no big deal. "It happens." Then he moves around me to get past.

While he makes his way back to his room, Bowie's ears perk from where he was lying on the ground. Barking, he shoots up, suddenly wide-awake, and races to the front window.

"What is it, bud?" I follow him.

Outside, Leslie stands on her front lawn, two other people talking with her. Squinting, I get a better look and recognize Beth and Alex, the couple who live to the right of her. They're newer to the neighborhood. Been here about three years or so. They've got small kids, and my guess is that they're in their early thirties, although I've only had a handful of shallow conversations with them. Leslie got her claws into them early on, and then their initial friendliness turned sour.

From this vantage point, I can tell Leslie is doing most of the talking, which isn't surprising. Her hands fly through the air, punctuating each syllable, as if she's miming. Her hand suddenly stills, her index finger pointed straight at me. All three heads swing in my direction. I feel like I'm on display, my window a stage, the lamp in the corner a spotlight. Face flushing, I turn away.

"Come on, Bowie," I say, my tone wavering slightly.

The policeman's eyes bore into mine, accusation thick in his gaze. Fear licking down my spine, I chose my words carefully. But all the lies in the world couldn't wash away the guilt, couldn't take away the knowledge that I was to blame.

Hudson re-enters the room wearing the same T-shirt, but has switched out the flannel pants for a pair of jeans. His hair's neater than before: he's just brushed and gelled it. "Ready?"

"Yep. Can you drive?" I ask. It's getting dark, and my vision isn't what it once was, especially at night.

"Sure," he says.

The chatter across the street floats toward us. When I glance up, I'm relieved to see all three of them retreating into their own homes. *I guess the gossip session has ended.*

"Wanna take your car? Mine's a mess."

"Maybe you should clean it," I chide.

"Yeah. Maybe," he says with a hint of sarcasm.

I yank my keys out of my purse, and then drop them into his waiting palm. "Okay. We'll take mine."

"Where to?" he asks as he reverses the car out of the driveway.

"Let's go to Paesanos," I say.

"Paesanos it is." Hudson flicks on the blinker.

I settle back into my seat, clutching my purse in my lap, and already dreaming up what I'll order. I often order the spaghetti carbonara, but I think I'm leaning toward the tortellini tonight.

A wisp of bold yellow catches my eye. We are coming up on Molly's house. I straighten up, pointing to the crime tape. "Do you remember that girl Theo introduced us to? That's her house."

He slows the car to check it out, eyebrows rising. "The one with the crime tape?"

I nod, waiting for him to give me any indication that he might have seen her after Friday night. Had Theo tried to hook them up the way he promised?

But he doesn't offer up any information, simply asks, "What happened?"

"She died," I whisper, although I'm not sure why. The crime tape blurs as we pass by.

"Are you serious?"

I nod again.

"How?"

"No idea," I say. "Her friend found her body this morning."

"Oh, my god. That's wild."

Silence falls over the car, as if neither of us knows what to say now.

Death has a way of doing that. Shocking you into silence.

I'm grateful when we pull up to the restaurant.

At Paesanos, they seat us at a little pub table near the front window. It's warm again tonight, so I'm grateful for the AC spilling from the vent above us. The place is packed, every table filled. The sound of laughter, chatter and dishes clinking floods the room. Warm light glows.

"I've come here with friends before, but I don't think I've ever been here with you," Hudson muses aloud, staring down at the glossy menu in his hand.

"Yeah, your dad wasn't a big fan," I explain, closing my menu and placing it on the table. I already know I'm ordering the tortellini. "But Suzanne and I used to come here all the time."

"Suzanne." Hudson smiles, and I'm certain he's remembering a funny story with her. She has that effect on people. "How's she doing?"

"She's doing really well. Same old Suzanne."

Our drinks arrive, and then the waitress comes to take our order.

"Is she still running that bar?" Hudson asks after the waitress leaves. He lifts the frosty mug of beer to his lips, foam sticking to his beard when he draws it back.

"Yep. No doubt she'll be running that place until the day she dies," I say, and then cringe, thinking of Molly. What was she doing when she died? I run my fingertips along the stem of my wineglass.

"Man, I haven't been there in years. Does it look the same?"

I take a sip, lower the glass, then shrug. "I'm not sure. I haven't been there in years either."

"Why not?" he asked. "You used to hang out there all the time."

"Exactly. Back when I was in the band," I say. "Now it reminds me of a life I no longer have."

After Darren's diagnosis, I was home taking care of him and rarely went out at night. He'd retired from the state, and his pension had kicked in. That, along with the royalties I still received from the songs I've written, kept me going financially, so I didn't have to go out for work anymore.

In the months following his death, I would sometimes go to the club to see Suzanne. But being there made me sad. Too many memories. Besides, Suzanne and I get together regularly for lunch or breakfast, and we talk on the phone all the time. I don't need to see her at the bar.

There was a time when I went out almost every night, but lately, I've become a homebody.

"We should go," Hudson says abruptly.

Curious, I peer up at him. "What?"

"Yeah, you and me." He points back and forth between us. "We should go."

"Really? You'd want to go to the bar with your mom?"

"For sure."

The waitress returns with our food. After thanking her, I pluck up my fork and spear it through my steaming pasta. Hudson picks up a piece of his pizza, bites into it.

After swallowing, he wipes his mouth with a napkin. "Let's go tonight."

"What?" His words were muffled behind his napkin, and I'm certain I misheard him.

"Yeah, we should go after dinner," he says as if he's already made the decision.

"I don't know." I uncross my legs under the table, bounce the toes of my shoes up and down on the floor.

"C'mon, it'll be lit."

Lit? "I don't know about that."

He laughs. "You gotta live a little, Mom."

I'm about to protest again, but I don't want to erase the broad smile from his face. I also have no desire to cut our night short. It's the first night in many that he hasn't been out with friends. I have him all to myself. "Okay, but I don't wanna be out too late." I have to maintain some semblance of control. I know how late Hudson usually stays out.

"Me neither. I have to work in the morning."

From over Hudson's shoulder, I'm distracted by a family entering. The little girl talks loudly, her lips moving swiftly, reminding me of how fast Kendra used to talk. I recognize the look on the mom's face—semi-interested, semi-annoyed. Returning my attention to our table, Hudson is leaning over his plate, clamping his mouth over another large piece of pizza.

I'd been about to say something, hadn't I? Or ask him something? What had we been talking about?

I rack my brain, but it's blank.

Sighing, I take a bite of my pasta, savoring the creaminess of the sauce, the richness of the flavors.

"So, we're on, then?"

"On for what?" I ask after swallowing.

"The Tavern after dinner?"

Oh, that's right, we'd been talking about stopping by the Full Moon. "Sure," I say, even though I'm not sure at all.

When Hudson pulls into the parking lot of the Full Moon Tavern, I hold tightly to the door handle. Hudson guides the car into an empty space, and I instinctively find Suzanne's pale green pickup truck in the far corner near the employee entrance.

I see the ghost of my former self, helping the guys load equipment into the van after a gig. Sitting on the edge of Suzanne's pickup truck, smoking a cigarette, puffs of smoke evaporating into the black night sky. Laughing with Suzanne as she regales me with stories of customers' outrageous demands. The guys teasing each other, laughing and joking as we headed to our cars. A slap on the back, "Good job tonight." A round of winks. Smiles. Thumbs-up.

And Mac. Always Mac.

Following me to my car. Whispering in my ear.

Then heading to his car alone, a swagger in his step.

But he was alive. So alive.

Hudson turns off the engine, opens his door. A rush of evening air pours in, smelling familiar, of nights gone by. I tighten my grip on my door handle, wondering why I'd agreed to this. We could be on our way home, to warmth and wine and Bowie.

A couple emerges from the doorway, the girl stumbling slightly, the guy steadying her with a hand at her elbow. I swallow hard. This was a mistake.

Hudson appears at my window, cocking his head and throwing me a questioning glance. Through its giant picture window, the front of the bar looks exactly the way I remember it. Stained wood and large glowing sign. I'm being silly. Drawing in a breath, I release my death grip. Hudson reaches out, opens the door for me.

"You okay?" he asks.

"Yeah." I climb out of the car and follow Hudson inside.

The bar is pretty dead. Then again, what had I been expecting on a Sunday night? There's no band playing. Instead, the music is being piped in through the speakers. Some eighties station. The nights when our band played, this place had been packed. Wall-to-wall people gyrating and drinking, the smell of beer and sweat so strong it gave me a headache.

But other than the emptiness, nothing has changed. Still the same old mahogany bar, sticky black bar stools, small pub tables, a stage set off to the side. Same dim lighting, and neon sign blinking in the window.

"Valerie!" Suzanne flies out from behind the bar, tinkling like a wind chime. "And Hudson, too?" She hugs us both. "You should've told me you were coming by."

"It was kinda last-minute."

"I twisted her arm." Hudson winks.

Suzanne smiles, nodding knowingly. "I believe it. I've been trying to get her in here for years." Then she looks around, almost regretful. "There's no band tonight."

"That's okay," I assure her with a dismissive flick of my wrist.

There is a devious twinkle in her eye as she sweeps her right arm out, Vanna White style. "Unless you wanna sing a few tunes."

"Oh, no." I shake my head.

"Come on." She waggles her brows.

I try another tactic. "I don't even have an instrument or anything."

"I can fire up the karaoke machine."

"Yeah, Mom. Do it." Hudson nudges me in the arm with his hand, but I can't tell by his tone if he's teasing me or not.

Either way, it's a hard pass.

"You should get up there. Show 'em how it's done." Mac nodded toward the stage, where an ancient woman wearing a crop top and a leather mini-skirt was butchering *"Like a Virgin."*

"No, I don't think so." I played with the straw of my drink.

"C'mon, I bet you kill at karaoke."

"I don't know." *Leaning down, I take a sip of my martini.* "I've never done it."

"You've never done karaoke?" *Mac's hand stilled on my thigh, a secret thrill. I tried not to think of when Darren had last done that. I tried not to think of Darren at all.*

"Karaoke is supposed to be fun and silly." *I laughed.* "Something you do on a drunken night with friends. You're not supposed to, like, show off or try hard."

Mac leaned back in his chair, looking me up and down as if appraising me.

How much am I worth? *I sometimes wanted to ask when I caught him doing that.*

Pitching forward, he slid his hands further up my bare leg. A slow smile spread across his face. "What if we sang something together? Come on. Just for fun."

There was a quiver low in my belly as his fingertips slid under the edge of my short skirt.

"Karaoke's not my thing," I say.

"But you're so good at it." Suzanne smiles. "Remember that time you and Mac did that song from *Grease*?" She snaps her ring-laden fingers. "What was it?"

"'You're the One That I Want,'" I mumble, feeling Hudson's eyes on me.

Mac's the only person who could ever coerce me into doing karaoke.

"Yes!" She stops snapping and punctuates the word with a fist in the air. "You guys were great!"

"Thanks," I say and then lightly laugh. "Well, we better order our drinks. We can't stay super late."

"Oh, yes. Of course." Suzanne moves to the side, placing a palm on my back and gently guiding me forward. "Sit at the bar, and I'll grab Jerry."

Suzanne's husband, Jerry, had been tending bar here since they'd opened. I'm glad to see that hasn't changed.

As I swing my leg over one of the bar stools, Suzanne squeals. "Do you still like sangria? 'Cause Jerry made one today that's to die for. You have to try it."

I giggle. I'd forgotten what Suzanne was like in her element. "That sounds great."

"Um…" Hudson raises his right hand as if he's a student in class. "I'll actually just take an IPA."

"Okay, we've got a double or a hazy on tap."

"I'll take the hazy."

"Great. I'll go tell Jerry." She sweeps away from us swiftly, a hurricane of bracelets, perfume and flowing clothes.

"See? Aren't you glad we came?" Hudson scoots his stool forward, leaning his elbows on the bar.

"Yeah, actually, I am." I glance around the room, at the sparse patrons, some at tables, some standing against the walls, a couple sitting down the bar from us. I don't know any of them, and yet they seem familiar. My people. The kind I spent most nights and weekends with for years.

This bar was like a second home to me.

But that feels like a lifetime ago.

"Valerie Jacobs!" Jerry's voice rings out. He's aged, the front of his hair balding, the top thinning. I remember when it was thick and long, and he wore it in a ponytail Suzanne loved to twirl on her finger. Spidery wrinkles sprout from his eyes and gather around the corners of his mouth. His nose is bulbous with a hint of purple on his skin. But his smile is as big as ever, his eyes still friendly.

"Hey, Jerry," I say as he makes his way over to us. "How've you been?"

"Can't complain."

I smile, thinking his catchphrases haven't changed.

He sets a glass in front of me filled with purple liquid, fresh fruit floating on top.

"Yum. That looks amazing," I say.

He narrows his eyes, studying me a moment. Then he says, "How is it that you haven't aged at all?"

His penchant for flattery hasn't changed much either. "Seems like he's fishing for a big tip, huh, Hudson?" I joke, side-eyeing my son.

"No way!" Jerry's eyes grow wide. "This is little Hudson?"

"I'm assuming by that moniker, you're not going to say I haven't aged at all," Hudson teases, and in that moment, I know why I said yes to coming here with him. He puts me at ease.

"No, you've definitely aged," Jerry says. "Last time I saw you, you were sitting at the end of the bar, doing homework while your mom had sound check." He lifts a frosted glass onto the bar, beer foaming down the sides, and slides it in Hudson's direction.

Hudson picks it up, brings it toward his lips. "Thank god those days are past us." Then he takes a long sip.

A couple across from us motions Jerry over. The woman's laugh is loud and high-pitched like the shriek of an electric guitar. And she clearly finds the man she's with to be hilarious, because she's been laughing nonstop since we got here. I remember ladies like her when we performed, their screechy giggles mixing with the music.

The sangria is syrupy-sweet on my tongue. I bite into a tart berry, and the sourness hits me in the back of the throat, a sharp contrast to the sweetness of the wine. It's delicious, and I take another sip. The next few berries are not quite as tart. The song switches to "Straight Up" by Paula Abdul, and my body instinctually sways, my feet tapping to the familiar rhythm.

"Good, right?" Suzanne sidles up next to me, head nodding toward my drink.

"Hmmm," I murmur, my mouth full.

"He's been making 'em all summer, and we've been selling 'em like hotcakes," she says.

"That's great." I attempt to take another sip, but only ice hits my lips. "Oops. All gone." When did that happen? My body is warm and tingly, like I'm submerged in a warm bath. Catching Jerry's attention, I ask for another.

"I know you can't tell tonight," Suzanne says, "but business has been really picking up lately."

"That's great," I say.

"Yeah." She glances around. "Sunday nights are usually pretty dead, but you should come back for trivia on Tuesday. This place'll be packed then."

"Trivia night?" I look at my friend, surprised. It doesn't seem like something she'd think of.

"It was Tony's idea. He's the new manager I hired. Young guy. He's been livening things up."

"Oh, that's right. You've told me about him." Suzanne doesn't bring up the bar often when we hang out or talk on the phone. She knows it can be a touchy subject with me. But since it's such a huge part of her life, it usually comes up in conversation at some point. Scanning the room, I notice the subtle changes I'd overlooked before. On the surface it all appears the same—Suzanne's eclectic aesthetic. But the light fixtures are new and modern. Even the bar stool I sit on is sleek and shiny, not chipped and antique like it used to be. The stage has been refinished. And on the far wall is a bulletin board behind glass, listing upcoming events and bands.

That must've been the new manager's doing. It's clear now more than ever that this place has outgrown me, moved on to bigger and better things. Not that I'd ever planned to perform again. Here or anywhere, but it still makes me sad.

Sullenly, I suck down more of my drink.

I'm starting to feel it, my head fuzzy. I clutch the edge of the bar to keep from toppling over.

There is a catch at my thumb as if a splinter has embedded itself in my flesh. I lift my hand. Underneath, initials are carved in the wood. Childlike block letters. I smile, remembering Hudson as a child, hunched over this bar, pencil on paper, math book opened near his elbow. Sounds spin around me: the guys setting up their instruments, bantering loudly to be heard above the racket of amps being turned on, cords plugged in.

I finish off my drink. A couple makes out in the corner, and my eyes linger a beat too long. The woman notices. Scowls. Cheeks warming, I look away. A man by the door saunters toward me. My heart stops.

Mac.

He grins, waves.

For a moment, I'm frozen. Paralyzed with shock.

What is he doing here?

It's been so many years.

But then I snap out of it. Regaining composure, I wave back. "Mac," I call out.

"What, honey?" Suzanne's fingers are warm on my arm.

"Mac," I say, continuing to wave.

But he looks over my shoulder as if I'm invisible. How does he not see me?

Desperation blooming in my chest, I scramble off the bar stool. But my foot gets caught and I lose my balance, my body teetering.

"Mom!" Hudson lunges forward, his arms coming around me. His hold is strong as he rights me, and for a second I lose my breath. Blinking, I catch sight of Mac again. Only this time it's clear that it isn't him.

His hair is slightly darker. His eyes not quite right—too almond-shaped and lighter in color. His jawline too sharp.

But the biggest difference is that he's alive, and Mac is not.

I wriggle out of Hudson's grasp, feeling stupid. "I'm okay. Just lost my balance." With my palm, I smooth down my hair. Inhale and exhale through my nose. I've read that's supposed to slow down your heart rate. It's not doing the trick right now. Mine is clanging in my chest, a full-blown drum solo.

Suzanne claps me on the back. "I told you those sangrias were good."

"Yeah." I force a wobbly smile, but my voice is shaky, and I can tell by Hudson's pensive expression that he notices it.

When Suzanne leaves, Hudson says, "Hey, Mom, can I ask you something?"

"Yes." I sit taller.

"Why haven't you seen a doctor about your memory issues?"

I shrug. "'Cause it won't make a difference."

"But what if it does?"

Narrowing my eyes, I take another pull from my drink. "Did Kendra put you up to this?"

He shakes his head.

"I know you guys are worried about me. I felt the same way when my mom was sick, and I pushed her to see a doctor. But it didn't help."

"Yeah, I get that. But if it were me, I'd want to see a doctor." He lifts his beer, bringing it to his lips and taking a large gulp.

My head feels like a balloon, full of helium, released and floating up in the rafters.

"I'm gonna go to the restroom," I mutter and quickly scurry

away from Hudson's prying eyes. I can still feel the heat of his stare on the back of my scalp, though.

In the bathroom, I run cold water over my hands and press my palms to my cheeks. As I study my reflection, I see Mac behind me, his dark eyes roving my body. Coming closer, he nuzzles my neck, the warmth of his breath skating over my skin. His hands slide up my back, fumbling with my bra clasps. I suck in a breath and squeeze my eyes shut.

When I open them, the memory of Mac is gone, replaced by a woman in skinny jeans and a halter top slipping into one of the stalls. Exhaling, I dry off my hands. After regaining composure, I head back out.

Suzanne is now talking with a group of women around a circular table in the corner. I pass her and I'm almost to the bar when I stop short. Hudson is talking with someone. From the back I can't tell who it is.

"...you and that girl last night?" I catch the tail end of a question the strange young man is asking Hudson.

"What girl?" I ask, curiosity getting the better of me.

"Oh, hey, Mrs. Jacobs," the young man with the heavy-lidded eyes and shaggy hair says.

"Mom, you remember Browning?" Hudson points to his friend.

"Ah, yes." How could I forget this kid? He and Hudson were always getting into trouble together when they were younger. Any time I got a call from the principal's office, I could pretty much guarantee Hudson's explanation would involve something about Jared Browning. "Hi, Jared."

Struggling to get back onto the bar stool, I say, "I want to hear all about this girl. I didn't even know Hudson was dating."

The annoyed expression on Hudson's face tells me that he was hoping I'd forget his friend's question. A fair assumption, lately, I guess. But this is a conversation I'm deeply interested in.

"I'm not." Hudson subtly shakes his head at Jared.

"C'mon, man, you were with her last night," Browning says, clearly not taking the hint. "The one at Midtown Saloon. What was her name? Holly, or something."

Holly. *Molly?* Heat rushes to my skin. Hudson was with Molly last night.

The night she died.

Hudson's face is red. It may be from the alcohol or how warm it is in here, or it could be something else.

"It was nothing," he says more to me than to Jared. "We just ran into each other at the bar."

"Didn't look like nothing to me," Jared said, throwing Hudson a wink.

My stomach sours, and this time it's not from the sangria.

"Was this before or after the fight?" I ask with a laugh to make it seem like an offhanded question.

"Fight?" Jared looks at Hudson, obviously confused.

"Yeah, you were in the bathroom," Hudson says. "It's not a big deal." Then he catches my eye. "We really need to get going." He looks pointedly at his friend. "Gotta be up early."

"Oh, right. The job," Jared says. "Yeah, you better not let me down. I stuck my neck out for you, bro."

"I won't." Hudson claps Jared on the back, then faces me. "Ready?"

"Yep." Reaching under the bar, I snatch my purse off the hook and stand. After saying goodbye to Jared, I go in search of Jerry and Suzanne. As I weave my way through the tables, I think about how this place feels both familiar and not at the same time, kind of like Hudson.

10

My head is pounding, my mouth paper-dry. Damn those sangrias. I sit up in bed, rubbing my temples. From Hudson's room, I hear shuffling, slamming, cursing under his breath. After sliding off the bed, I amble out of my room and down the hallway. His door is open, and he's on the ground, peeking under his bed.

"Everything okay?"

He gets up too fast and hits the side of his head on the bed frame. "Ouch." Sitting back, he rubs the spot. "Yeah, I just can't find my employee parking badge."

"The tag on your key ring?" I try to picture it, to recall if I've seen it lying around. It was small, rectangular, black on one side and a barcode on the other.

He sucks in his cheeks in frustration. "I've looked everywhere."

"Want me to help you look?" I kind of hope he'll say no. My headache is progressively getting worse. I'd expected him to be gone by now. Thought I'd have a quiet house to my-self this morning.

"Nah." He grants me my silent wish. Clutching the edge of his bed, he pulls himself to a standing position, then rakes his fingers through his hair. "I'm running late. I'll just have to park somewhere else today."

After snatching his keys off the dresser, he says goodbye, then hurries down the stairs and out the front door. As I make my way down toward the kitchen, I notice the little specks of gray clay on the stairs and in the entryway. Hudson's been leaving a trail of them in his wake since getting this job. *If only he'd clean them up himself,* I think sourly as I pour myself a tall glass of water and take an Advil.

Ahh, the house is finally silent.

I slowly make my way back up the stairs, glass of water in hand, dreaming of a long, hot shower. I'm about to head into the bathroom and turn on the water when my phone blares on the nightstand.

It's Suzanne. I'm sure she's calling about last night, and I almost don't answer, but that's just delaying the inevitable.

"Hey." Sinking down onto the edge of my bed, I press the phone to my ear.

"Hey, girl," Suzanne's raspy voice fills the line. "How ya feelin'?"

"Been better," I answer honestly.

"I bet." She laughs.

I want to join in, but don't dare. The Advil is just kicking in, but the headache's not gone yet.

There is a beat of silence before Suzanne says, "Well, I just wanted to check on you. Make sure you were okay."

"I'll survive," I say with a shrug. "Not like it's the first time I've been hungover, and it probably won't be the last."

"Yeah, right." Another chuckle, only this time it's lukewarm.

My muscles tighten.

"But...um...are you sure that's all that's going on?"

"What do you mean?" I chew on the end of one of my nails.

"It's just you were acting kinda strange..." The sentence trails off as if she had planned to say more and then changed her mind.

"Oh, really?" I pinch the bridge of my nose. "Well, like I said, I had a little too much to drink."

"No, it wasn't that...um... I feel like..." She pauses. "Did you think you saw Mac?"

Heat rushes to the surface of my skin. "Oh, yeah, no, I just saw someone who looked a lot like him. Brought me back for a minute, I guess."

"Seemed like it was more than that," she says.

This is exactly the reason I've been avoiding Suzanne lately. She knows me too well.

"Have you thought about maybe talking to someone?" Suzanne adds before I can say anything to defend myself.

"Like a therapist?"

"There's nothing wrong with seeing one."

"I know," I say. "I have seen one."

"And you've talked about Mac's death?"

"I mean, maybe not specifically."

"I think it might be good for you to talk to someone about it."

"I don't know, Suzanne. It's been ten years."

"Exactly," she says, and that simple word shoots through me. But she doesn't get it. No one does.

"I'm fine, Suzanne," I say.

There's no way I can sit in a therapist's office and relive that awful night. Recount what I saw. What *he* did. What *I* did. Even all these years later, it feels like a fresh wound, gaping and oozing.

I see it at night when I lie in bed, playing out like a movie behind my eyelids. The memory so crisp and clear, it's like it happened yesterday.

Our whole relationship feels that way. Sometimes I think that what I had with Mac was more real than anything else I've experienced. I had a life—a marriage and a family—with Darren, and yet my memories with him often pale in comparison to the ones involving Mac.

I'd had a crush on Mac from the minute I'd met him. I knew it was wrong. But I couldn't help it. I was drawn to him like a catchy song. One that you don't want to admit you like, but every time it comes on the radio, your body betrays you—dancing and singing along.

Mac was good-looking in an edgy, dangerous, almost confusing way. His features weren't the kind usually associated with good-looking men. His jaw was too severe, his eyebrows bushy, his nose crooked, his eyes dark with a tiny scar above the left brow. But for some reason, all those things together worked. And not just for me. Girls fawned all over him at every show.

It was rare to meet a woman who didn't think he was hot.

When we first started playing together, Mac and I did nothing but flirt. I told myself it was natural and innocent, not hurting anyone. But deep down, I knew that wasn't true. It was leading to something. And if I'd been honest with myself back then, I would've admitted that I wanted it to.

We crossed the line about two years in. It was after a show. We were riding the high of the applause and compliments of the bar owner when he paid us. In the parking lot, I'd said goodbye to the guys and headed for my car. I'd almost gotten inside my vehicle when Mac ran after me.

"Val, you dropped this." He was holding a glittery bracelet.

I glanced down at my wrist and then at the bracelet. "That's not mine."

"Oh. Sorry. It looked like something of yours."

I laughed. "No, it doesn't. I wouldn't be caught dead in something like that. Too much glitter."

"But you love glitter."

"Correction: I love sparkle. Jewels. Diamonds, that kind of thing. Not cheap glitter."

A bemused smile spread slowly across his face. "Got it. You have standards for your sparkle. No cheap glitter for this girl." The smile vanished, replaced by Mac's deep-thinking expression. He reached up to touch his chin. "That's it. The missing lyrics for the song I've been working on."

I laughed, knowing what song he was talking about. One we'd been struggling with about a girl ditching her ex to find true love.

"She's got standards for her sparkle. Diamonds and jewels. Cheap glitter will never do," he sang out.

"I like that," I said slowly, repeating the last line, "Cheap glitter will never do." And then I added, "That's all she's been offered by you."

He was quiet a moment. "I feel like we had a line like that already, though."

I bit my lip. "Maybe. I can't remember all of the lyrics right now."

"I've got them back at my place. Why don't you come over, and we can hammer this out?" The words were right, professional even. Mac and I spent a lot of time writing songs together in a professional capacity. But never late at night after a gig.

"Tonight?"

"Why not? The ideas are flowing. What better time?" He leaned against my car, his face so close to mine I could feel the warmth of his breath.

He wasn't wrong. We'd been stuck on this song for a while, but I also knew that wasn't why he was inviting me over. The truth was written in his eyes—the way they drank me in greed-ily. It was there in his body language, the way he angled his shoulder into me, allowing his arm to fall so his fingertips grazed my side.

I swallowed hard and nodded. "Okay. Sounds good."

"That's my girl." Pushing off my car, he winked, swag-gered off.

When I got in my car, I thought about calling Darren and telling him I might be a little late, but decided against it. He was probably already in bed, and if he wasn't, I didn't feel like getting the third degree. At least, those were the reasons I gave myself. But I knew it was because hearing Darren's voice might have stopped me.

And I didn't want to stop.

I kept up the professional pretense for the first few minutes at his house, sitting on the piano bench and rifling through his notebook. But then he slid onto the bench next to me, so close our thighs touched. Lowering one hand, he let his palm fall to my bare leg. Goose bumps rose on my skin.

"I always love when you wear this skirt."

"I know," I said. "That's why I wore it." Darren hated it. Said it was too short. That men could probably look up it while I was singing. But Mac always complimented me on it.

"Really? You wore it for me?" There was a teasing lilt to his voice, and I could tell he wasn't sure if I was messing with him or not.

I turned to him, my face serious. "Yes, Mac, I really did."

His hand slid higher up my thigh. I leaned into him, an invitation.

That was all it took. His free hand lifted to catch the side of my face. When his mouth met mine, his kiss was greedy. Hungry.

We didn't make it to the bedroom. I straddled him right there on the piano bench. Later, we joked about how fitting it was that our first time was in the place we'd so often made magic together—just in a different way.

I could've stopped it at any time. Put on the brakes. Bailed.

But I never really wanted to.

"Okay, I'm sorry," Suzanne says quietly, pulling me back to our conversation, to her suggestion that I talk to someone. "I shouldn't have overstepped. I just wanted to call and make sure everything was all right."

"It is," I assure her, knowing it's a lie but not wanting to burden Suzanne. I've been relying enough on Kendra—and now I have to lean on Hudson, too. No need to drag her down with my issues as well.

After hanging up, I take another sip of my water and glance around, trying to remember what I'd originally come up here to do. My gaze falls to my unmade bed. Absently, I walk toward it. Fingering the edge of my comforter, I know this isn't what I'd been planning to do when Suzanne called. Still, I make my bed, hoping the simple act of doing something will trigger my memory.

It doesn't.

As much as I hate to admit it, I know I'm getting worse.

I head downstairs, make myself a cup of tea and meander into the family room. In the corner, by the large bay window, sits my baby grand piano. In the early morning sunlight, the dust is more visible than usual. It's been neglected lately. I can't remember the last time I sat down and played.

It holds too many sad memories.

But after talking to Suzanne this morning, I feel like playing it. I set down my mug and move toward the piano. Pulling the cover up, I'm greeted by a row of ivory keys. As I rest my hands on the keys, my signature red lacquered nails sparkle—I still get a manicure every two weeks. Beneath them, my hands are weathered, covered in age spots and spidery blue veins.

I rack my brain for a song I know by memory. One of my favorites comes to mind. A song Mac and I wrote together over fifteen years ago called "Heart Sky." I play through the first verse and chorus. The piano is out of tune, and my voice is rough, out of practice. But it doesn't matter to me right now. Closing my eyes, I conjure up the image of playing this with the band. I can feel the beat under my feet, the energy from the audience. When I reach the bridge, I falter, pausing, my fingers hovering. As hard as I try, I can't remember the chords. It's like I've hit a wall.

Frustrated, I shove back, stand up and close the lid with a little too much force.

Then I think more about Hudson's suggestion to see the doctor. If there's even the slightest chance someone can help me, I have to take it. Right?

I click into my contacts, look up Dr. Steiner and dial.

The first thing I notice when I turn the corner onto Molly's street is the news van. I tug on Bowie's leash, thinking we should go back. But curiosity propels me forward. The reporter is one I've seen before, but I can't remember her name. It was Darren who used to watch the news all the time, not me. Blonde. Pretty. Young. Today she sports a black-and-white pinstriped pantsuit, her hair twisted into an updo. She stands in front of Molly's house, holding a mic in front of her face, a cameraman poised a few feet in front of her.

Neighbors gawk from their yards, or peek through their blinds. When I get close enough, I catch the tail end of the reporter's words.

"...rocked this quiet community with the news that police now believe Ms. Foster's death to be a homicide." I nearly stumble over a crack in the sidewalk, jerking Bowie's leash by accident. "This morning, the Sacramento Police Department released a statement asking the public for help in learning more about the circumstances of her death. We will be sure to share more information with you on this developing story as we have it. This is Bethany Smith, reporting live..."

Her words become white noise as I hurry forward, head ducked, trailing after Bowie.

Homicide.

The word plays in my head like a refrain, punctuating each step I take.

Homicide.

Homicide.

Homicide.

It wasn't an accident. Not suicide or a health crisis. Molly was murdered. My fingertips run along Bowie's fur. His tail wags, and he scoots a little closer. The warmth of his body seeps into my thigh.

When Darren passed away, I was often afraid to be alone in my big house, especially at night. Then I'd remind myself that this neighborhood has always been relatively safe. We had the random robbery, car break-ins, bikes taken from a driveway.

But murder?

This is the first one I've known of.

I'd only met Molly the one time. We weren't friends or even acquaintances. And yet, it's hard to believe that she's gone. Unfathomable that a week ago I saw her alive and breathing, and now she isn't. Death has always been hard for me to process. Most things in life aren't so final.

There are always second chances.

Forgiveness.

The rising of the sun bringing a new day.

Most things can be righted.

Except for death.

Once someone is gone, that's it. There are no more opportunities.

At this point in my life, I'm well-acquainted with death: my mother, Heather, Mac, Darren. Death and I are old friends. And yet, I never find it any less shocking when he shows up.

I hurry home with Bowie, where I pour myself some coffee and set an English muffin to toast.

I wonder how Molly was murdered. The reporter hadn't said. Gunshot?

Stabbing?

Strangulation?

The pads of my fingers run along the skin on my neck, tracing my trachea. Not being able to breathe has always been my biggest fear. Gasping for air to no avail. The helplessness, and terror. But worse, the knowing.

Panic sweeps over me at the thought. I shake my head. Clear my throat. Jump out of my skin when the toaster pops and, finding that I'm not so hungry after all, I feed the muffin to Bowie instead.

I hope it was more humane than that for her. Gunshot. Quick and painless. Would I have heard it? Would I have recognized the sound if I had? I wonder why the police are keeping it from us. Why tell us it was a homicide and then nothing more? A woman was killed so close to my home. A single woman like me. We have the right to know what happened.

My laptop is open on the kitchen table from when I'd been paying bills yesterday. A few folded papers and torn envelopes sit cluttered around it. Shoving them to the side, I plunk down into the kitchen chair. The screen before me is black, my own reflection appearing in it. I place my hands over the keys, but they don't move. Oh, god. I can't remember how to log on.

Mom sat on the couch, staring at the blank television.

"Mom?" I touched her shoulder. "You okay?"

"I wanna watch something," she said.

"Okay." I glanced down at the remote in her trembling hand. *"Well, put something on."*

"I don't remember how to."

My chest tightens. No, this can't be happening.

I just used the computer yesterday. I know what to do.

But still, my hands don't move.

My mind is completely blank.

I'm about to call Hudson when my fingers finally start to work, touching the mouse pad and bringing me to the lock screen. It only takes me a few seconds to remember the password. But the panic lingers in my uneven heartbeat, the trembling in my bones.

Ignoring it, I type "Molly Foster" into my browser's search bar. A dozen articles immediately populate. I click on the first one. Written by a local news station, it's filled with everything I already know.

Her name.

Where she lives.

The friend finding her body.

The police suspecting foul play.

A number to call with any information.

I scroll down, clicking on the next few articles, but they're identical. Biting my lip, I stare out the window, my hands lying idly on the keyboard. It's Monday, already gorgeous out, and as usual, Leslie sits on her front porch, mug in hand. I have no doubt Beth or Shelly will mosey on over for a dose of morning gossip any minute. I've wanted nothing to do with the silly neighborhood gab sessions for the past ten years. But this morning, I feel a stab of envy. Does Leslie know something I don't? Something I can't find online?

No. How could she?

I know how she used to get her information. Back when

114

we were friends. From James. He'd been a detective for Sacramento County. But after they split up, he transferred to a department in the Bay Area. And I doubt they talk anymore. Their divorce was anything but amicable.

I turn my attention back to the computer.

I must've inadvertently tapped something, because I'm not looking at the article. I've moved below it into the comment section. I scroll through some of them, and they're pretty much what I expect.

"So sad."

"Wow. Much too young."

"Prayers to the family."

But then I reach one that stops me cold.

"That bitch got what was coming to her. She was nothing but a tease."

Asshole.

Back in my performing days, I met a lot of guys like him. Men who thought I owed them something for the money and time they'd spent on our shows. As if the music wasn't enough.

I distinctly remember one man cornering me after a show, and when I politely asked him to leave me alone, he'd said that I'd been flirting with him with my eyes the entire show. He was too dumb to know I could barely see the crowd through the stage lights. Most shows, when I sang, I looked like I was smiling at everyone, but I didn't even see them.

The username of the person who wrote the vile comment was "Anonymous."

Of course. Coward.

The words are so hateful, I try to imagine the anger he must have felt to spew such vitriol about a dead woman. I don't know that it's a man, but I'm assuming. Could he have been involved? Is that what happened? Molly rejected a man and he lost it? The scenario plays out in my mind, an enraged man wrapping his hands around Molly's neck and squeezing hard. And that's when a long-forgotten memory surfaces.

I heard a rattle. Then a scrape and a stomp, followed by an ear-piercing scream.

All coming from upstairs.

My shoulders tightened. What now? I'd just finished cleaning up a vase Hudson had broken. God, those two had been fighting constantly lately. Darren criticized me for letting them duke it out. "Are you the parent, or are you eight, too?" he'd asked only days ago after sending Hudson upstairs for yelling at his sister on my watch—but I was at my wit's end. I had half a brain to let them kill each other.

The noises stopped suddenly, blanketing the house in silence.

That was what made me leap up. As annoying as all the noise was, that was typical. Silence meant something was wrong.

I tore up the stairs and raced into Hudson's room. He was over his sister, his hands wrapped around her neck as she clawed at him. Hudson had always been big for his age—and strong.

"Oh, my god. Stop!" I hollered, prying his fingers from her neck until they finally came loose. I grabbed Hudson by the shoulders, yanked him back. "What the hell is wrong with you?"

"She started it!" my son insisted.

"Yeah, right." Kendra's voice was hoarse.

"I don't care who started it. You don't lay hands on your sister like that," I snapped.

Hudson crossed his arms over his chest, glaring at his sister. She stuck out her tongue. Beneath my fingers, I felt his muscles clench.

"Hudson, you're in time-out. Kendra, you can go."

As Kendra left, I stared in horror at her reddened neck and wondered what would have happened if I hadn't come in when I did.

I click out of the comments and refill my glass of water. As I sip it, Jared Browning's face emerges in my mind like a reflection in moving water. It takes a minute for the entire memory to become lucid—seeing him at the Full Moon Tavern and having a conversation. Had he really said that Hudson was with Molly the night she died?

Bro, stop hitting me up or I'm gonna block you.

The text I'd seen in his phone was from someone named Blondie. Molly was blonde. And it had come in the night she died. At what time, I'm not sure. I hadn't thought to check the time stamp.

The "bro" part reassures me a little. Don't guys call each other bro? And if it is from a girl, doesn't the bro greeting mean they were friendly?

I feel like maybe I'm reading too much into the text. It could have been playful or teasing, not necessarily ominous.

I think about Hudson's infectious laugh and charming smile, and how much he puts me at ease. And not just me but everyone around him. When he was younger, his teachers always told me he was a joy to have in class. His baseball coach said he was a natural-born leader.

I know people are different at school and on a baseball field than they are in romantic relationships. But for years, I saw the way he was with Heather—back when they were friends and then when they started dating. He was nothing but sweet and gentle with her.

It's actually how they became such good friends.

"Hey, Mom, can Heather ride to school with us tomorrow morning?" Hudson asked the Tuesday night of Heather's first week at his school.

I knew Leslie didn't work, so I wondered why she couldn't

take her. She hadn't mentioned anything to me, and we'd just spoken that morning.

"Sure," I said. "Is everything okay with her parents?"

"Yeah." He frowned, running a hand through his unruly hair. "It's not because of her parents. It's because of the kids at school."

"What about them?"

"Some of the kids are really mean to her."

"Why?"

"I don't know, 'cause they're stupid." He shrugged. "But I just thought if she rode to school with me, I could protect her."

I smiled. "That's really nice of you, Hudson."

He'd spent the next seven years being Heather's protector and friend. That's one of the many reasons it was so hard to reconcile the way Leslie turned on him after that fateful night in October.

Sweet and kind—that's the boy I've always known. And there's no way that boy hurt Molly…or anyone, for that matter.

He was only a child when he and Kendra fought. And, knowing her, she probably did instigate it.

I am still curious about this Blondie person, though. So I log back on to the computer, click into Facebook. After I type Hudson's name in the search bar, multiple accounts come up. It's easy to find his bearded face among the thumbnail photos. I go into it. In the past his account had been private, but today it's public, so all of the posts and pictures are readily available. Maybe he won't friend me, but whatever, I can still see all of his stuff. I'm practically giddy, my hands shaking as I scroll the page. I find pictures of him and his ex, who I now know is named Natalia. That had been one of my guesses, right? She's pretty. Fresh-faced. Tanned skin. Black hair, not blond. So most likely not the Blondie person in his phone. Unless he's being ironic? I peruse the photos. Hudson looks happy, and it makes me wonder what happened between them. I try to remember if he ever told me why they broke up. If he did, I don't recall it.

Below one of the photos of them in a restaurant, surrounded by a few friends I don't recognize, Natalia has commented, "Such a fun day!"

Smiling inwardly, I continue scrolling. There's a grouping of photos posted by a guy named Chase Folley, and they appear to be from a party. Hudson has been tagged in a few. Natalia is beside him in all three. When I enlarge one of them, my stomach knots. Natalia's expression is off. She looks uncomfortable. Hudson's smile is tight, his face slightly red. His hand is clutching Natalia's shoulder so tightly his knuckles are white. I swipe my fingertip over the screen to remove a smudge and then realize there isn't one. The dark spot under Natalia's eye is on the actual picture. A bruise?

I click on her name, and it routes me to her account, but it's private. Disappointed, I head back to Hudson's page, stare at the picture a little longer. Perhaps it's not bruising. Maybe it's a shadow. I click on the other photos, zooming in to one that has a good view of her face. It's a bruise all right.

When Kendra was around six years old, she'd been trying to do a handstand in the middle of the family room near where I was seated, reading a magazine. She fell over, her heel launching itself into my face and giving me a black eye.

Accidents happen.

Natalia's black eye doesn't necessarily mean anything. It's her expression that unnerves me.

The ringing of my phone causes my heart rate to spike. Exhaling, I pick it up.

"Kendra," I answer hurriedly. "I've been trying to reach you since yesterday."

"I know. I'm sorry. I had a test and a double shift, and Mason's teething. Anyway, what's up?"

"Did you hear about that girl? The one Theo works with?"

"Oh, my god, yes. He told me. Isn't it awful?"

"So awful," I agree. "And now they're saying it's a homicide."

"I know. It's so scary," she says. "And so weird that we just saw her last Friday."

A chill runs through me. I hug myself.

"Do you know if Hudson ever made his move? Or talked to her?"

Her question throws me. "No, but I mean, how would he have even been able to?"

"I don't know," she says. "I'm sure he didn't. I was just curious. He was clearly interested, and she did tell us where she lived."

"What are you saying?"

"Nothing," she says defensively. "I was just curious." A pause. "Look, I gotta get going. Talk to you later, Mom."

I've done it again. Upset her.

"Kendra?"

But she's already hung up.

Facebook is still up on my computer. Curious, I type Molly's name in the search bar. There's a list of Molly Fosters, but her smiling face greets me at the top. Unfortunately, like Natalia's, her account is private. I can only view her profile pictures. All but two are smiling selfies. One of them is of her and a group of girlfriends wearing bikinis, holding cocktails and sitting on a beach. The last one is of her and a guy. I sit forward. Does she have a boyfriend?

I look at the date. Almost a year ago.

I sink back into my seat. Probably not relevant, then.

And didn't that neighbor of hers say she'd had guys over a lot? The picture wasn't romantic. Two smiling faces in close proximity. No indication that it was a love interest. Could be a friend or a brother, even.

Shaking my head, I log out of Facebook. I have no idea what I'm hoping to accomplish, anyway. Reaching out, I pick up my water and take a sip. It feels good as it slides down my throat.

I close my laptop and stare out the front window. My online snooping has gotten me nowhere. I'm still as lost as I was when I started. The answers I'm looking for, clearly, aren't on the computer. I stand, my hand alighting on the kitchen window.

"He was clearly interested, and she did tell us where she lived."

Kendra's words float through my mind, a not-so-subtle accusation. But she's wrong. There's no way Hudson was at Molly's house.

Right?

"I saw her with some guy yesterday, though. Some young guy with a big beard."

But what if he was?

Even if he didn't kill her, with his past, the police will think he did.

"I just can't find my employee parking badge."

My stomach plummets. Is it possible that he was in her house, and that's where he lost his parking badge?

This morning when I passed Molly's house, the crime tape had been taken down. And I'm sure the news crews are gone by now. Police presence has all but ceased in the neighborhood. Over the years, I've watched enough crime dramas to know that they've probably confiscated all of the evidence in Molly's home by now. But even if they saw the parking badge, they wouldn't necessarily think it meant anything. They might think it's Molly's.

As long as they don't scan it or look into the barcode. Once they find out it's for parking at the mine, it won't take more than a minute to connect it to Hudson.

I can't let that happen.

If Hudson was with Molly the night she died, and if he

went to her house and lost his badge there, I have to find it before the police do.

I should wait until it's dark, but I'm too restless. After putting on my shoes, I hurry outside. It feels weird walking down the street without Bowie. Halfway to Molly's, it dawns on me how silly I look. How conspicuous. When a car drives by, I lower my head. My heart pounds loudly in my chest.

Turn around.

Go home.

Unable to make my feet obey my thoughts, I continue on. I'm wearing joggers and a T-shirt, sneakers on my feet. My hair is pulled back in a ponytail at the nape of my neck. To anyone passing by, I look like someone on a brisk walk. Sure, I don't have Bowie, but who says I can't go on a walk without my dog?

Air flowing a little more freely through my chest now, I hurry forward. If I stay calm, this'll be easy.

The mailbox with the flag on it is before me. I glance subtly up at the houses to the right and left of Molly's. Quiet. Blinds closed. I peer across the street. No prying eyes there either. Probably all at work. Thank god it's Monday.

Eyes tracking the street, I move stealthily forward, ducking into the side yard. Movement tickles the corner of my right eye. Carefully, I turn my head. Through the leaves of a nearby bush, I see one of the elderly neighbors I spoke with the morning Molly died. Her kitchen window overlooks Molly's side yard. She appears to be standing over her kitchen sink, and by her movements, I'd guess she's scrubbing a pan or something difficult to clean. I wonder about the man she saw with Molly on the day she died. Was it in Molly's home? Outside?

I should have asked more questions.

Lowering my body, I hunch over and walk below her window, careful to keep myself concealed behind the large bush. The backyard is enclosed by a tall privacy fence, its gate closed with a simple latch. Once I'm safely inside, I heave a sigh of relief and stand up straight.

The yard is small—a patch of grass and a cement patio. The grass is yellow, and weeds line the fence. On the patio sit a couple of plastic chairs, surrounded by a few planters spilling over with red geraniums and something pink I don't recognize.

I make my way across the dead lawn to the back door. I'd been expecting a slider, but it's a regular door. And it's locked tight. I make my way to the other side of the house and come upon a high window. Even on my tiptoes I can barely reach it. There's no way I'm getting inside through it. I blow out a frustrated breath. Clearly, I hadn't thought this through before racing over here. How will I get in?

Rounding the corner, I find myself on the back patio again. I glance down at the potted plants, green leaves and colorful petals springing out of the soil. It's odd how she didn't care for her grass, but she did care for the plants on her patio. Maybe as a renter, she didn't feel obligated to maintain someone else's yard? As I'm staring into the planter, something catches my eye. A rock nestled beneath one of the plant stems. But not a normal rock. It almost appears to be plastic. I reach out and pick it up, hoping my hunch is right.

I roll it over in my hand. Sure enough, there is a cutout on the bottom, lid secured. I open it, revealing a key inside. Shocked, I palm the key. It can't really be this easy, can it?

I hurry to the back door and jam the key in the lock. It slips in easily, and I turn the knob. My heart is pounding erratically in my chest as I open the door and step inside. I can hardly believe I've made it in so quickly.

It smells bad, like mold or spoiled food, reminding me that there has recently been a dead body in here. My stomach churns, the nausea I felt last week returning momentarily, and for a split second, I want to flee. Remembering Hudson and why I'm here, I swallow hard, determination propelling me forward. The first thing I'm struck with is the mess.

It's obvious that no one has been in to clean since the police left. Magazines litter the coffee table, and a few lie open on the carpet. Knickknacks, a couple of remotes and an empty cup are also on the ground. Footprints of all shapes and sizes are stamped into the ivory carpet. I wonder if the items on the ground were knocked over in a struggle or if the police knocked them over while they investigated. Either way, I don't want to disturb anything. I keep my eyes peeled, scanning the carpet, the tables, the countertops for Hudson's pass.

The walls are relatively clean. So probably not a gunshot or stabbing, right? Wouldn't there be blood all over if that were the case? Unless the police cleaned it. Yes, I suppose they could have. I don't know much about how police process crimes.

I don't know if she was killed in this room, of course. The neighbor only said that her friend found her. Not where. And the news so far had given the barest of details. Wincing, I peek down the hallway. What if there's blood all over the hallway or one of the bedrooms?

Shivering, I peer longingly over my shoulder to the back door. The thought of what I might find in the rest of the house almost makes me jump ship.

Almost.

But I've never been a quitter. And I've already come so far.

Molly had good taste in home decor. Boho chic, with pops of bright color, baskets and macramé hanging planters. Her couch is a muted gray with bright orange pillows, a teal throw blanket. She's got one of those chairs that hangs from the ceiling that are popular right now.

The family room and kitchen are separated by a counter and two bar stools. A small hallway leads past the kitchen and to the front door.

I start to walk toward the bedrooms when I'm struck with a sudden dizziness. Reaching out, I press my palm to the wall and breathe in deeply. It takes a few minutes to steady myself. My head is still a little fuzzy when I push off. It's probably the smell…or knowing what's taken place in here. Exhaling, I steel myself for what's ahead and continue on. The walls are bare. One bedroom is completely empty other than a few storage boxes, a desk in the corner, some papers and a closed laptop sitting on top. The bathroom resembles mine. Curling iron on the counter, tangled cord piled up alongside an array of hair products. Makeup brushes and palettes load the other side.

The bedroom at the end of the hall must've been Molly's. The bed is unmade, the white down comforter flung to one side. The walls in here are bare as well, and I realize that the only painting I saw was the one in the family room. She must not have lived here long.

There is a framed picture on one of her nightstands, though. It's a family photo. Even though Molly is much younger in it, I recognize her immediately. The other people must be her parents and, by the looks of it, a brother—but I don't think this was the guy in her profile picture.

I lean in to look more closely and feel something under my shoe: on the ground near my feet lies a lilac G-string. Face hot, I turn away from it. There are some dark dots in the carpet. Crumbs, maybe. I had noticed an open bag of Oreos on her nightstand. For someone so good at decorating, she did seem to be a bit of a slob. Something gold and shiny winks at me from under the dresser. Not a badge, but still, it catches my eye.

I know I shouldn't mess with anything, but I have a fluttery feeling in my gut and can't help snatching it up: a gold watch, large face and band. A man's. Something about it is familiar, but I don't know why. Hudson isn't historically the type for nice watches. I turn it over in my hand. There is an inscription on the back that reads "777."

What does that mean?

It seems foreign, and yet something deep in my gut tells me it's not.

I'm racking my brain to figure out if or where I've seen it before when my cell phone rings in my pocket. A startled squeal escapes through my lips. Heart hammering, I shove the watch into my free pocket and yank my phone out of the other one.

Kendra.

I hesitate, wondering if I should ignore it. But what if it's an emergency? She never calls me twice in one day, and especially not after the way we left things in our last conversation.

Pressing the cell to my ear, I say, "Hello."

"Mom?"

My pulse quickens at her panicked tone.

"Mom, I need you to come over right now."

I whirl around, heading quickly out of Molly's room. "Is it Mason? Is he hurt?"

"No. Mason's fine. I need you to watch him."

It hits me then. "Are *you* hurt?"

"It's Theo. The police…they brought him in for questioning."

"For what?"

"The murder of Molly Foster."

11

Dazed, I hang up.

Why would the police be questioning Theo?

"Molly and I work together."

Is there more to it than that?

My head swims. I squeeze my eyes shut to keep from falling over. When I open them, I'm momentarily startled by my surroundings. *What the hell am I doing here?*

This is a terrible idea. What had I been thinking?

Backing out of the room, I walk down the hallway with the bare walls and into the messy family room. Then I stop short. I haven't found Hudson's badge. Should I keep looking?

Kendra's panicked tone rings out in my mind. Her rushed words.

"I need you."

As I hurry out of Molly's house, the memory of Hudson saying almost the same words to me ten years ago chases me down the street.

★ ★ ★

It was a cold October night, a week before Halloween. Kendra and Hudson had gone out earlier in the evening. I'm embarrassed to admit, I didn't ask a lot of questions. Hudson had said he was going to an early Halloween party with Heather, and that was good enough for me. Kendra had told me she was going out with some friends. I honestly didn't think they were going to the same place. They rarely hung out together, but again, I didn't ask. Darren was the one who liked all the details. I never needed them.

I was living in a fog of grief over Mac's death. I spent that evening eating Chinese food out of a container alone while rewatching the movie *Face/Off* for the dozenth time. Darren had drunk himself into a stupor and then passed out.

I went to bed fairly early, but then tossed and turned for a bit before falling asleep. When I did, I fell hard and deep. That's why I didn't hear my phone at first when it rang. When I did awaken, it was by Darren's rough hand, shaking my shoulder.

"Your phone," he said, his voice groggy.

It was past midnight. Who would be calling?

The kids.

Were they still out?

My pulse spiked.

"Hello," I answered.

"Mom," Hudson's voice was strangled, panicked. I glanced over at Darren, who was already starting to fall back asleep. For being such an involved parent during the day, he was sure a disappointment at night. It was the same when they were infants. I'd be rudely awakened by a baby's wails only to find Darren snoring away, not a care in the world. I'd feel nothing but resentment for him as I peeled myself from the sheets and slunk down the hallway toward the nursery, where I was greeted by a red-faced crying baby. Then again, it was Darren who got up for early-morning feedings while I slept in, so I suppose it was a wash. I just couldn't see it at the time.

"Yes? It's me." I sat up straighter in bed.

"Mom," he repeated, and now there was no doubt something was very wrong. My son was fifteen, not two. His days of repeating "Mom" over and over had long past. "I need you to come quick. Something bad happened. I can't—" he choked "—I can't tell you. Just please come."

A thousand scenarios ran through my mind as I headed to the field overlooking the American River, where—I learned—my son, his girlfriend and their friends had been drinking and partying. But my imagination could never have prepared me for the truth.

Kendra is waiting for me at her front door when I arrive. Probably wondering what took me so long. I can usually make it to her house in less than ten minutes. But I don't usually have to sneak out of a house I've broken into and run back to mine before coming over. I barely have time to walk into the entryway before she thrusts Mason into my arms. She's wearing jeans and a blazer, flats on her feet, a purse hanging from her shoulder.

"He's just been fed," she says, palming her keys and moving around me. "I don't know how long I'll be. But I'll keep in touch."

"Wait." I turn, wishing I could reach out and grab her arm, but mine are securely fastened around Mason. "Where are you going?"

"The police station." She says it like I'm daft.

I open my mouth to ask more questions, but she's already stepped outside, the door closing loudly behind her.

Mason coos in my arms. Kicks his pale, chubby legs. I bounce him up and down as I stare out the front window.

Kendra backs her car out of the driveway. Her mouth is set in a hard, determined line. My stomach twists as I try to work out what's going on.

Does Theo have something to do with what happened to Molly?

I think about how uncomfortable he'd been in the hospital when Kendra had been in labor. The sight of Kendra in pain distressed him—and he didn't have the stomach for the mess, the blood. A couple of times I thought he'd pass out. I mean, he practically gags every time he changes Mason's diaper.

And it's not just bodily messes that gross him out. Glancing out at the pristine front lawn, I think about how he and Kendra hired a landscaper the moment they moved in here.

Theo doesn't like getting his hands dirty.

He always drives the speed limit, and according to Kendra, he never even partied in high school. Didn't drink until he turned twenty-one.

He's not a risk-taker.

He's stable and responsible, matter-of-fact, logical. All the things Kendra wanted from a husband. I've never seen him lose his temper, and I've been around in times when he probably should have. After Mason was born, I helped around their house a lot. Kendra picked and nagged at him incessantly during those days, and they were both exhausted, running on almost no sleep. But still, he kept his cool. It's only been recently that I've even seen them argue openly. He did appear frustrated with Kendra the other night, but I understood that. She could wear anyone down. Besides, he didn't raise his voice and I never thought he was in danger of exploding on her. I've been around men who were loose cannons before. Men who had anger and violence simmering under their skin.

That wasn't Theo.

Before they got married, I warned Kendra that I didn't see a lot of passion or enthusiasm from Theo. She scoffed at that, saying that life wasn't a sporting event. She didn't need a cheer-leader. She needed a partner. It wasn't exactly what I meant, but by her response, I could tell we desired very different things from a romantic relationship.

No, there's no way Theo did anything to that girl. Besides, what would his motive be?

Turning away from the window, I rain down soothing words of love onto Mason's head. I sink down into the leather recliner, pushing off with the toe of my shoe, causing it to rock gently back and forth. Mason nestles into my chest, a squishy ball of softness that feels like heaven in my arms.

In front of me sits the sleek granite coffee table, decorative gold shapes (octahedrons, Kendra once told me) and a planter sitting on top. Beyond that, the leather sectional couch, piled high with throw pillows in muted tones, matching with the large painting of the New York skyline on the wall. Next to it is a tall wicker basket filled with fuzzy throw blankets. Kendra's house is the opposite of mine. Modern and trendy. Darren would've loved it.

I don't, but it certainly fits Kendra and Theo.

"I'll never understand what it is about this house that appeals to you," Kendra said shortly after Darren's death. It was right after she'd tried to convince me to downsize, and I'd shot her idea down flat.

"It has character," I said, immediately knowing it was the wrong way to go.

Kendra's nose scrunched up. "It's old. Everything in it is old."

"Antique," I corrected her. "There's a difference."

"Dad hated this house, too," she said, looking at me as if to gauge my reaction.

If she was hoping for shock, she wasn't going to get it.

"Yeah, I know," I said, and it was her face that flipped from smug to surprised.

"You knew?"

"Of course I did."

"And you made him live here, anyway?"

I laughed. "I didn't make him do anything. We chose together to buy this house and stay here. Marriage is full of compromise."

"Seems Dad was the only one compromising," she muttered, and as much as I wanted to tell her that wasn't true, that she had no idea how much I'd compromised for Darren, I kept my mouth shut. She was grieving. Let her think what she wanted.

It wasn't her business, anyway.

When I peer down at Mason, his eyes are closed, his eyelids fluttering as if dreaming. I stroke his head and continue rocking. Kendra doesn't like when I hold him through a nap, but I have no desire to put him down. Besides, he looks too comfortable to move.

On the wall nearest the hallway, Kendra has hung a collage of family photos, all in matching frames, of course. It was an idea she got off of Pinterest. I stare at the newest one—a photo taken out in a large, leafy field, the sky sun-streaked, burnt orange and yellow hues mixed with the bright blue. Kendra holds Mason in her arms, his legs dangling, his face forward. Theo has his arm resting on her shoulders. All are smiling broadly, even Mason. The photographer was good.

A car engine roars out the window. I whip my head in the direction of it, knowing rationally that it won't be Kendra, but hoping it will be. I wonder what the police are asking Theo. Is Kendra in with him or waiting out in the lobby?

Mason stirs, his fisted hands rubbing over his eyes, but he doesn't wake. My legs are wearying of the constant rocking, but I don't dare stop. When my own kids were babies, this was my least favorite part of the day. It felt like a waste of time to sit and rock them to sleep. I'd be restless, my mind a revolving door of all the things that needed to be done. All that I could be doing. Funny how differently I feel about my grandson.

Then again, life isn't so busy anymore.

I find my own eyelids drooping slightly. Still rocking, I lean my head back and close my eyes for a moment.

I'm startled awake by a car door slamming, followed by Mason whining. *How long have I been out?*

Blinking, I lift my head from the chair. Mason stares up at me, blue eyes large and round. The front door pops open, Kendra stepping through. Hanging her purse on the hook near the door, she looks at Mason and me, raising her brows.

"Well, someone had a nap," she says sourly.

I smile. "We both did, actually."

She doesn't smile back. "Yeah, I can see that."

Mason's eyes track his mom as she makes her way over to us. She bends down, gripping her son's hands and shaking them gently. "Hi, there, little man. Looks like Grandma spoiled you, huh? Now you'll expect to be held every time you nap. It'll make it twice as hard for Mommy to get you down in your crib." Even though her words are laced with sarcasm and irritation, she keeps that soothing, high-pitched tone reserved for Mason.

Why is she acting so normal? You'd think she returned from the grocery store, not the police station.

"Where's Theo?" Outside, the sun is going down, the sky beginning to darken.

"He's stopping at the store on the way home. We're out of diapers." She plucks her son from my arms, drawing him into her bosom. "I bet you're hungry," she says in a singsong way.

I follow her as she carries him into the kitchen. "Kendra, what happened at the police station?"

"Just a few routine questions." Patting Mason's back, she peers over her shoulder. "They questioned all of Molly's work colleagues. Standard procedure, I guess."

"Oh." Leaning against the doorway, I cross my arms over my chest. "That makes sense."

Kendra lowers Mason into his high chair and buckles him with a loud snap. "I'm sorry I made you come all the way over here. Theo didn't need me. I just overreacted."

"Well, that's understandable. It's not every day your husband gets questioned in a murder investigation."

"True," she says absently while spooning pureed sweet potatoes into a bowl and stirring it with a tiny spoon. "How are things at home…with Hudson?"

"Good," I say, pushing off the wall and stepping further into the kitchen. "He's working now."

"Oh? That job he was telling us about? With Jared's uncle?"

"Yeah," I say.

She nods, loading up Mason's spoon. "Well, at least he's doing something." After depositing it into her son's mouth and wiping the excess with a rag, she says, "And how have you been feeling?"

"Pretty good," I say, and I'm about to tell her about my upcoming doctor's appointment, but she stands abruptly.

"Oh, I wanted to tell you about something." She moves across the kitchen and flips open the laptop on the kitchen table. "Remember when I told you about the research I'd been doing on the correlation between gut health and the brain?" I follow her. As her computer roars to life, I see all of the tabs across the top of the screen. They're all open to articles about Alzheimer's. My heart pinches. She's so dead set on helping me. I don't have the heart to tell her about my appointment.

She'll no doubt insist on coming. And it'll get her hopes up. What if there's nothing Dr. Steiner can do? What if there's nothing any of us can do?

I remember how devastating it was for me when my mom was going through it. How helpless I felt.

I can't do that to Kendra.

She points to the screen. "This article is all about diet and how it can affect your brain. I'm gonna email it to you, okay? I can even help you put together a grocery list and menu for the week if you want. I'm sure with Hudson there, you're not eating the best."

She's not wrong. I've eaten out more lately than I have in a while, but I shake my head. "I've been eating fine."

Kendra is quiet a minute as she goes into her email. "Okay, I just sent it. Read it and let me know what you think."

I place a hand on her shoulder, ignoring how her muscles tighten beneath my touch. "Thanks, Kendra. I appreciate it."

"Sure." Mason whimpers from his high chair. "Sorry. Mommy's coming." She closes her laptop and stands.

Hudson will be home soon, and I want to talk to him before he goes out with friends or holes up in his room for the night.

"If you don't need anything else, I'm gonna take off," I say as she resumes her seat in front of Mason's high chair.

"Okay, thanks, Mom." She smiles at me while bringing the tiny spoon filled with orange mush up to Mason's lips. His mouth opens wide, then closes around the spoon.

"Anytime."

After kissing my grandson's cheek and offering Kendra a swift hug, I head outside into the cool night air, unable to shake the funny feeling that Kendra isn't telling me everything.

12

Over a simple dinner of grilled cheese sandwiches and tomato soup, I tell Hudson about my day. Well, minus the part about stalking his Facebook page or breaking into Molly's house, that is. I do, however, share about my upcoming doctor's appointment, which he's very excited about, and then the part about watching Mason while Theo was questioned in relation to Molly's murder.

With my empty spoon suspended over my bowl, I watch for his reaction.

He's just taken a bite from his sandwich, a string of cheese tethering him to it momentarily. When he sets the sandwich back down on his plate, the cheese lingers, hanging like a snagged thread that needs cutting. Wiping it off with a napkin, he says, "Yeah, it makes sense that they'd question everyone she worked with."

"Everyone? How much could Theo know about her? Do you remember if Theo mentioned their being in the same department or sharing a project or something? You don't think it's weird?" I'm rambling, I know, but I haven't been able to shake that funny feeling.

"I wouldn't worry about it. I mean, have you seen Theo's scrawny arms? There's no way he could strangle someone to death with those." He lets out a noise that's a cross between a laugh and a grunt as if to emphasize how preposterous it sounds.

My spoon pauses mid-scrape inside the bowl. "How do you know Molly was strangled?"

He slurps up a spoonful of soup, then licks his lips. "Um... I don't know. I must've read it somewhere or heard it on the news."

I'd been searching for the information for hours. There's no way I missed it. But I must have. How else would Hudson know? And how could he talk about it so nonchalantly?

He shoves the remainder of his sandwich into his mouth, crumbs decorating his beard.

"Why didn't you tell me about seeing Molly Saturday night?" I ask, staring down and swirling the spoon nervously in my bowl.

There's a long pause, and then he shrugs. "Wasn't important."

I look up. "You saw a woman on the night she was murdered. How is that not important?"

"I saw her for like two seconds."

"That's not the way Jared made it sound."

Hudson shakes his head. "*Jared* doesn't know what he's talking about."

I'm shocked at how unaffected Hudson seems by this whole thing. Picking at the skin on my finger, I take a deep breath and then ask the question that's been burning inside me for days. "You didn't go to Molly's house, did you?"

His eyes flash. "Of course not. Why would you ask that?"

I almost tell him about what Molly's neighbor said but decide against it. He'd feel betrayed. And probably angry. Guys with beards are a dime a dozen these days. Why would I automatically make the leap to Hudson?

There is one more question that's hot on my tongue, though. It burns to be asked, and I can't keep it inside anymore. "Who's Blondie?"

He seems stunned for a second, as if unable to keep up with the subject change. "Huh?"

I sigh, my shoulders dipping. "I…um…you got a text the other day and your phone was out…in view… I didn't mean to look." Who's the liar now? "But I saw a name. Blondie. So, I was just kinda curious who that was. An ex or something?"

"Oh." He shakes his head, the fog clearing, and a smile emerges on his face reminiscent of the way the sun peeks out of the gray mist. "No. That's my buddy Steve. He's blond, and years ago I started calling him Blondie as a joke. We like to give each other shit. You know, mess with each other."

I nod. So maybe that text was nothing more than his buddy razzing him. A response to some teasing text thread. An inside joke I wasn't privy to.

Groaning, I run a hand over my face. "I'm sorry. I don't know why I'm acting like this. Just freaked-out by this whole thing, I guess."

Hudson's face softens. "I get that, but you have nothing to worry about. You're safe. I'm here."

I force a nod and a smile before dropping the subject, never admitting to him that it isn't me I'm worried about.

I can't get my conversation with Hudson out of my head. How could he know Molly was strangled? I still haven't been able to find the information anywhere.

And I'm not sure I buy his explanation about the text.

I stop in front of Hudson's room. Hesitate. Glance around.

The AC kicks on, and I flinch, even though I know Hudson is at work. I hear Bowie walking around downstairs. In the distance, there's the sound of drilling. Someone must be getting work done on their home. But other than that, it's quiet. Swallowing hard, I step forward, turn the knob and swing the door open.

Hudson's bed is unmade, discarded clothes lie on the floor and empty water bottles line the dresser. I stand at the edge of the room, a conflict raging inside of me. I've never liked snooping in my kids' things. My mom was a big snooper. In my teenage years, it wasn't uncommon to come home from school and find the items in my room moved around, sometimes even reorganized.

"Well, it's my room," she said as justification when I called her on it. "I pay for it. Therefore, I can go in it whenever I like."

Technically, Dad paid for it, but I knew better than to say that. Instead, I started hiding the things I didn't want her to see. My journals. Pictures. And as I got older, cigarettes, fake ID, letters from boyfriends.

I told myself I'd never be that kind of mom. The kind that enters her children's rooms uninvited and goes through their things.

But this is different. Hudson is no longer a child. He's a grown man living in my home. He's clearly keeping things from me, and I have every right to know what they are.

I step further in. The bottoms of his pants are coated in white clay. His shirts are splattered with it. God, he gets that stuff everywhere. Sometimes after he showers, I still see it clinging to strands of his hair. Next to his clothes are a few gum wrappers and a bag of Doritos. Something tugs at the back of my mind, instant and jarring like that time Darren and I went parasailing and the guys on the boat thought it was funny to yank on the rope. I blink, willing the fog of dementia to lift. What am I looking for? What am I expecting—fearing—to find?

"Have you seen Theo's scrawny arms? There's no way he could strangle someone to death with those."

On the dresser, I find a stack of receipts. Gas. Food. When I come across one from Midtown Saloon, I scan it. It's dated the night of Molly's murder. Hudson had bought several IPAs, and one cocktail. Was the cocktail for Molly?

I picture them together. Laughing, talking and drinking. Her asking if he'd like a nightcap and him following her back to her place.

"Of course not. Why would you ask that?"

But I don't think he ever would've told me he saw her that night at all if not for Jared's slipup. What if he's lying to me about this, too?

The closet door is slightly ajar. I open it all the way, revealing the scratches on the interior. I imagine someone's fingernails raking over the wood, splinters embedding in their skin, under their nails. Reaching out, I trace them with the pads of my fingers. As my fingers dip into them, I realize they're deeper than I'd originally thought. I'd always imagined with morbid curiosity that Grace had made them, but it's hard to believe that her tiny hands could've dug this far into the wood. I picture her inside here, crouched down, crying and clawing at the door.

My body involuntarily shivers. Hugging myself, I avert my gaze from the scratches, forcing my thoughts to the present.

A jacket is hung next to a couple of flannels. A pair of tennis shoes sits on the floor. A guitar is propped against the wall. I didn't notice it the last time I was in here. I pick it up, perch on the edge of the bed and strum it lightly, wondering if Hudson still plays. As a child, he'd shown a brief interest in it.

One afternoon when Hudson was around nine, Mac and I

were writing a song together at my piano. We were in the zone. In the middle of making magic. It was one of my favorite things in the world, watching a song take shape. Words on a page that sprout wings, take flight.

As a new idea hit, I leaned down to press my fingers to the keys when Hudson broke out in song from the hallway. Something silly about snails and rat tails, his voice slightly off-key, his exuberance stealing away my train of thought. Mac laughed. I frowned.

"Hudson, that's not funny," I scolded when he appeared in the doorway. He pressed his lips together, but still they shook. I stood and shooed him out, anyway. "Go outside. I'm working right now."

Eyes downcast, he scampered from the room.

"Sorry about that," I said to Mac before sitting back down.

But Mac shook his head. "You know, I think he just wants to be included."

"Well, his father can include him in whatever he's doing." I tried to hum what we'd come up with, grasp the words that had been on the tip of my tongue moments earlier, but it was gone. "Damn it!"

"I'm sure it'll come back to you." Mac smiled. "And I bet if you spent some time teaching your son music, he might leave you alone when you're working. He just wants you to pay attention to him."

Darren and I had had similar conversations, but for some reason, when Mac said it, I actually heeded the advice. That evening, when I tucked Hudson in, I brought my guitar and let him stay up late strumming A and G. And that Christmas, I bought him his own guitar. I rarely saw him play it, though, his interest in music waning as his love of baseball grew.

Looking away from the guitar, my eyes skate over the remainder of his floor.

In response to my strumming, Bowie has run in, tail wagging. I don't want him tracking hair in here or knocking anything over. Then Hudson will surely know I've been snooping. I get up, gently placing the guitar right where I found it. I leave the closet door ajar just like it was moments ago. Then I carefully back out of the room, closing the door behind me.

Back in my room, I pick up my hamper and head downstairs to the laundry room. I sift through my clothes, checking all the pockets before throwing the items in the washer. In the pocket of my jeans, my fingertips sweep over something hard and smooth.

The watch from Molly's.

In all the chaos of having to race out to watch Mason, I'd forgotten about it. I hadn't even really meant to take it, but now that same feeling of familiarity hits me again.

I throw my jeans into the washer and slam the lid shut. Then I hurry to my computer and google "777."

The search brings up a zillion hits on some model of airplane. For a brief second, I wonder if Molly was seeing a pilot, but that seems like a ludicrous mental leap, so I adjust my search: "777 meaning." Google repopulates with article after article about angels, 777 being the number of reassurance that your angel is guiding you on the right path.

I frown, perusing further.

The only other thing I can find regarding the number is that it means "luck."

Neither of these explanations is particularly helpful either. I stare down at the face of the stolen watch, my blurred reflection looking back at me. Why is it so familiar? And what does it mean that I found it in Molly's house?

I wish I may, I wish I might
Have the wish I wish tonight.

"Let me out!" I screamed and screamed until my throat was shredded and raw, until the words came out soft and feathery, the beating of a butterfly's wings. I pounded my fists against the door in tandem, but it was no use.

All I'd succeeded in doing was bruising my small fists.

I could hear Andie's breathing. The steady rhythm of her footsteps outside the closet door as if she was that tiger at the zoo, pacing back and forth in the cage. Restless. Angry. Standing guard.

In frustration, I dragged my fingertips across the wood, splinters embedding themselves underneath my nails, and piercing the flesh. I did it over and over, until the grooves were so deep I could fit a finger inside.

I was the one who started this. She'd kept telling me what to do, and I didn't want to listen to her. I was tired of it, but I should have known better than to challenge her.

"You're not the boss of me!" I'd screamed.

"Oh, yeah?" she'd countered before grabbing me.

I'd done my best to fight her off, but she was bigger than me. I'd managed to land a single punch right in the center of her chest, momentarily knocking the wind out of her. I felt stunned but proud. For a second, I thought I'd finally done it. Gotten the best of her.

But that's when she shoved me in here.

"I *am* the boss of you!" she'd shouted through the door.

It was dark and smelled like mothballs and dust. Old clothes. Stinky shoes.

It had been hours now. I wanted out. But I was exhausted.

I sat back, resting my head on the wall. I had no choice but to give in, to let her win.

But it was the last time.

I was done being the prey.

13

I stare at the profile picture of Natalia. Almost an hour ago, I'd sent her a private message through Facebook. I'd kept the message light, explaining who I was and that I just wanted to talk about her relationship with Hudson. So far there'd been no response. I don't know why I'm surprised. I'm her ex's mom. What did I expect? But I can't get that picture of her with a black eye out of my head. I need to know how she got it.

I need to know my son didn't give it to her.

And it's not like I can ask Hudson.

I get that she doesn't owe me an explanation, but that doesn't stop me from wanting one.

Discouraged, I log out and push away from the table.

Leslie stands in the middle of her lawn, chatting animatedly with Beth. A couple of times her head bobs in the direction of my home. I frown and turn away from the window. The gold watch lies on the table, a reminder of what I stole from Molly's. And for what?

In all my searches today, I've come up empty. The answers aren't in this house. Not on the computer or in Hudson's room.

As much as I hate to admit it, my son is a stranger to me. There are so many years I wasn't a part of his life. His ex-girlfriend could fill in some of those gaps.

With determination, I walk across the kitchen to the junk drawer. I pull out a steno notebook and flip through the first few pages until I find the one I'm looking for. For the past few years, I've kept track of all the phone numbers I've had for Hudson. All the ones that had shown up on the caller ID when he'd phone. Many of them have been disconnected or belong to someone else. But I could never bring myself to cross them out or get rid of the sheet. They were a connection to my son, and deep down, I thought I might need them one day. If something bad were to happen to him and his cell was turned off again, I thought they might come in handy.

This isn't exactly what I had in mind.

The first number is his current one, but the three below that are from when he was with Natalia. With slick, shaky fingers, I dial the first one. Almost immediately, the little song comes on betraying that I've reached a number that has been disconnected.

Heart sinking, I try the next one.

This time it rings and rings. I'm about to hang up when a woman's voice comes on the line.

"Hi, you've reached Natalia. Leave me a message." It's so quick I'm caught off guard by the beep. It takes a second to get my bearings. Think of what to say.

When I finally do speak, it comes out hurried, a burst of words, gelling together like melted candy on a sidewalk.

"Hi, Natalia. It's Valerie, Hudson's mom. I really need to talk with you. Can you give me a call?" I rattle off my number and hang up, kicking myself for not giving more of an explanation.

I glance at the time. It's already late afternoon, and my stomach growls. I scour the contents of the fridge. Hudson will probably be home shortly. I haven't even thought about dinner. After closing the fridge door, I scan the take-out menus stuck to the front, trying to think of what I feel like eating.

The ringing of my phone startles me.

My heart picks up speed when I see that it's the number I just dialed.

"Hello?" I answer, my voice shaky with anticipation.

"Did Hudson put you up to this?" a woman's voice snaps, her words hard. *Natalia.*

"Um…no, he—"

"Because that's a clear violation of the restraining order," she continues.

My spine straightens. "Restraining order?" I repeat as if the words can't be right. "You have a restraining order against Hudson?"

"He didn't tell you?" She laughs bitterly. "Why am I not surprised?"

"W-why do you have one? What did he do?"

"I shouldn't even be talking to you," she says. "I only called back to tell you to leave me alone or I'm calling my lawyer."

"Wait," I say louder than I meant to. "Natalia, please. Hudson has no idea I'm calling. I just want to ask you a few questions."

"I'm sorry. I can't do this." The phone clicks in my ear.

I stare at it in shock.

Behind me, Bowie breathes hard as he enters the kitchen. Probably ready for his dinner. In a daze, I walk slowly to the cabinet and scoop out a cup of dry food. But when I turn toward his bowl, a gasp leaps from my throat, and the plastic cup slips from my fingers, crashing to the floor, dry food littering the hardwood.

In Bowie's mouth, punctured between his teeth, hangs a deflated pink ball.

I can't sleep. Natalia's words keep playing through my mind. *Restraining order.*

Restraining order.

Every time I do catch a few moments of slumber, I dream of Natalia's black eye, Hudson looming over her, hands wrapped around her neck.

Lying in the dark, clutching the edge of my comforter, I tell myself it could be nothing. A big misunderstanding. Or perhaps Natalia is being overdramatic. I don't even know her. But even as I think it, I know it's silly. Restraining orders are a huge deal. People don't get them for no reason.

I wanted to ask Hudson about it over dinner tonight. We got Chinese takeout, and I stared intently at my chopsticks, attempting to formulate a question that was subtle and organic. One that wouldn't arouse suspicion. I couldn't come up with anything.

The point of calling Natalia was to get answers. Instead, I'm left with more questions.

They spin in my brain like a clothes dryer, leaving me nauseous and disoriented. Blowing out an exasperated breath, I sit up. In the weeks after Darren's death, I suffered from insomnia. Suzanne had bought me a bottle of melatonin and some sleep-aid tea. It did help a little. Maybe it will tonight, too.

Tossing and turning is getting me nowhere. I've even tried counting, but the numbers morph into disturbing images of Heather's lifeless eyes or Mac's bloodied head. I need to quiet all the thoughts in order to fall asleep.

After sliding out of bed, I pad out of the room. The deflated pink ball lies flat in the corner. When Bowie dragged it into the kitchen earlier, I'd been so stunned by the phone call, I hadn't seen which direction he'd come from. I had the vague sense that I'd heard him on the stairs, though. Had he found it upstairs? Or was it possible he'd had it the whole time, stashed away in some corner of the house?

More questions without solid answers. I seemed to be drowning in them lately.

When I get to the bottom of the stairs, heavy breathing reaches my ears. It's coming from the family room. I creep forward, moving toward it, picturing six-year-old Grace in her frilly red dress, the one she's wearing in the photo most of the papers printed in the wake of her death. I half expect to see her ghost standing in the middle of the family room, her pink ball round in her hands.

Instead, I find Hudson, curled up on the couch, sound asleep. He has the comforter from his bed upstairs wrapped around his body. Aside from the bushy beard, he looks almost childlike with his body tightly coiled, his mouth parted, his eyes squeezed shut.

It's puzzling. Why does he keep coming down here at night?

Did he sleepwalk again?

Or is there more to it than that?

There are clearly things going on with him. Things he isn't sharing with me. And I won't rest easy until I know what those things are.

14

After parking my car, I adjust the sunglasses on my nose and pull my hat further down my forehead. Glancing around, I open the car door and step out. The lot is pretty full, most of the spaces taken. But only a few people are outside, a family talking near an SUV, a homeless man standing in the corner of the lot, leaning against a grocery cart full of his belongings, and a young woman walking swiftly past me, purse tucked under her arm.

The front of the record store is all windows. It's not very busy inside, only a few people scattered throughout. When I was younger, I'd spend hours in stores like this, listening to demos and perusing the aisles. But with the invention of streaming apps, times have changed. I still have my old record player, and I pull it out occasionally. There's nothing quite like the sound of vinyl. Most of the time, though, I listen to music on my phone. All my CDs are boxed up in the garage. I never pull those out. No reason to.

I see Natalia through the window. She's behind the register, helping a customer. I've never met her in person, but I recognize her instantly from her photos.

It hit me as I lay in bed last night, unable to fall asleep. The way to track Natalia down. To force her to talk with me. Hudson had given me the clue I needed in our first conversation about her. It was when he'd called me out of the blue to say that he was moving in with his new girlfriend and that he now had a reachable phone number. I hadn't talked with him in months. He sounded happy. Grounded.

At the time, I felt relieved and hopeful.

"How did you two meet?" I'd asked him, adjusting the blanket over my legs. Bowie stirred on the couch by my feet.

"At Chill," he'd replied.

"What's that?"

"A record store here in Oakland."

He'd been in Oakland for almost a year then. It was a long time for him to stay put. He'd never invited me for a visit, so I had no idea what kind of place he was living in. It was probably best that way, though. When he was living here in town, I had a terrible habit of showing up at his place unannounced to help out or clean up or just check on him. He didn't like that. Maybe once he was settled in with his new girlfriend, they'd have me out.

"A record store, huh?"

"Yeah, she's a manager there."

"God, I haven't been to a legit record store in forever," I said, staring at the television I'd muted when the phone rang. Monica and Rachel from *Friends* mouthed words animatedly in the middle of their New York apartment. "Do people still buy records?"

"I do," he said, sounding slightly offended. "Often. That's how we got to talking. She said I was her favorite customer."

I could hear the smile in his voice, and it made me smile, too.

My skin itches underneath my top as if I've broken out in hives. This happens sometimes when I'm nervous. The first couple of times Flight of Hearts performed in front of an audience, I thought I'd scratch my skin right off. I take a step backwards, almost falling off the curb and onto the hood of a parked car.

Last night, in the darkness, safe under the covers in my bed, this had seemed like a good idea. Necessary, even. The pictures of them on Facebook stirred up so many questions. And now that I know about the restraining order, it's clear that Hudson's been keeping things from me. I need honest answers, and I feel like she's the only one who can give me them. But outside in the harsh light of day, I realize that this is a very bad idea.

I could really mess things up for Hudson. Maybe even be in violation of the restraining order. It was a thought that had crossed my mind during the hour and a half drive, too. I even turned around a couple of times, the rational part of myself screaming out what a big mistake this was.

Now I'm wishing I'd listened to that voice of reason.

I'm ready to now.

Smoothing down my hair, I turn, intending to head back to my car. But then Natalia steps outside, pack of cigarettes in hand. She can't know what I look like, I think as she walks in my direction, taking a cigarette from the pack. Not unless she did get my message and saw my profile picture. Or if Hudson had ever shown her one, and that's doubtful. But when she brings the cigarette up to her lips, her eyes meet mine. Her mouth hinges, her hand lowering.

"What are you doing here?" Her expression is one of desperation, possibly even fear.

Does she think Hudson is with me? That this is some kind of ambush?

I hold up my hands, showing my palms, as if in surrender. "He has no idea I'm here. I just need to talk with you."

She shakes her head, her hands trembling as she shoves the cigarette back into the pack. "You shouldn't be here."

"I know. I know." I stay where I am, scared to move a muscle. As if she's a stray cat I'm afraid will run away. "And I promise I'll never contact you again after today if you just answer a couple of questions."

She cocks her head to the side and narrows her eyes. "Is that a threat?"

"No. Of course not." I sigh. "Can we please start over?"

She backs away. "I don't think so."

I'm losing her. "Wait. Please," I call, but she isn't moved. "He's living with me."

I've piqued her interest. "I just… I…um…need to know what he's capable of." God, I'm the worst mother on the planet. Maybe Kendra is right about me. I look around. If Hudson ever finds out about this, I'll probably lose him forever.

What am I doing?

"Fine." She turns, blowing out a breath. "But I only have a few minutes." I follow her as she moves down the side of the building until we're standing outside the range of the windows. Propping one leg up, she places her foot against the wall. "And I'm having a smoke." She places a cigarette between her lips and lights up. There is a tattoo on her lower arm. At first I only catch the edge of it, a black swirl. It takes a moment to see what it is. A pair of angel wings. I briefly wonder at its meaning, liking it much more than the foreign words inked on my son's body. She raises a brow. "Shoot."

"Huh?"

Now both brows go up. "You said you had some questions."

"Oh. Right." Well, there's no backing down now. As much as I think this is a mistake, I know I'll kick myself if I let this opportunity go. I ask the question that's been plaguing me all night. "Why'd you file a restraining order against my son?"

She lifts her chin, blowing a steady stream of smoke into the air above my head. It lingers for a moment before dissipating. "I didn't want him contacting me anymore."

Clearly. I bite back a snarky remark and instead say, "Right, but why? What had he done to you?"

Taking a long drag from her cigarette, she studies me. In person, there's a hardness to her that the photos don't show. Her under-eye makeup is a little smeared, and her thin lips are painted in a dark maroon color that causes her pale skin to look even lighter. She has a nose ring, but not on the side. It's in the center, hanging down. It looks uncomfortable. Tattoos line her arms, which are exposed under a retro Metallica T-shirt. Her hair is pulled up in a messy ponytail. Online I'd assumed she was younger than Hudson. Up close, I'm now guessing they're the same age, or she may even be older than him.

"Did Hudson tell you I'm a big fan?"

It takes me a minute. "Oh." I point to my chest. "Of me, you mean?"

She nods. "Well, of Flight of Hearts, but yeah."

"No, he didn't."

"It's how he got me to go on a date with him. Told me you were his mom." She flicks ash onto the concrete. "I thought it was pretty cool."

I wonder why Hudson hadn't told me that. Fans are hard to come by these days. I would've liked knowing I had one.

"I'd just gotten out of a relationship. My ex cheated on me. And Hudson was just so…"

Charming? Sweet? Good-looking?

"Into me."

Okay. Not what I was expecting.

"It felt good, you know, to be with someone who liked me so much. Someone who liked me, maybe more than I liked him." Her eyes cut to me to gauge how I take this news, her taking advantage of Hudson's feelings. I say nothing, keep my listening face blank. "I thought it was perfect. Thought he'd never cheat on me." She looks me in the eye. Frowns. "Turns out, there are worse things than being cheated on."

A chill runs up my spine, despite the fact that it's not cold at all today. I hug myself. "What do you mean?"

"Hudson was scary jealous. He never wanted me going out with friends. Hell, he didn't even like me coming to work. He used to hang out here…kinda like you're doing now." My face flames. "Thought I was gonna have to quit after we broke up because he wouldn't stop coming by."

"But you didn't," I point out. Hudson must not have been that scary. She wasn't exactly hiding. "You didn't even change your phone number."

"I almost did. Almost moved out of my apartment, too, because he kept showing up there. Almost changed every goddamn thing about my life. But then he would've won, you know? And I was like, screw that." She throws the cigarette on the ground and stomps on it with the sole of her checkered Vans. "That's why I filed the restraining order. So I could keep my life and not have to worry about him harassing me anymore." Stepping around me, she says, "Break's over."

"Did he ever hurt you?" I ask before she can walk away. "Physically, I mean." The image of her bruised face fills my mind.

"I gotta go," she says impatiently without slowing down. "Don't come back here." Then she disappears inside, leaving me standing alone in front of the store, still as confused as ever.

After a few seconds of standing in bewilderment, I blink. Turning, I stare through the window of the store. At first, I don't see Natalia. She's not at the register like before. But then I find her, in the middle of one of the aisles, talking to a customer. She's pointing to something, an album maybe. When she smiles and pushes a strand of hair back, I can sort of see what Hudson must have seen. I try to picture him in place of the customer, but end up frowning.

My conversation with her has tainted my view of my own son. The way she described him is in direct conflict with my own memories—the boy who needed an extra hug before I would leave him, the one who would tuck his hand into mine when he was afraid. Her words are also a stark contrast to the man living with me now who buys my groceries and takes me out to the bar to help cheer me up. I hate that she's changed things for me. I hate that I'm seeing him in this new, jarring light.

"There are worse things than being cheated on."

The recollection of the words she spoke, sparks a long-forgotten memory of a few days before Heather's death.

It all started when I stubbed my toe. Cursing under my breath, I located the culprit. Hudson's Nikes.

We were having Leslie and James over, and I'd cleaned the entire house earlier. Lord knows, Leslie's house was always pristine. I'd told the kids to keep it that way. Was that really too big of an ask?

With a frustrated grunt, I snatched up the pair of shoes and marched up the stairs. His door was closed, but I was so annoyed I didn't bother knocking. If he wanted me to follow his rules, he needed to follow mine.

Shoving open his door, I dropped the shoes on the ground. They fell at an interval, each thudding loudly. I looked up wearing a triumphant smile, which quickly died when I noticed Hudson wasn't alone. A girl was draped over him like a blanket. Her hair was messy, and lipstick trailed up her face. The shade blooming on Hudson's mouth like a Popsicle stain perfectly matched it.

"Oh, my god. I'm so sorry," I mumbled, backing out of the room and firmly closing the door.

It's not like I'd never walked in on Hudson in a compromising position. Darren had been threatening lately to take his door off the hinges, but Hudson always talked him down, saying we knew Heather—we could trust them together.

But that girl in there was not Heather.

Natalia spots me through the glass and I wonder how long I've been standing here, lost in my memories. She purses her lips in a look of annoyance. I've long overstayed my welcome. Head down, I scurry to my car. Once inside, I secure my sunglasses on my nose and take a deep breath. I never should've come here.

If Hudson ever finds out, he'll be livid. And if I messed things up with the restraining order, I'll never forgive myself.

A restraining order. How absurd is that? It still boggles my mind. Before this week, I thought only scary guys had those taken out against them. Drug dealers, mobsters, violent men. Not someone like Hudson. As I pull out of the parking lot, I wonder if I know my son at all. Is he really the possessive control freak Natalia described? Or is he the sweet young man who looks after me? Is it possible to be both? My head swirls.

I flick on my blinker, preparing to merge onto the freeway. My heart stops when I peek into my rearview mirror. Hudson is behind me.

Not directly behind me, a few cars back.

A second ago, I caught a view of the side of the vehicle when it changed lanes from the middle over to mine.

I squint. Is that really him? It looked exactly like his car, but I couldn't make out the person in the driver's seat. It was definitely a man, though. I could tell by the build. But now I can't see the car at all.

What if he saw me leaving the record store? He'll know why I came here. What other reason would I have for hitting up a record store? Chill, no less.

No, there's no way that's him. It's the middle of a workday. He's at the mine in Vista Falls. That's the opposite direction from Oakland. There's no way he's out here.

Once I've safely made it onto the freeway, I glance once again in my rearview mirror. There's no trace of Hudson's car in any of the three lanes behind me. I heave a sigh of relief, even though anxiety still clings to my chest. I'm not sure if it's the possibility of that car having been Hudson's or simply the vestiges of guilt over what I did today. What I did was irresponsible. Stupid. So unlike me.

Is this part of the disease?

Mom did a lot of things that were out of character for her after her diagnosis.

Yes, that has to be it. A symptom of my disease, nothing more.

I'm not acting rationally. I never would've done this if I was. Still, I can't ever let Hudson know about it.

I stop for gas on my way home, and the scent of it paints my fingertips long after I leave the station. It's an errand I hate, and I often wait until I'm about to run out before stopping. Today was no exception. I'm fairly certain I was minutes away from ending up on the side of the road. For most of our marriage, Darren filled my tank for me. The first time I had to go on my own after he got sick, I burst into tears at the pump. The attendant came over to see if I needed help, but I shooed her away. Customers gaped at me from their respective cars. I ended up only filling a quarter of my tank before jumping in my car, too embarrassed to continue. In my haste, I forgot to unhook the nozzle, and it broke off, hanging from my car as I started to leave. Obviously, I noticed immediately, and pulled over. After paying the gas station for the damages and our mechanic to get rid of the dents in the side of my car, it ended up being an expensive trip to get gas.

When I get home, Hudson's car is parked along the curb. The same car I thought I saw two hours ago in Oakland. The car I thought was in Vista Falls, parked in front of the clay mine, and couldn't possibly be following me. And yet, here it is.

Uneasiness returns to my chest, making itself at home.

It's only two-thirty. Typically, he doesn't get home until close to four, sometimes later if he works overtime.

Inside, I find Hudson standing over the kitchen counter, eating a sandwich. His head bobs up when I enter the room, and he eyes me curiously. There are crumbs all over the counter, along with the opened loaf of bread and lunch meat, as if he'd made the sandwich in a hurry.

"You're home early," I say, unable to look at him. "No overtime today, huh?"

"Nope," he responds around a mouthful. "Where were you?"

Do I detect accusation in his tone? I can't tell. "Um…just running errands." The lie tastes bitter on my tongue, like cheap coffee with no cream. I continue to stare at the ground.

He drops his sandwich onto a paper towel, and then wipes his hands on his pants. "I'll help you bring stuff inside."

Is he calling my bluff? "N-not that kind of errands." His eyebrows lift. "I had to get gas and stuff like that." At least now I'm partially telling the truth.

"You should've told me. I'd have done it for you."

His words stop me in my tracks. Does this sound like a

mean, terrifying individual? I think about how Natalia glared at me when she caught me staring through the window. Not just then, but through our entire conversation, she'd been aloof, bordering on rude and disrespectful. It's the only interaction I've ever had with her. I know nothing else about her. Maybe she's the one with problems. The unstable one. Maybe she filed a restraining order out of spite, to blacken his record, cost him legal fees. She could've been lying about the entire thing.

I don't like siding against someone who might be a victim. But am I going to trust a complete stranger's assessment of my son over my own? I never should've talked to his ex.

Guilt spreads through me like a rash. I can't take the way he's looking at me. I'm worried I'll spill everything. "Um…" I rub my temples. "I have a bit of a headache. I think I'm gonna go lie down."

He nods, his forehead pinched, the corners of his lips curled downward in a look of concern. This is who my son is. Concerned. Caring. Shame on me for thinking otherwise.

And there's no way he was following me around. He was at work and then he came home and had lunch. End of story.

I start to walk out of the kitchen when an insistent scratching noise catches my attention, followed by a distressed bark.

Bowie.

The dog door is latched closed. I never lock it during the day, and certainly not if he's out there. Another bark.

"You locked Bowie out?"

Hudson shrugs, offering up no explanation. Maybe he's embarrassed to admit to me that he's scared of Bowie. But I wish he would so we could talk about it. I know Bowie would never hurt him, but I get that seeing a kid get his face attacked could color all of your future interactions with any dog.

Plus, Hudson's never had a pet. Well, unless you count

Chompers. Standing at the door, my mind flies back to when Hudson was ten.

Leaning down, I brushed the hair from Hudson's forehead and pressed my lips to his warm skin. He always ran hot. When he was an infant, I was constantly freaking out, thinking he had a perpetual fever. Straightening up, I whispered, "Good night" and was about to reach for the light switch when I glanced down into Chompers's cage.

Hudson had gotten the hamster a few months ago after begging for one for ages. So far, he'd been taking great care of it, making sure Chompers was fed and had clean water. He and Darren had even cleaned out the cage a few times together. I was proud of what a great job he was doing taking care of an animal. And honestly relieved the job of cleaning out sawdust reeking of pee hadn't fallen to me when the novelty of a new pet had worn off.

Now I paused: Where was Chompers? Usually, he was pretty active when I tucked Hudson in, as he came more alive at night. His cage was filled with cubbies and wheelie gadgets—all the things they urged us to buy at the pet store. Narrowing my eyes, I peeked around each of the obstacles, but there was no sign of the hamster.

"Hudson? Where is Chompers?"

He clutched the edge of his blanket with both hands, and his bottom lip trembled.

My heart sank.

"Hudson?" I inched away from the wall.

"I don't know." His voice was small and scared. "He wasn't in his cage when I came back up here after dinner."

When Hudson got Chompers, my only rule was that he wouldn't let him out of his cage. I didn't want to wake in the middle of the night to find a hamster in my bed. The thought alone made my skin crawl. Now, as I scoured Hudson's floor, my neck and chest became a flaming inferno of stressed-out itchiness.

"Why didn't you say anything?"

"I didn't want to get in trouble." He sat up in bed, his eyes watery. "I promise I had his cage locked. I don't know what happened."

I stared at him a moment and then sighed. He was only ten. Maybe that was too young to be responsible for a pet. Once I left his room, I told Darren, and together we spent the evening searching for Chompers.

After a few hours, we gave up. We left some piles of food out to tempt him into emerging, but the outlook seemed bleak. Darren was convinced he'd died in the walls chewing some wire, and tasked me with telling Hudson the bad news in the morning.

"He'll take it better coming from you," he said, although I wasn't sure that was true. I agreed only because I'd felt bad about how much time I'd been spending away from home lately.

Darren went to bed earlier than me that night—per usual. I stayed up late, watching TV. Around eleven, I'd gotten hungry for something salty and junky, so I snagged a bag of the kids' chips we bought to pack in their lunches, stood in the kitchen crunching away, watching a light come on upstairs in Leslie's house and then go out a minute later. Someone getting themselves some water, maybe. I smiled. It was so nice to be friends with our neighbors.

When the baggie was empty, I slid open the kitchen trash can. It's not like Kendra or Darren would've cared about my late-night snacking. But this was the last bag of nacho cheese Doritos, which were Hudson's favorite. I wasn't about to give myself away as the thief. I shoved the crumpled chip bag a layer or two down in the garbage, gingerly placing another piece of trash over it, when I saw something brown. And fuzzy.

I shoved a few wrappers and an empty milk carton out of the way until it came into full view.

Chompers.

His body was stiff, head cocked at a wrong angle.

I swallowed a shriek, not wanting to wake the house; wrapped him in a paper towel while trying not to gag; and said a few words—"Sorry, little guy"—before burying him properly in the big garbage can outside.

When I asked Hudson about it the next morning, he said he had no idea how Chompers got there. But I knew that wasn't possible. A hamster doesn't get into the trash and die all by itself. I didn't have the heart to tell Darren I'd found the runaway. He would've flipped out.

The only person I did tell was Mac, who assured me I didn't need to worry. Said that Hudson had probably just squeezed the hamster a little too hard in exuberance or let him out and accidentally stepped on him. Most likely it was an innocent mistake, and at this point, Hudson was too afraid to come clean. *What kind of kid kills his own hamster, right?*

I'd believed Mac back then. But what if he'd been wrong? What if Hudson had hurt Chompers on purpose? What if this was a sign I should have taken seriously?

I'm doing it again. Going down this rabbit hole. What is wrong with me? Maybe paranoia is all part of the Alzheimer's. I should probably bring it up at my doctor's appointment.

I unlatch the door, and Bowie rushes through it, relief evident in his aggressive tail wags. Without a word to Hudson, I head upstairs, my trusty dog at my heels.

15

I'm out of lunch meat. Frowning, I stare down at my half-made sandwich. Cheese, lettuce, mayo, bread, but no meat. I've ransacked the fridge. It's gone. Hudson must have eaten the entire package.

"That boy is gonna eat us out of house and home," Darren used to say when Hudson was a teenager.

I guess not much has changed.

Closing the sandwich, I resign myself to eating it as is. Taking a bite, I wonder where Hudson went. He was gone by the time I returned from my walk this morning. It's Saturday, so I doubt he's working.

I take another bite, the flavors instantly catapulting me back to childhood. Growing up, my family didn't have a lot of money, and often my mom would make me cheese sandwiches. I picture her in our old, tiny kitchen, standing over the counter, taking slices of white bread out of the crackling cellophane wrapper. My children had no idea what it was like to grow up that way. For all their complaining about how they were raised, they hadn't wanted for anything.

I know I'm not like Leslie or Beth. I didn't take to motherhood naturally.

I wasn't one of those girls who grew up fantasizing about getting married and having kids. I dreamed about being famous. Performing on Broadway. Being the lead singer in a popular band. These were the things I strived for.

Bright lights, creativity and excitement. I had no desire for a family. Large or small. It was Darren's dream. He's the reason we have our two.

I'm the reason we don't have more.

My mom stayed at home. Took care of me and my dad. Watching her made my skin itch, my chest tight. All of her days revolved around maintaining our home, keeping Dad and me happy. Weeknights were spent in the kitchen, cooking and cleaning. Saturdays she ironed all of Dad's shirts and work pants. Sundays she prepped meals for the week. She didn't seem to hate it, though. I thought I would shrivel up and die if I had her life.

Then I met Darren. We were both seventeen. I sang at the wedding of a family friend. "All I Ask of You" from *Phantom of the Opera*, accompanied by a string quartet. I still remember what I was wearing. A navy dress, matching pumps. I felt so grown-up.

At the reception, Darren approached me. He was cute, dark hair curling over his collar, giant chocolate eyes. Not hot like some of the guys at my school—he did have this funny crook to his nose—but he had a genuineness they didn't. A calming presence. Nice smile. He stood before me in black pants, a collared shirt, one hand tucked in his pocket.

"You have an amazing voice," he said.

It was the best compliment he could have given me. Lots of boys told me I was pretty, but I wasn't interested in hearing that. My dad told my mom she was pretty all the time, patting her condescendingly on the head. His good little wife, looking pretty on his arm, and taking care of him. I never heard him say that she was smart or talented. He didn't even know that she had a creative side. Once, I found a few sketches she'd done tucked away in a junk drawer.

"Oh, they're nothing." She'd waved away my interest in them. "Just a silly hobby."

But it wasn't silly. She was good.

Too good to spend her days tending to my dad's needs instead of her own.

I wanted a man who saw me as more than a pretty girl. I wanted someone who saw my talent.

"Thanks." Smiling, I pushed the toe of my pump along the ground.

"What do you say? Wanna dance?" he asked, his arm sweeping out toward the dance floor.

"Sure." His hands were strong on my back, and he smelled good, a cologne I couldn't place. But I decided in that moment it was my favorite.

At the end of the night, I thought he might ask for my number, but he never did. Then he left with his parents, and I figured I'd never see him again. Sacramento is a large city. It was rare to bump into a friend or acquaintance at the store or out around town. What were the chances I'd run into him? I didn't even know what part of town he lived in.

But then a month into junior college, we ran into each other in the quad at lunch. This time he did ask for my number. A year later, I got pregnant with Kendra. I had no one to blame but myself for that. I'd been frequenting open mic nights, Darren's eyes bright with love and locked on mine as

I sang, a second drink in his hand for me when I'd wrapped up, and I'd end up staying out so late I often forgot to take my pill in the morning. Some weeks I missed more than I took.

I didn't know the first thing about babies. I'd never been a babysitter, except when pressed into service by my mother's friends—and even they seemed to know I was only suited for short emergency errands. Even with my dolls, I never nurtured or cared for them. When other little girls were carrying their baby dolls and holding them close, I was lining mine up in rows to sing to, a makeshift audience.

I'd never wanted to be a mom. I wanted to be a star.

Despite that, I love my kids and I did the best I could. I only hope one day they'll see that.

Finishing off the sandwich, I carry my empty plate to the sink and turn on the faucet. Water washes the crumbs away, leaving it clean, slick. I notice soil under a few of my nails as I put the plate into the dishwasher and wonder with an uneasy shiver where it came from. Then I remember that I'd spent the morning making a new succulent arrangement. After washing under my fingernails, I wipe my hand on a towel. The AC clicks on overhead. Goose bumps rise on my flesh. I head upstairs to grab a sweater. When I reach the top, I glance down into the living room. Bowie's sound asleep in his bed near the piano, sunlight from the window glistening over his fur. He's curled up, not a care in the world.

Must be nice.

Once inside my room, I look around, but my mind has gone blank. Why had I come in here? I rewind. Making a sandwich. Out of lunch meat. Right, I need to add that to my grocery list. But that's in the kitchen. What did I need to do in my room?

I stand in the middle of the room, looking around and hoping something in here will jog my memory. Nothing does.

Buzzing comes from my pocket. I pull out my phone.

It's Kendra.

"Hey, Mom. How is it going?"

"Good," I say absently, still trying to figure out what I need in here.

"Have you had a chance to read that article I sent?"

Oh, shoot. The article about the correlation between memory and healthy eating. "No, not yet. But I will today. It's actually perfect timing 'cause I need to go grocery shopping. I'll read it this morning before finalizing my list." I doubted there was anything on there that I didn't already know, but I'd humor Kendra.

"Yeah, please read it. I think it'll be helpful," she says. "Anyway, I have to go in a minute. But I wanted to see if you could watch Mason on Monday."

"Monday?" I hurry down the stairs and into the kitchen to look at the calendar. My doctor's appointment is Tuesday, but I have nothing on Monday. "Yeah, that works."

"Great. Theo will drop him off at like 7:30 in the morning."

"Okay."

"Make sure you write it down," she says, but I already am.

"I did."

"Good." A pause. "Hudson's working on Monday, right?"

An odd question, but I answer honestly. "Yes."

"Cool."

I hang up, wondering what that was about.

"Mom!" Kendra screamed my name so loudly, I was surprised the windows didn't shatter. Her voice carried all the way down the stairs to where her dad and I were watching TV. Though it wasn't loud enough to wake Darren, who was snoring away in the recliner. Exhaling, I stood, shoulders already tensing. I'd finally sat down to relax after a busy day. I didn't appreciate the interruption. Slowly, I

climbed the stairs. When I reached Kendra's room, she pointed at her floor and said, "Look what Hudson did!"

Her room was like a scene in a horror movie. Severed doll heads and headless bodies littered the floor. They weren't Barbie dolls either. Barbie heads would've been easy to pop back into place. These were her fabric dolls. The ones she'd had since she was little. In between the heads and bodies, gauzy cotton spread over the hardwood like decorative spiderwebs for Halloween.

"Hudson!" I admonished my little five-year-old, feeling both fascinated and petrified, and snatched his safety scissors from where they lay on the floor. How safe could they be if they were sharp enough to wreak this kind of damage? "Why would you do this?"

Crossing his arms over his chest, he glared at his older sister. "I didn't want to play house. She made me. It's her fault."

As I set the phone down, I hear the front door open. Bowie barks. I step into the hallway as Hudson enters the house holding a bag of groceries in his hand. Bowie runs to him, barking and leaping around. Hudson shields his body with the grocery bag.

"Bowie, no!" I holler, making my way down the stairs. My eyes meet Hudson's. "You went grocery shopping?" It was like pulling teeth to get him to come with me as a kid. He'd moan and drag his feet. I rarely made him, unless Darren wasn't home to watch him. It wasn't worth it.

Shrugging, he goes into the kitchen, sets the bag on the counter. "I saw your list."

"Thanks." Reaching inside the bag, my fingers light on a package of sliced turkey. I feel bad for getting irritated with him earlier. I never should've let Kendra get in my head about him. Their issues were nothing more than a case of sibling rivalry. My relationship with Hudson has always been different from theirs. Separate. I know him in a way Kendra doesn't.

It's not like I'm blind to his flaws. He's not perfect. But he's sweet. Always has been. He makes mistakes, screws up from time to time. But he always makes up for it.

"What have you got there?" It was late, the sky outside dark. Hudson's room was dimly lit, the lamp on his dresser offering the barest yellow light. He hid in the corner, slumped over something he didn't want me to see. I'd told him to get ready for bed ten minutes ago. He was wearing his Batman pajamas, and as I got closer, I caught the faint smell of toothpaste on his breath.

"Hudson? Let me see." I lowered myself down to his level.

He turned, lifting up what he'd been hiding. It was one of Kendra's dolls. He'd attempted to reattach her head with duct tape. It almost worked, too, except he'd accidentally put it on backwards. It was creepy, the way the doll's face came out of her back, her head slightly askew and bobbing with each movement of Hudson's hands.

Forcing a smile, I gently patted Hudson's hair. "That was nice of you to try to fix Kendra's doll, but why don't you go ahead and put her down now, okay?"

Frowning, he nodded.

My heart pinched. He might have done a bad thing earlier, but he was trying to make up for it, and that's what mattered.

"I'll tell you what," I said while guiding him toward his bed. "Tomorrow we'll go to the store, and you can help me pick out a couple of new dolls for Kendra, okay?" His lips curled upward at the corners. He seemed much more content as he nestled into his pillow. As I tucked him in that night, the doll with its head on backwards stared up at us from where it lay on the floor. I shivered, unnerved by its black beady eyes and crooked neck.

"I'll bring in the rest," I say, following him outside.

Across the street, Leslie's front door pops open. Hudson's bent over, grabbing a bag out of his trunk. A man steps onto Leslie's front porch. He has a large build, salt-and-pepper hair.

Hudson stands, cocking an eyebrow. "Leslie's got a boyfriend?"

"Not that I know of." I haven't seen a guy over there in years.

I squint. "Is that James?"

"You think?" Hudson squints, too.

"It looks just like him." A few pounds heavier, his hair more gray than brown, but definitely him.

"Maybe." Hudson shrugs, moving around me.

The longer I look, the more I'm sure.

But what's he doing there?

He looks in our direction, and I lift my hand and wave. We hadn't ended things as badly as Leslie and I had. In fact, he and I had had a mildly pleasant conversation the week he moved out. But today he doesn't return my wave. Instead, his attention is fixed on Hudson's back as he carries a bag of groceries up the front stairs.

16

Mason babbles from his playpen, kicking his legs high up into the air like he's doing infant yoga. His bright blue eyes stare up at the vaulted ceilings. Kendra has class this morning, and Theo is at work. Mason is wide-awake right now, but I doubt it will last long. According to Theo, he hasn't been sleeping well. Which means nobody is.

"You look tired," I observed when Theo slumped in the front door this morning, Mason in one arm and the diaper bag in the other, a yawn on his lips. "Mondays are always rough, huh?"

"It's not just that. I was on kid duty last night since Kendra was up late studying for a test she has today." He thrust Mason into my arms, visibly relaxing once I had him in my grasp. "On her nights, Kendra's been taking him on long drives to settle him. But I tried last night, and it didn't work. Kid was up all night playing and talking."

"Are you not sleeping well?" I say to Mason now. He gig-gles in response.

Giggling back, I hurry into the kitchen to make him a bottle. After scooping in the formula, I turn on the faucet and wait for the water to warm. Glancing out the window, my mouth dries out.

Leslie is on her front porch, holding a coffee mug, just like every morning. Only this time, she's not talking with a gaggle of gossipy neighbor women. She's talking with a cop.

Mason begins to whimper.

The water pours out of the faucet, turning so hot it steams up toward my face.

But I can't move. I'm frozen, transfixed, as Leslie points toward my house, the policeman's gaze following her hand. It's like déjà vu. Like we've traveled back in time ten years.

Mason's crying intensifies, snapping me out of it.

"Grandma's so sorry, honey," I holler from the kitchen, turning the heat down on the faucet. "Just a minute. I'm al-most done." Once it's mixed and shaken up, I hurry to him. After scooping him up, I carry him to the couch, then nes-tle him in my lap and pop the bottle's nipple into his mouth.

He drinks greedily, his hand playing with the bottom edge of my sleeve.

My back is to the window, so I can't see Leslie any longer. But it's probably for the better. I try to focus on my sweet grandson. Up until a month ago, I used to watch him a lot. A few times a week, at least. Kendra swears she doesn't need as much help now. But I know better. She's worried about my memory lapses. I only have a few hours with Mason as it is, so I plan to savor it. Not let Leslie get in my head.

Breathing deeply, I settle into the couch cushions, readjust-ing my arm a tad. Mason has gotten a lot heavier lately.

It doesn't take long for Mason to fall asleep, nipple falling out of his pursed mouth. A dribble of milk travels down his chin. I wipe it with my fingertip, having forgotten to grab one of his washcloths before sitting down. I don't have the heart to move him. Plus, it's not like I have anywhere to be. So I secure my hold on him, staring down at his sweet, sleeping face. His eyelids flutter as if his dreams course below them.

I gently touch his chubby cheeks with my knuckles, and he puckers his little lips, making me smile.

An authoritative knock at the door breaks the spell. I flinch. Mason stirs.

Twisting around, I look out the front window. Leslie is on her porch alone. And the cop car is still parked at the curb.

My stomach knots.

Pressing Mason close to my chest, I stand, watching his face. He continues to sleep in my arms as I walk steadily to the front door. Through the peephole, I see a man wearing a collared shirt.

Swallowing hard, I swing the door open with my free hand, clutching tightly to Mason with the other.

"Can I help you?" I speak quietly so as not to wake Mason.

"Yes, hi. Mrs. Jacobs, right?"

"Yes, but you can call me Valerie." Mrs. Jacobs will forever be associated with Darren's mom in my mind. When the kids were little, I always insisted their friends call me Valerie. The other moms preferred their children call me Mrs. Jacobs, thought calling me by my first name was disrespectful. I never understood that. My name was Valerie. Why couldn't they call me that?

"Valerie, I'm Detective Daniels. I've been talking to some of your neighbors about Molly Foster's case." He flashes a badge.

I nod, relief flowing through me. He's probably just talking to all the neighbors, same as the police did with her coworkers. I'd talked to both Kendra and Theo about his interview with the police, and the questions were all benign.

How well did he know her?

Did he know of anyone who'd want to hurt her?

Had she been acting strangely in the days before her death? That kind of thing.

"Sure… I doubt I'll be of much help, but I'm happy to answer any questions you might have," I say.

"That's kind of you, but I'm actually looking for your son, Hudson."

All the relief I'd felt is sucked out of me. "Hudson? Why?"

"Just have some questions I need to ask him."

"Well, he's at work right now, but he wouldn't be able to help you, anyway. He didn't know Molly."

"Really?" Detective Daniels's eyebrows jump up. "A couple of your neighbors said they saw him talking to her in your front lawn, actually."

I shift Mason's position. "Oh." Damn Leslie. She must've been spying on us again. "Um, yeah, the other night my daughter and her husband were over for dinner with me and Hudson. We were sitting on the porch having dessert when Molly jogged past. Apparently, she works with my son-in-law and he introduced her. To all of us."

"Who is your son-in-law?"

"Theo Pritchett."

He jots something down—Theo's name, I assume—then looks back up at me. "Then why did you say Hudson didn't know her?"

My skin flushes. *God, now I sound like a liar.* "'Cause he didn't. I mean, we all met her that one time, but that's it."

Mason blinks his eyes, stirs, then nestles back in. I wish he'd wake up and wail so loud it'd force the detective to leave.

"And he never saw her after that?"

I open my mouth fully intending to say no, but then clamp it back shut, thinking better of it. If he's asking the question, he may already know the answer. Lying will only make Hudson look guilty, and maybe even me by association. Besides, I know Hudson is innocent, right? I found no evidence of him at Molly's. Maybe the truth will set us all free.

"I believe he was at Midtown Saloon on Saturday night with a friend, and she happened to be there."

"Do you know if they spoke? Shared a drink? Do you know if he went back to her place afterward?" His tone is matter-of-fact, regardless of the fact that he's asking a mother about her son's sex life.

I think of the neighbor. The one who said she saw a young man with a beard at Molly's. Has Daniels talked with her? Even if he has, it doesn't prove anything. A young man with a beard could be anyone.

"No, he didn't," I say.

"Are you sure about that?"

"Yes, I am." Mason slips a little from my grasp and I hoist him upward. At that moment, it finally happens. His face screws up, his skin red as he opens his mouth and starts to cry. I throw the detective an apologetic look. "If that's all, I really need to go."

He reaches into his pocket and pulls out a business card. Then he juts out his hand. "When your son gets home, can you have him call me, please?"

"Sure." I take the card.

Hudson stares at the card in his hand. I'd caught him on his way out the door to go out with friends, since I'd been changing my clothes when he returned home from work. Mason had drooled all over the shirt I'd had on earlier. "Why does he need to talk with me?"

"He was just interviewing everyone in the neighborhood, I think."

"He talked to you?"

I nod.

"Then why does he still want to question me?"

Sighing, I know I have to come clean. "He knows you saw Molly Saturday night."

His eyes darken. "How does he know that?"

"I'm sorry, Hudson." I grimace. "I didn't have a choice."

"*You* told him? Why would you do that?" His tone is hard, his voice rising.

"I got the feeling he already knew. Lying would only make you look guilty."

"How would he already know?"

I shake my head. "Not sure, but Leslie was talking to him before he came over here. I saw her pointing. And he knew about us—you—meeting Molly on Friday night."

His teeth grind together, the vein in his forehead throbbing the way it does when he's upset. "I should've known this had to do with Leslie. She's never gonna leave me alone, is she?"

Bowie enters the room, and my fingertips graze his fur. "I wouldn't worry about it. You have nothing to hide, so just call Detective Daniels and tell him what you know."

"Yeah, okay." Distractedly, he shoves the card in his pants pocket. "I'll do it tomorrow." He reaches for the door handle. "I won't be home too late tonight."

His words replay over and over in my mind as I watch him leave through the beveled glass of the front door, his body multiplying and morphing, a trick of light.

"She's never going to leave me alone, is she?"

Ten years is a long time. I've often hoped that, as the years went by, she'd end up dropping her vendetta against Hudson. Against our family. But instead, it seems to get worse.

After Hudson's car pulls away from the curb and drives down the street, I put on a pair of shoes and a warm jacket. Then I head outside and stalk across the street.

It's time Leslie and I had a little chat.

The neighborhood is quiet, dimly lit by the streetlamps when I traipse over her front yard to knock on her door. The air is cool, and smells sweet and dewy.

"What are you doing here?" Leslie asks when she answers, her expression guarded as it flicks over my shoulder. Her arms instinctively wrap around her body, shielding herself from me, I guess. As if a thin woman in her fifties is some grave threat. I almost laugh.

But on the walk over, I'd vowed to play nice. So I stifle the laugh and force a cordial smile.

"I thought we could talk."

Her eyes narrow. "It's late."

"I know. That's how important this is to me." I can tell by her expression that she isn't swayed in the least. "Please, Leslie, I just need a few minutes, and then I promise I'll leave you alone."

A teakettle peals from the kitchen. She hesitates, her feet shifting toward the sound and then back to me. Finally, she sighs. "Fine." Without welcoming me in, she pivots and hurries toward the kitchen, leaving the front door wide open.

After glancing around, I step inside, closing the door behind me.

Not much has changed since the last time I was here. Her style has always been outdated. As if she has never moved past the eighties. In her living room, she still has the same white wicker furniture, the beachy paintings on the walls, teals and salmon pink in watercolor. A fern spills out of a seashell planter, while a giant potted palm leers tropically from the far corner. I've always abhorred this coastal crap. We don't even live near the beach.

When I enter the kitchen, the puke-yellow walls greeting me, Leslie stands over the counter, pouring herself a cup of tea. She doesn't offer me one.

"Okay." She cocks one brow. "You've got three minutes." It reminds me of something she'd say to Heather when the kids were younger.

"Leslie, you're wrong about Hudson. You always have been." My elbow brushes the leaves of a pothos that's hanging from the ceiling. *God, it looks like a plant nursery in here.* Leslie has always loved plants, but it seems she's gone a bit overboard lately.

"If that's all you came here to say, you've wasted your time."

"Come on, you know Hudson...or, rather, you knew him when he was younger. He was over here all the time. You loved him." My throat itches. So does my nose. It's got to be all these plants. I'm slightly allergic. That's why I only plant succulents. That and I'd probably kill them, forgetting to water them.

Her face remains unchanged. "That was before."

"I know how hard it was to lose Heather, but—"

"No, you don't," she snaps. "Don't come in my house and tell me what it feels like to lose a child. You have no idea. You have both of yours." Her hands tremble at her sides. Her lips waver.

I swallow hard, giving her a few seconds. "You're right. I don't fully understand your pain, Leslie. But I loved Heather, too. So did Hudson. It was hard for all of us when she died."

"He didn't love her. He killed her."

"You know that isn't true. He didn't hurt Heather, and he didn't hurt that woman—Molly. He could never hurt anyone," I say, desperately needing her to hear me. "What happened to Heather was awful, but it was an accident. Even the police think she just got too close to the edge and fell."

"He pushed her," she says with so much force, a little spittle leaves her mouth and lands on her skin.

"There's no way he pushed her, Leslie. I'll never believe that," I say. "And you need to stop punishing him for something he didn't do. Leave him alone. Move on. Stop spreading rumors and talking to the police about this new case. He had nothing to do with it, and all you're doing is messing with an investigation and stopping them from finding the real killer."

"Who says that's what I've been doing?"

"I know you have. The police came to my house to talk to Hudson right after talking to you. I doubt that's a coincidence."

"Why do you even care what I say? If he's so innocent, why does it matter who I talk to?"

"Because I know that if enough people talk, the innocent can be made to look guilty. It happened to me with Mac. You remember that, right?" We'd been friends then. I'd confided in her.

She narrows her eyes, but slowly nods, giving me this one mercy. Behind her head, her favorite mugs hang from hooks under the cabinetry.

A deep sadness fills me for what Leslie and I lost. The years of friendship we could have had if not for what happened on that fateful October night.

Standing in her kitchen now, I wonder, as I have many times over the years, if there was ever anything I could have said back then that would have mended things between us.

But when she looks at me, her lips a tight line, angry tension drawn around her eyes, I know that there wasn't. Losing Heather changed Leslie irrevocably. It destroyed her marriage, even. If her relationship with James couldn't survive, why would I assume ours would have?

For years, I've wished I never would've let the kids go out that night. I wish it even more in this moment, staring at the face of my former friend. I see a flicker of something about to loosen and give, and I can't help but aim for that crack in her armor. I wish I could draw my former friend out, the one who believed in me and my family.

For a brief moment, I see us the way we once were. Sitting in this very kitchen, laughing and talking over steaming cups of tea. Leslie was the only friend I trusted to talk to about Darren's drinking, and my fear that I wasn't a good mother. She'd listen without judgment, place a hand on my arm and tell me that everyone's life was hard, and that we all were doing the best we could.

Was it really so outlandish that I'd expected some of that support and understanding after Heather's death?

Shaking my head, I force myself back to the present. To the situation at hand. "I saw James over here. Why else would you be talking to him if not to share with him all of your theories about Hudson?"

Her softness turns hard again. "Pretty sure your three minutes are up."

Nodding, I back away from her counter, desperate to be out of here, anyway.

I turn, fleeing from the house, the plants and the memories.

17

I'm hunched over Heather's lifeless body. Blood pools from her head, rivulets of scarlet staining the floor. My shoes are splattered in the sticky liquid, and when I pull back, my palms are coated with it. Horrified, I squeeze my eyes shut. When I open them again, I'm surrounded by plants, thick and green. They close in around me, the leaves tickling my skin. I shove them away, my nose itching, my throat scratchy. One of the leaves crumbles beneath my touch, and I look to see that the plant is yellow, brown at the edges; dying.

The toe of my shoe hits something hard and unmoving. The body at my feet is no longer Heather's.

It's Mac's.

I'm startled awake by a loud thud. My eyelids flip open. Sweat coats my skin. I look down at my hands in the moonlight filtering through the curtains. They're clean. White. Dry and in desperate need of lotion, but thankfully, not covered in blood. Mac's lifeless eyes staring up at me linger in my mind, and I suck in a much-needed breath.

Another thud. I shoot up in bed. *Grace?*

I look around, truly expecting to see a child at the foot of my bed, that bubblegum-pink ball in her hand. Darren always thought my fascination with Grace was unhealthy. Kendra, too.

"Don't you think it's creepy? Believing that you live with a child's ghost?" they'd both asked me over the years.

But I don't. I find comfort in knowing she's here with me. That I can count on her, almost like my own guardian angel.

When the noise repeats, I realize it's more like a slam than a thud. Bowie's ears perk, his head lifting. I toss my covers off and slide out of the bed. Bowie leaps down and follows. When I go into the hallway, it's cold. Colder than it should be in here. And I smell damp outside air. *Is a window open?*

Hudson's door is ajar. It creaks and sways like a child's playing with it.

I peek in, squinting across his dark room. No Hudson.

I thunder down the stairs. The breeze hits me at the bottom. A startling whisk of cold. My hands skate up my arms as if to erase the goose bumps. I find the culprit. The front door is wide open, the wind slamming it repeatedly into the wall of the entryway. My chest tightens. I touch Bowie's mane.

"Hudson?" I call out, my voice wavering.

My heart hammers in my ears as I inch forward, my eyes and ears open.

"Hudson," I say again, this time more firmly. Still no response.

The porch is empty, wind rattling the chains of the bench swing. My hands are cold and clammy, my nerves shot. Did someone break in? Are they inside? I turn, thoroughly expecting someone to be there, a large figure camouflaged in all black, thick gloves ready to grab me. But thankfully, no one's there.

I step onto the porch, the boards rasping beneath my bare feet. The darkened street is quiet. I scan the front lawn, and then my gaze shoots across the street.

That's when I spot Hudson. He stands rigid, shirtless, his back to me. And he's in the middle of Leslie's lawn.

Oh, my god.

What is he doing out there?

Springing into action, I sprint down the front steps. Bowie runs beside me, the metal on his collar rattling. The wind whistles through the trees, leaves skittering on the asphalt like tiny insects. I run as fast as I can over my front lawn, ignoring the dampness soaking into my feet. Then I hurry across the street and leap onto Leslie's front lawn.

Hudson stares blankly at Leslie's front window, his eyes hollow, his pupils still.

He's sleepwalking.

I know better than to startle him in this condition, but I do need to get him back inside.

"Hudson, come on." I gently tug on his arm while scouring the neighborhood, praying no one sees us. I can't imagine what kind of rumors would start swirling tomorrow if anyone did. "We need to go." Wrapping my arm around his waist, I maneuver him to face the opposite direction. He allows me to lead him, and we take a few steps forward.

"Mom?" Hudson blinks, coming out of his trance. Confused, he looks at me. "What's going on?"

"You were sleepwalking."

"But why here?"

"I don't know." I shake my head. I hear car tires buzzing, an engine rumbling. I reach for Hudson's hand, more desperate now. "But we need to get off Leslie's lawn…before someone sees us."

"I think about her all the time, you know." It's like he doesn't hear me.

"Leslie?" I frown.

"Heather."

"Oh. Right." The screech of a tire in the distance makes me flinch. "Well, of course. I get that."

"I haven't told you everything…" he blinks "…about that night. About what happened."

My stomach bottoms out. Hudson's teeth chatter. "Listen, we can talk about this later. We need to get inside." Sensing his hesitation, I grip his arm tighter. "Now. Come on."

The moonlight across his face resembles a cut. A clean slice. His eyes darken, but he nods, and follows mutely. I whistle to Bowie as we cross our yard, and he crashes out from beneath the porch where he'd been sniffing around. When we make it back inside, I slam the door closed and lock it. I dare one more glance out the window at the quiet, empty street, and then blow out a long, deep breath, expelling everything from my lungs. The soles of my feet sting from the cold. I press them into the entryway rug, grateful for the warmth of it.

"Mom?" Hudson's voice cuts into the silence.

I shake my head. "It's late. We should get back to bed."

Bowing my head, I make my way to the stairs, keeping my eyes trained on my bare feet and red lacquered toenails. The words I refuse to let him speak follow me all the way up the stairs.

Hudson was waiting for me when I drove up. He stood in the gravel lot alone, far from his friends. In the distance, I saw a bonfire blazing. I hadn't been up to the bluffs overlooking the American River since my own high school days. Clearly the local teenage choice for a parent-free hangout spot hadn't changed in decades. Getting out of the car, I heard loud chatter and music, smelled wood smoke.

He was trembling, his teeth chattering, his shoulders shaking.

I took them in my hands, looked into his eyes. "What happened?"

"It's Heather. She—she fell."

"Where is she?" I glanced around. "Is she okay?"

He stared at me a moment without speaking. My chest tightened. Then his head slowly swiveled back and forth, his eyes filling with tears.

He craned his neck to look over his shoulder, a shaky arm lifting to point toward the cliffs. "We were talking by the river, you know, up high. She was drunk. And yelling. One second she was there, and the next—I tried to help…" His voice cracked; his words trailed off. I felt a rush of sick fear, questions burbling up: What was she yelling about? Where is Heather now? Then he looked into my eyes, desperate for me to believe him. "It was an accident."

And that's when I knew Heather was dead. "One second she was there, and the next…" My mind filled in the blanks. The next, she was falling. If she'd slipped from the edge and hadn't been lucky enough to catch one of the craggy pines that grow on the bluff, the drop was severe—there was no way she survived a fall from that height. Panic and grief kicked up inside me, but I forced them down. This wasn't the time. My son's future depended on what happened next.

I swallowed hard. "Have you called the police?"

"Not yet."

My chest expanded. I thought of Mac, of the police skewering me with personal questions, of the cruel suspicion with which my bandmates and friends and total strangers treated me. There was still time for Hudson.

"Mom, I'm scared," he said.

"I know," I said. "I promise it'll be okay."

I believed him when he said it was an accident.

★ ★ ★

When my alarm blares, I roll over, confused as to why it's going off in the first place. I don't usually set it. My internal clock usually wakes me up in time for my walk. My eyelids are heavy, as if glued shut. I thrust my arm out and hit the snooze button. When it goes off again, I successfully pry one lid open, and that's when I see the Post-it Note that reads, "Dr. Steiner, 9:00 a.m."

I stare up at the ceiling and contemplate canceling. After finding Hudson in Leslie's yard, it took me hours to fall back asleep. And when I did, it was fitful and riddled with nightmares. I'm so tired. The last thing I want to do is sit in Dr. Steiner's waiting room, only to be brought back to his office to be poked and prodded and asked degrading questions about my mental state. I can't think of anything worse.

"Aren't you a pretty girl?" Mom reached out to touch a tendril of Kendra's hair. "You look a lot like my daughter. Have you met her?" Her watery eyes swept the room. "I think she's around here somewhere. Always off playing, you know?"

Kendra's lower lip trembled as if she might start crying. She wrinkled her nose and glanced up at me, a desperate plea in her eyes. My heart ached. Kendra would've loved my mom if only she'd known her when her mind was sharp. Not only were we strangers to my mom, but she'd become a stranger to us. And that filled me with extreme sadness. It's an odd sensation to mourn the loss of someone who is still alive.

That's something I never want for Hudson and Kendra, or even Mason, for that matter. Mind made up, I force myself out of bed and drink a gallon of coffee while getting ready. I'm running a little behind, but miraculously make it to my appointment on time.

Dr. Steiner asks me some basic history, runs through a few cognitive tests—can I read the time on an analog clock? How many animals can I name in sixty seconds?—and then sends me to the lab for blood work. He also schedules me for an MRI tomorrow morning.

As I drive home, I'm more hopeful than I've been in weeks. Suzanne is right. Medicine has advanced since my mom was sick. Dr. Steiner explained that once all my results come in, there are medications he can prescribe me that will help. There's still no cure, but there may be options to slow down the disease. And isn't that worth a try?

There is a lightness in my step that has been absent for weeks when I stop at the store to pick up a few items I'm out of. Once inside, I fish in my purse for my list, the one I always keep tacked to my fridge. The one I distinctly remember grabbing before I left the house this morning. But I can't find it.

"Excuse me." A lady speaks from over my shoulder. She holds the hand of a young boy. He sort of reminds me of Hudson when he was younger. Hair mussed, cowlick sticking up, a mischievous grin on his face.

"Oh, sorry." I move out of the way so I'm no longer blocking the entrance and continue rifling through my purse. I find receipts, a few stray mints, a lip gloss, my signature red lipstick, a miniature hand lotion. It must have been slightly open, because it's slick and slippery. Lotion coats my palm. After wiping it off, I continue my search, but don't find my list.

Maybe I didn't grab it this morning. Perhaps I'm remembering a different morning. I had been in a hurry today. So it's possible I grabbed it only to drop it somewhere.

Biting my lower lip, I try to remember what was on it. There were only a few items, but at least one of them I need for dinner tonight. What am I making again?

I can't even remember that.

"Ma'am, are you okay?" A girl wearing a name tag that reads "Stella" sidles up to me.

"Mom, are you okay?" I touched her arm and she flinched, her eyes clearing as if coming out of a trance.

"Yeah." I blink. "I'm fine." God, I must look ridiculous, standing at the entrance of the store, staring off into space. Securing my purse on my shoulder, I turn and walk back out to the parking lot. Once inside my car, I lean my head into the seat and groan.

Thank god I went to see Dr. Steiner today. If only I'd gone sooner. If only I hadn't been so stubborn.

Emotion bubbles up in my throat. My eyes are hot. I breathe deeply in through my nose and out my mouth a few times until I feel more steady. Then I shove the key into the ignition and turn it, music immediately surrounding me. I have it on an '80s station, and as I drive out of the parking lot, a familiar Madonna song plays, instantly putting me more at ease.

When I pull into my driveway, I notice a group of neighbors congregating across the street. Irritation instantly strikes. But then it wanes when I realize Leslie isn't in the circle, and no one turns in my direction. So this gossip session clearly isn't about me or my family. A couple of ladies I don't know talk with Beth. Their chatter travels across the street, a jumble of words punctuated with laughter. I briefly wonder who their poor victim is this time.

It's odd that Leslie isn't a part of the gab session. She usually has FOMO about stuff like this. When I reach my front door, I peer over my shoulder, expecting to find Leslie's face peeking out of the front window or her door popping open as she steps outside, hurrying to Beth's to join in. But her blinds are all closed, her front porch empty. She wasn't outside this morning when I left either.

Strange.

Maybe she's out of town or something. But as I unlock my front door, I notice her car sitting in the driveway. It's her lawn that calls out to me, though, the image of Hudson standing in the middle of it, blanketed by darkness.

After discarding my purse and shoes near the door, I head into the kitchen. Sure enough, I find the grocery list on the kitchen table. So I *had* taken it off the fridge. It just didn't make it into my purse. I scan it briefly.

Milk.

1 yellow onion.

Mild Italian sausage.

Oh, right. I had planned to make pasta tonight. The onion and sausage are what I needed to grab at the store. If only I could have remembered while I was there. Dropping the list, I head toward the cabinets. Finding a few cans of Campbell's and some bread, I decide I can always do a soup and sandwich night. I don't feel like heading to the store again.

Sinking down into a kitchen chair, I log onto the computer.

I can't get the image of Hudson in Leslie's lawn out of my mind. It's been plaguing my thoughts all day and night. Why would he sleepwalk over there? In my search bar, I type, "Causes of sleepwalking."

I click on the top article and skim through it.

Genetics is listed as the top cause. I don't know of anyone in my family who sleepwalked. But maybe in Darren's. He never mentioned it, but that doesn't mean anything. Darren's parents were pretty private. They always acted like they were so close, but no one ever talked about anything important.

Sleep deprivation is one that surprises me. It would stand to reason that if someone had been sleep-deprived, they'd be out like a light, not walking around. But what do I know? Hudson has been going out a lot at night, and getting up early to go to work, but I don't think I'd categorize him as sleep-deprived.

Alcohol is listed. Hudson has been drinking a lot. But nowhere near what his dad used to drink, and as far as I know, Darren never sleepwalked.

Stress is one I always knew about. When Hudson first started sleepwalking, his pediatrician had asked me if he'd been stressed. Since he was only a child then, I'd scoffed at the question, but looking back, I realize he had plenty of reasons to be stressed. We'd recently moved into this house, and I'd been gone more with the band. All of that might have been stressful for him, and I simply hadn't appreciated that at the time.

But is he stressed now?

Maybe.

I blow out a breath and minimize the article. Within minutes, I find myself back on Hudson's Facebook page, scrolling through pictures of him and Natalia. The pictures hit me differently now that I've met her. No longer do they seem as happy and in love as I'd led myself to believe when I perused them the first time. There are hints of Natalia's discomfort in her expressions and body language. It's subtle—a downcast tilt of her mouth, a shifting of her eyes, a dipping of one shoulder to keep it from touching his.

In one picture he appears to be holding her arm tightly, as if to keep it in place. But that isn't what stops me in my tracks, causing my breath to hitch in my throat. It's what's wrapped around his wrist.

A gold watch.

Heart pounding, I hurry up the stairs and into my bedroom. After flinging open my nightstand drawer, I fumble around for the watch I found at Molly's. Palming it, I race back to the computer. I zoom in to Hudson's hand and hold up the watch. The larger I make the photo, the grainier it becomes, making it hard to tell if it's the same. But it could be.

I haven't noticed him wearing a watch, but then again, he's often in long-sleeved shirts. Flannels, mostly. So maybe the watch has been tucked underneath it. The more I compare the two, the more I'm sure it's his. I scroll through more photos, but Hudson's wrist is never in the frame.

I turn the watch over in my hand, my fingertip tracing the "777" engraved on the back.

Hudson isn't the kind of guy to believe in angels, and I don't think he's into numerology. I freeze, remembering the tattoo on the lower part of Natalia's arm. The one I saw when she lifted the cigarette to her lips.

Angel wings.

Maybe she got him the watch.

Stomach knotting, I stare at Natalia's bruised face, then look to the watch on Hudson's wrist. The one that matches the one I hold.

"There are worse things than being cheated on."

The watch is heavy in my hand. I shove it in my pocket, and shut the laptop with more force than I mean to.

My knees crack as I stand up. My throat is parched. I need some water. Walking to the fridge, I pass the front window. Leslie's porch is still empty. Blinds closed. Car in the driveway. An involuntary shiver works its way up my spine.

18

Bowie wakes me with a nudge and a light bark. I blink a few times, my eyelids heavy, and roll over. The room is light. Sunny.

What time is it?

I squint against the blurriness, colors blending like an impressionist painting. I blink a few more times, home in on my alarm clock.

10:00 a.m.?

I never sleep this late.

A dull ache spreads across my forehead and pokes at my temples.

I hope I'm not getting sick again.

In my bare feet, I shuffle out of my room and down the stairs. Hudson's bedroom door is open, his room empty. I try to remember where he is and can't. Panic washes over me at the realization that my mind is completely blank. I rack my brain for what I did last night or what day it even is, and nothing.

Nada.

A blank piece of paper with no words.

Mouth drying out, I continue past his room. Bowie follows me as I clamber down the stairs, my feet thudding like a horse on a track. When I reach the kitchen, I check the calendar, follow the x-ed out days to the new fresh one. Wednesday. That's what day it is. Hudson is working. I have one appointment later.

I grab a glass, fill it with water and take a sip. Down my vitamins.

It's nothing, I tell myself. I've just woken up, and it took a few minutes to get my bearings. It happens.

I'll never forget how delirious Hudson used to be when he woke up from his naps. *What time is it, Mommy? Is it tomorrow?*

As the panic subsides, the water helping my headache, last night comes flooding back. Nothing earth-shattering. A quiet dinner at home. Turkey sandwich and a can of soup. Hudson didn't join me for dinner, said he'd eaten a late lunch at the job site. Before he'd headed out to meet his friends, I'd asked him if he'd called Detective Daniels and he said, "Nah, I don't think I need to."

"I really think you should. We have no idea what Leslie said to him. You know what a gossip she is."

He touched my arm lightly before heading out the door. "It's okay, Mom. You don't need to worry about Leslie."

I hardly agreed, but he seemed so at ease and confident that I wanted to believe him. Perhaps my chat with her had made a difference. But how would he know that?

After dinner, I binge-watched *Unsolved Mysteries* until going to bed. Maybe that's why I'm so on edge. I knew better than to watch those kinds of shows late at night, especially when I was home by myself.

I put some food out for Bowie and change the water in

his bowl. Then I pull a carton of eggs out of the fridge. As I crack them, I have the strange feeling I'm forgetting something. Something important.

Washing my hands in the sink, I glance out the window. Leslie's front porch is empty again, envelopes stuffed in the mailbox, the blinds still closed. It's so odd. If she's not out of town, what's going on?

Maybe she's sick. It's that time of year. Honestly, I'm not feeling great this morning. Also, my allergies are worse in the fall, and Leslie's constantly surrounded by all those damn plants. Yeah, that's probably it. She's probably inside lying in bed and drinking tea, nursing an illness.

Illness.

Doctor.

Maybe…do I have an appointment today?

I walk to the calendar, and search for today's date.

11:30 a.m., MRI.

I have a sense, like a dream that escapes you upon waking up, that I've looked at this already. How could that have slipped my mind?

Thank god I checked the calendar when I did, while there's still plenty of time to eat breakfast and get ready.

I can't wait to get some answers, and hopefully meds that actually work. I know Kendra means well, but I'm not sure her vitamins and probiotics help at all. If anything, I feel worse since I started taking them. Then again, I guess that is the way the disease works.

As I whisk the eggs, I spot Beth walking across her yard and into Leslie's. I watch curiously as she goes up the front steps and knocks on Leslie's door. A few seconds go by, and then she knocks again. As she waits, she runs a hand through her hair, paces back and forth a few times. Then she pulls a phone out of her pocket and dials before pressing it to her ear.

I continue watching as I pour the egg batter into a sizzling skillet. As I push the spatula around, Beth hangs up her phone, shoves it back into her pocket and then walks slowly back to her own house. I can't tell if she actually got a hold of her or not.

After eating breakfast, I head upstairs to get ready. I take a shower, dry my hair and apply minimal makeup. Then I put on a pair of jeans, a long sweater and my favorite brown booties. I pick out dangly earrings and a long necklace, and then realize they're going to make me take them off for the MRI, so I hang them back on my jewelry rack. It's rare that I go anywhere without jewelry on, and I feel naked without it.

In the entryway, I snatch up my purse and keys. After flinging open my front door, I freeze, my blood running cold.

An ambulance is parked in Leslie's driveway. Déjà vu strikes me as I watch the paramedics rolling a stretcher into the back.

It has to be Leslie. She's the only person who lives there.

In a daze, I watch the paramedics close the doors to the ambulance and drive off.

Many neighbors are outside, standing on their front lawns, staring at Leslie's house. Gaping, I stand in the middle of my doorway, as if I'm a tree planted here, unsure of what to do. Beth notices me. Her mouth moves, and then her husband Alex's head bounces up in my direction. I shrink back momentarily, but then lift my chin.

Oh, screw it. I have every right to know what's going on.

I'm done cowering.

Drawing in a breath, I lift my chin and jog across the street.

"What's going on?" I ask the minute my feet hit their grass.

Their lips are pursed in suspicion.

Oh, come on.

"Is Leslie okay?" I press.

Beth shakes her head, her eyes filling with tears. "She's dead."

My stomach bottoms out. "Dead?"

She nods, her lips trembling. Alex puts his arm around her shoulders.

"Oh, my god. Do they know what happened?" I ask. Two women hurry up behind us, startling me—more members of Leslie's morning coffee huddle. My approach has clearly emboldened them to leave their yards and come closer, too.

"I went over to check on her this morning," she says. "Normally we talk every day, but she never came out of her house all day yesterday or this morning, and I was worried. After knocking for a while and calling her a couple of times, I finally dialed 911. When the paramedics got here, they found her unresponsive." Fresh tears fall from Beth's eyes. Her husband draws her close, and she sobs into his shoulder.

I stare at Leslie's house, taking in the stuffed mailbox. "So the last time you saw Leslie was Monday?"

"Yeah." Beth nods against her husband's shoulder. The other ladies nod as well. "At book club that night."

Swallowing hard, I feel queasy.

I might have been the last person to see Leslie alive.

It's getting dark, the sky a deep charcoal, tumultuous and cloudy like plumes of smoke. The moon is an eerie bloodred tonight. It seems oddly fitting. Hudson isn't home, and he's not returning my texts or phone calls.

Worry churns in my gut.

The television plays quietly in the corner, but I'm too distracted to pay attention to it.

Hudson is usually home by now. Where could he be? Even when he goes out with friends, he comes home to shower and change first. I turn, my face appearing in the glass, ethereal and blurry. Beyond that, Leslie's house is dark, except for the automatic porch light. It's that damn light that causes my eyes to well with tears. Something about it still turning on even though the rest of the house is dark fills me with extreme sadness. Even though she's not there to sit outside and gossip with her neighbors, it still illuminates the space. An ache spreads through my chest.

I've always found it odd how life goes on, many things operating like clockwork, even when someone passes away. Even when the lives of those around them are at a standstill.

I picture Leslie the way she looked when I first saw her, young and idealistic, dirt coating her palms and residing under her fingernails. I see her progression over the years, her working in the yard, her sitting on her front porch, cup of tea in hand. The year Heather died, she let all the plants in the beds go wiry and unwatered. James moved out at the end of the summer, dragging his bags across the brown grass.

A tear slips down my cheek, and I wipe it away. We may not have gotten along recently, but we were friends once. It's hard to accept that she's gone.

"I haven't told you everything about that night." The words Hudson said to me while standing in the middle of Leslie's front lawn float through my mind.

I pick up my phone and shoot off another text to Hudson: Where are you? Call me. It's an emergency.

My fear escalates as the minutes tick by. Have the police picked him up? Did he panic—did he bolt?

Have my suspicions about him been justified?

I'm about to try him again when lights appear in the window, sweeping over the pane and then clicking off. I pitch forward, my breath caught in my throat. Hudson's car parks along the curb. He quickly pops out of the driver's side and makes his way hurriedly up the front stairs.

Reaching for a tissue, I pat at my damp cheeks and wipe under my eyes. When I pull back my hand, the tissue is streaked

with snail trails of black mascara. I sniff as the door is force-
fully thrust open.

Hudson shoots into the room, wild-eyed. His shirt is mot-
tled with brown mud, and dirt cakes his forearms and fingers.
He stares at me as if he's checking for wounds.

"Are you okay?"

I don't know how to answer that. Physically, I guess I am,
so I hesitantly nod.

He steps further into the room. "Then what's going on?
You said there was an emergency."

"There is. It's just not involving me."

"Huh?" A breath bursts from his mouth, the rush of adrenaline dissipating.

"Leslie's dead," I say, not wishing to delay the inevitable.

"What?" He falls into the couch like his knees buckled.

I nod. "They found her body earlier today."

"H-how?"

"I don't know. But on the news, they're already calling it
a homicide."

He gathers his beard in between his thumb and forefinger,
drawing it to a point at his chin. "When did she die?"

"The last time anyone saw her was Monday night."

His head snaps up. "Monday night? B-but that's when…"
Turning his head, he looks out the window, no doubt remembering how he'd been standing in the middle of Leslie's
yard late that night.

He looks scared, like a lost child. I almost don't have the
heart to ask him the question lingering on my tongue. But I
have to. "Hudson, what did you mean when you said that I
didn't have to worry about Leslie anymore?"

"Oh, my god." His eyes bug out, his lips curling downward
in an expression of betrayal. "Do you think I hurt her? Is that
why you were blowing up my texts, because you think I had

something to do with this?" He stabs his fingers through his hair in obvious frustration.

"I simply asked a question," I say, as calmly as I can. I've poked around enough—he deserves the chance to explain it himself.

His eyes meet mine, and he shakes his head. "I just meant that the police didn't suspect me of Molly's murder anymore."

"Who told you that?" It's not the impression I got from my conversation with Leslie.

"I heard it from Leslie."

"You talked to her?"

"Not exactly," he says. "I overheard her talking to a couple of her friends the last time I went jogging—so, Monday morning before work."

"What exactly did she say?"

"I only heard a little bit. One of my AirPods had fallen out, and I was searching in the grass for it when Leslie and her friends came walking down the sidewalk. I ducked down behind a tree so I wouldn't have to talk to her. And at first all I caught was something about fingerprints not being in the system. And then Leslie was saying that the police found out Molly had a boyfriend."

"Who?"

"No idea." He scrunches up his face. "They walk fast."

Blowing out a breath, I sit back. If this is true, then it changes everything. Whoever killed Molly had the motive and practice to kill Leslie—maybe Leslie was starting to look into the boyfriend. Isn't the murderer usually the partner? I blush with shame for having thought it could be Hudson.

"That's why I didn't think I needed to call that detective. But maybe I should call him now."

"What? Why?" I ask.

"I was at Leslie's house that night. We both were. What if someone saw me?"

It's the same thing I'd been spinning about all day, but I'd looked around when I ran out to get him. I hadn't seen anyone. "I don't think anyone did," I say now, praying that I'm not lying to him. It was the truth, except for the fact that I have no idea how long Hudson had been out there. Could someone have seen him before I did?

"But we don't know that for sure," he says, as if voicing my internal concerns. "And everyone knows how much Leslie hated me."

"She hated me, too. She probably hated a lot of people. Doesn't make us all murderers."

He fixes me with an exasperated stare. "She'd accused me of her daughter's murder and had been harassing me for years. That gives me motive."

I recoil, his words like a slap to the face. "Don't say things like that."

"It's true." His jaw sets, his eyes narrowing.

"It's actually not. Heather's death was a long time ago. Leslie's the only one still talking about it. Your name has already been cleared. And it sounds like she wasn't accusing you of anything currently. There's no motive here."

"Either way, maybe I should just call the detective and tell him about sleepwalking over to Leslie's that night," he says. "Get ahead of it. Just to be safe."

"I don't think that's a good idea." I can't imagine how guilty he would look if he admitted to seeing Molly the night she died and then being on Leslie's property the night she died. Talk about circumstantial evidence. It'll be like a slam dunk. An open and shut case. They probably won't even look at anyone else. I feel queasy at the thought. If he stays quiet, they probably won't look into him at all.

"Isn't it better if they hear it from me?" Hudson continues.

"I think it's best if we lay low, wait for the police to come to us. Why draw attention to yourself unnecessarily?"

Hudson is quiet a moment, and then he nods obediently just like he did ten years ago.

"Does anyone else know?" I asked him when I arrived at the field that fateful night. "Where were your friends? Where's Kendra? Did she drop you off, or did she stay?" We were shrouded by trees and bushes, but I had to keep a lookout. No one could know I was here.

He shook his head. "No one was with us."

"But do you think anyone heard?" I hated asking the question, but I had to. "Did she scream?"

His teeth chattered, his hands moving up and down his arms. The skin on his face was a sickly gray color. He was in shock. "Um…no, it all happened so fast. I think she tried to scream, but then she was…gone." The last word was barely audible, partially cut off by a sob that tore violently from his throat. He looked dangerously close to puking, his body slumped over, his facial features scrunched together in a severe wince. "But it's so loud out here, I don't think anyone heard anything." He was probably right. Not only were the kids' chatter and laughter loud, but the wind was fierce, howling as it whisked through the trees. His eyes widened, another wave of panic hitting. "What if they think I did something?" His voice cracked. "I didn't do anything!"

"Okay, listen to me." I gripped him by the shoulders. "I need you to do exactly as I say, all right?"

He nodded, his eyes large round circles hypnotized with relief at someone else taking charge.

"Pull yourself together. Go find your friends. Share a beer—" I cringed…what parent told their fifteen-year-old to do that? "—and act normal. Mention that you've been walking around, mingling with the other guys. Say something about how you haven't seen Heather in a while. Then go find her friends. Find Katie. Tell them the same thing. Ask where she is." I squeeze tighter. "This is the important part. Make sure someone else finds her; have them call 911. At that point, call me and I'll come back."

His eyes flashed with something akin to terror. It reminded me of the night of my launch party. I wouldn't let him down this time. "Where are you going?"

"I won't be far. Only a few miles away. Out of sight."

He hesitated. His eyes were ringed in red, his cheeks damp. I swiped at his tears with my thumbs.

"You can do this."

He didn't look convinced.

"You need to go now before someone sees me." I released my grip. "You remember what to do?"

His head bobbed up and down again, slowly, almost unsure.

"Hudson?" I pressed, nervous.

"Yeah, I got it." This time he sounded more like himself. Assured. Maybe even a little annoyed.

"Okay. See you soon." I looked at him one last time before hurrying to my car. I thought of Heather, the little girl who had built forts in my backyard, done her homework at my dining table, sat with her feet in my son's lap while we all watched movies together—now lying lifeless and crumpled somewhere on the ground below me. And I prayed Hudson could pull this off.

When Hudson goes upstairs to take a shower, I head to the kitchen. If there was ever a night that called for wine, it's tonight. With slow movements, I get a wineglass down and place it on the counter. As I pour wine into the glass, I find my gaze once again darting out the window toward Leslie's house. It's like I'm unable to stop myself.

Back when we were friends, Leslie used to host a book club at her house once a month—well, clearly she still does. Or *did*. Anyway, I just haven't been invited in ages. But back then, for months, she tried to recruit me into it. Tired of turning her down, I finally gave in. Before the first meeting, I read the book and jotted down some questions. But about a half an hour in, I realized it was more of a wine club than a book club. The entire two hours were a drink-and-gab session. I think we talked about the book for a total of five minutes. I ended up attending for about a year, and the only time I remember Leslie being into the book was when we read *The Time Traveler's Wife*. She was always a sucker for romances.

After carrying my full wineglass into the family room, I sit on the couch and reach for the remote. Propping my feet up on the coffee table, I click the television on. In honor of Leslie, I find the Hallmark Channel. It's halfway through a romantic movie, but it doesn't take long for me to get the gist. A city girl with a high-powered corporate job is falling for a small-town boy who runs a farm. I nestle into the couch cushions and sip my wine. The movie doesn't exactly take my mind off of the day's events, but it is a welcome distraction.

Right at the moment when it reaches the conclusion and the guy and girl are about to kiss, I'm startled by a rustling noise outside. I sit up, feet slipping from the table. Footfalls ring out upstairs. I'd heard Hudson getting out of the shower a little while ago; now he moves about his room, floor creaking overhead. Maybe that's all it was. It seemed like it was coming from outside, but perhaps it was from upstairs.

I lean back, shifting to get comfortable against the cushions, when I hear it again.

No, it's definitely coming from outside.

I set my wineglass on the coffee table. The credits are rolling. I groan. After all that, I missed the happy ending. Standing up, I preemptively feel silly. Most likely, all I'm going to find is a squirrel playing in the bushes. A bird in a tree. Bill next door in the driveway between our houses, throwing something in the trash.

At the window, I lean forward, so close to the glass I can feel the cold seeping in, smell the dampness in the air. It's dark and hard to make anything out. We've never had great lighting on this street, and my own porch lights are dim. I make a note to talk to Hudson about replacing them, even though I still haven't given him that list of chores I made when he first moved in.

I squint, pressing my nose to the windowpane.

And then I hear it again.

Something glints, like the flicker of a light.

No, not a light. Something reflective.

Glasses?

I look harder.

Yes, glasses perched on a man's nose.

A man who's lurking in my front yard.

19

I duck down below the windowsill, hoping he hasn't already seen me. The man wears all black, so it almost appears as if his head is floating in the night sky. If it weren't for his glasses, I wouldn't have noticed him at all. It's unclear what he's doing, but he's near the side gate.

I clutch my chest, and my heart dances against my palms.

I picture the yellow crime tape encircling Molly's house; Leslie's body under a sheet, being wheeled out on a stretcher. Two suspicious deaths in my neighborhood in a week's time, and now a strange man is in my yard. Maybe this is the guy Leslie suspected.

"Hudson," I croak, but it's so soft I'm sure he can't hear me. I snap my fingers, hoping Bowie will come. Last time I checked, he was asleep on my bed upstairs.

I briefly wonder if Molly or Leslie had called out for help, and to whom. They lived alone, so there would've been no one there to hear them.

Up until a few weeks ago, I'd lived alone.

Heart rate increasing, I call out again, "Hudson!"

This time, the bedroom door opens, his head poking out, hair still damp, and my heart slows at the sight of him. I'm not alone. "Yeah?" His eyebrows rise when he takes in my demeanor. I must look ridiculous crouching down under the front window. "What's going on now?" It reminds me of how Darren would address the kids when he found them whining for the tenth time in one day.

"A man," I say insistently, pointing to the window above me. "In the yard."

He studies me a minute, then dips back into his room, only to re-emerge holding a wooden baseball bat. It swings at his side as he takes the stairs two at a time. "Stay here. I'll take care of it."

He bursts outside so fast that I can't stop him. It feels weird allowing him to walk into danger. I'm his mother. Shouldn't I be the one protecting him? But I know how silly that line of thinking is. Hudson is younger. Stronger. Double my size.

I lift my head slightly, daring a small peek out the window. Hudson stalks across the front lawn, bat by his side. I don't see the man in black anywhere. Hudson's going in the right direction, though. I crane my neck to follow him, but it's no use. He disappears behind the side of the house.

I wait, my face flush against the glass. Behind me, the Hallmark Channel is airing another romantic movie. Cutesy banter and cheery music are a stark contrast to the darkness outside, a strange man in my yard and my son going after him with a baseball bat.

I never should've sent him out there.

On shaky legs, I straighten up and hurry to the front door, where a pair of slippers is discarded on the ground. I shove my feet into them and step outside. Cold air smacks me in the face.

My leggings and my thin, short-sleeved T-shirt are no match for the chill breeze. Shivering, I bound down the front steps.

"Hudson!" I call out.

No response.

I reach the bottom. "Hudson!" I holler, louder this time.

"Right here."

My heart jumps at the sound of his voice, closer than I expected, but too calm to be in distress or danger. When I round the corner, he comes into view.

"Oh, thank god. You were taking so long, I thought maybe something happened to you." As my fingertips alight on his arm, I see the man standing behind him. I flinch.

"Mom, this is John. He lives on Twenty-First, around the corner." I know his words are meant to calm me, but they don't. Molly was probably killed by someone in the neighborhood. Why not this man? As my eyes adjust, I get a better look at him. He appears to be a little younger than me, dark hair, nondescript features, same height and build as Hudson. Normal, basically. I've probably seen him around and never noticed.

"Hi, John," I say, warily but politely.

"Sorry about scaring you. I was just out here keeping an eye on things. I thought I might've seen something in your neighbor's yard and needed a closer look. It was nothing," John says.

"He's part of the neighborhood watch," Hudson clarifies.

"Neighborhood watch?" I loosen my grip on Hudson's arm. "I didn't even know we had one."

"We didn't, but after...well...everything that's happened in the last week, we thought we should start one," John explains, and his words sting. No one had told me anything about it. "We're actually having a meeting tomorrow night, if you'd like to join."

"Where's the meeting?" I ask.

"At the O'Leerys'."

"The O'Leerys'?"

Why am I not surprised that it would be held at Beth's house?

"You're welcome to join us," he says again. "Seven o'clock tomorrow night."

"Okay, thanks." The cold gets to me, goose bumps rising on my arms, the tip of my nose wet. I sniff, dancing from one foot to the other in an effort to heat up. Thank god for the slippers, or I never would've made it this long.

Hudson puts an arm around me. "We should be getting inside."

"Sorry again about scaring you," John says as Hudson ushers me back to the house.

Once inside, my teeth chatter. Clearly awoken by all the excitement, Bowie jogs down the stairs to greet me. I sit on the couch and wrap myself in a blanket. Bowie curls up by my feet. Hudson props the bat against the wall by the front door.

"Where did you find that?" I thought I had donated all of his leftover sports equipment years ago—whatever he hadn't taken with him.

"It's mine." He turns it so the A's logo is visible. They've been his favorite team since he was a small child. Often, he and Darren used to sit on the couch, wearing matching A's jerseys, and watch the game together. "It was a birthday gift from Natalia." He moves away from the wall, and sinks down onto the recliner across from me. "And it's one of the few things I actually got to take with me when I left."

My heart rate has finally returned to normal, but his words strike me as odd, and I remember how little he brought with him when he moved in. "Why did you only take a few things?"

"Because that's all she'd let me take." He says it matter-offactly, but it's anything but. I've met Natalia. She's tiny. There's no way she could have stopped Hudson if he'd picked up a box and wanted to march out with it. How could she force him out without his stuff?

"What, did she, like, hold a gun to your head?" I joke.

"Pretty much," he says, bouncing his right leg up and down in agitation. "That chick's crazy." My mouth goes sour at the sound of that word from my son's mouth. "Like, for real. When she got mad, she lost it. The night she kicked me out, she was screaming and throwing things. She was so loud, the neighbor guy came over to see what was going on. Natalia immediately went into victim mode, and of course the neighbor bought it, so I got the hell out. Just took a duffel bag of stuff, along with my guitar. Luckily, the bat was in my trunk because I'd played ball with some buddies the week before." He strokes his beard. It's something he does a lot. I doubt he even notices. "I tried to go back later, but she wouldn't let me in. We had this chain on the door, and she had it locked. Probably could've busted the door in, but I wasn't gonna do that. I figured she'd come to her senses. But no, she didn't. She ended up changing the damn locks, so then I went to her store a few times. I just wanted the rest of my stuff, you know? But you know what she did?"

I did know, but I shook my head like I didn't.

"She had a damn restraining order taken against me! Can you believe that? All 'cause I wanted my stuff. I told you— chick's crazy." He leans back in his chair.

There's so much I don't like about what he said. Darren would call me crazy, too, whenever I'd get upset about something. As though his emotions were completely valid—he could get angry over the smallest things—but mine were unreasonable, hysterical.

But I do get why Hudson is so mad. I would be as well if someone held my belongings hostage.

And I'm glad that he finally came clean about the restraining order. Maybe he had no intention of keeping it from me. Maybe he just needed to feel more comfortable. He does seem to be coming out of his shell more, becoming more talkative lately.

"Why do you think she filed the restraining order, though? That seems really extreme, especially if she was the one acting violent?"

"'Cause that's what Natalia does. She likes drama. Playing the victim. When we met, she told me her ex cheated on her." He shakes his head, his lips curling in disgust. "But that was a lie. He never cheated on her."

"What?" She had told me the same thing. Had it really been a lie?

And if she'd lie about that, what else would she lie about?

"Yeah." He throws his hands up, his eyebrows rising in tandem. "I guess she did it for attention. I mean, I definitely felt sorry for her, and, yeah, I wanted to protect her. You know how guys are. We're drawn to that damsel-in-distress shit. And when she kicked me out, suddenly that neighbor guy was around all the time. I bet she did it to get her hooks into him, same way she did with me. He's probably over there right now standing guard, her personal watchdog."

It's quiet a moment. I want to say something helpful, but I have no idea what that is. So I finally settle on, "I'm sorry."

He shrugs in response.

I don't know Natalia, and in our one interaction, she didn't exactly win me over. But saying she took out a restraining order to get attention from another guy seems like a pretty weak defense. In raising my kids, I often found that their explanations were black-and-white—while the truth was somewhere in the gray.

Bowie stirs on the ground. I continue playing with the edge of the blanket.

"Are you really gonna go to that meeting?" Hudson asks, breaking the silence.

"I don't know." I frown. "I mean, I feel like I should. It's my neighborhood, and I have every right to know what's going on."

"Weird how they didn't invite you, though," he muses. Turning, he peers out the front window, his forehead creasing. "John didn't seem surprised when I went out there. Didn't even seem scared that I had a bat. It was almost like he was expecting me."

"Well, I mean, he had to figure we'd confront him if we caught him snooping on our property."

"Exactly," Hudson says. "So, why our yard? If he saw something in Bill's, why was he in ours?"

The hairs on the back of my neck stand at attention. "Good question. Better view?"

"Or is keeping an eye on us part of the neighborhood watch?"

Now I know the answer to Hudson's earlier question. "I guess I'll find out tomorrow night."

"So you are going?"

"I don't think I have a choice."

"Do you want me to go with you?"

I mull it over a minute and then shake my head. I'm sure Leslie has told them all sorts of bad things about me, but it's nothing compared to the gossip she's spread about Hudson. "No, I think it's best if I go alone."

Hudson studies my face a minute and then nods slowly, reluctantly. "Just be careful."

"I will," I promise him.

* * *

Hudson's words ring out in my mind as I knock on the O'Leerys' front door.

Be careful.

The door swings open. Beth stands in front of me wearing jeans, a flannel shirt, fuzzy socks on her feet. Her hair is pulled back in a messy ponytail. I feel overdressed in my skinny jeans, gray sweater and white Frye leather booties, accessorized with large dangly earrings and chunky bracelets lining my wrist. Then again, I've never known how to dress casually in social situations. I live in my joggers around the house, but whenever I leave it I like to dress nice.

"Is that what you're wearing?" Darren used to ask when I'd come down the stairs ready to go grocery shopping or run errands.

I'd glance down at my silky top and high-heeled boots or sandals, confused. "What's wrong with it?"

"Nothing, you look amazing, but look what I'm wearing." He'd point to himself, indicating his gym shorts and T-shirt, tennis shoes on his feet.

"Want me to change?" I'd ask, praying he'd say no. Other women rock sweatpants and T-shirts, some managing to appear glamorous in them, even. I don't. I feel most comfortable when I'm put together.

And tonight, I need to feel comfortable.

Upon seeing me, the smile on Beth's face slips, her mouth freezing around the word, "Oh." She's always been a little frumpy. Her brown hair is a drab color, and it's always in a ponytail. Recovering, she brushes back a strand of hair that escaped from her hair tie. "Hi, Valerie." She makes no attempt to move away from the door and continues to stare at me in confusion. "What are you doing here?"

"John told me about the neighborhood watch meeting. That's tonight, right?" I peer over her shoulder, hearing chattering from the other room. I purposely showed up a little late, not wanting to be one of the first to arrive.

"Oh, he did, did he?" She doesn't sound pleased.

"Yeah, when we caught him snooping on my property. It was actually very scary, since no one had made us aware of the neighborhood watch in the first place."

Her cheeks flush the tiniest bit, a wash of pink against her pale skin. "Well, John jumped the gun." It isn't an apology. It's also not an explanation. "We haven't even started the neighborhood watch program yet. I'm still in the process of registering and getting signs and information."

"But you're still having the meeting, right?" Again, I look past her down the narrow entryway and into the family room. From this vantage point, I can tell the O'Leerys' house is laid out similar to Leslie's, the front hall leading to the den, the kitchen immediately off to the right. It's decorated much differently, though. Beth seems to be into the farmhouse thing. Her walls are covered in whitewashed wooden signs that say things like, "Family," "Home Sweet Home" and "Gather."

A small group is huddled in the family room. I can't see everyone, but it seems to be ten to fifteen people. I recognize most of them from my walks or from seeing them gabbing on Leslie's front porch.

"Um...yes, but it's just an initial meeting, explaining our options, gauging interest." She crosses her arms over her chest, making no attempt to move out of the way.

It's irritating. It's not like I want to be here. I'd give anything to turn around and race back home. Run across the street. Bolt my door shut. Curl up with a blanket. But I came for answers, and I plan to get them. It's my only hope of finding out who really killed Molly and Leslie.

"Well, I'm interested." I clasp my hands nervously in front of me. Pressing my lips together, I glance at Beth's frowning face. "Are you gonna let me in?"

"I'm sorry, but I really just wasn't expecting you," she says in an apologetic tone, peering warily over her shoulder. I notice a few of her guests peeking at us, Shelly being one of them. Alex, Beth's husband, stands from an armchair like he's wondering if he should intervene.

"The meeting was open to the entire neighborhood, wasn't it?"

She nods. "But given your history with Leslie...and, well... you know..."

"No, I don't," I say, unable to give her the satisfaction of getting away with a statement like that. She should have to verbalize what she thinks, not force me to fill in the horrible blanks.

"Okay, I didn't want to say this." She stares down at her hands, but a small smile plays on her lips that betrays she's having more fun with this than she cares to admit. "But I think maybe the meeting will be a little uncomfortable for you."

"What do you mean?" My hands have become fists, my fingernails piercing the insides of my palms.

"I just...um..." She holds up her index finger the way a teacher does to an interrupting child. "Hang on just a minute, okay?" She peers down the entryway and hollers out, "We'll start in just a minute. Why don't you all get a drink and a snack?" Catching her husband's eye, she nods. "Alex, can you help with that, please?"

He nods, eyeing me suspiciously.

I swallow hard.

She turns back to me and sighs heavily. "I'm sorry, but I really don't think it's a good idea for you to be here. John never should've invited you."

"He also shouldn't have been snooping in my yard," I snap, stinging from the rejection.

"No, he shouldn't have been."

"Why was he?" I place a hand on my hip, cocking my head to the side.

She shakes her head. "Like I said, he must have jumped the gun. Or misunderstood. I don't know."

"Either way, I'm part of this neighborhood, and I have every right to be at this meeting." I hold my ground.

Beth presses her lips together, her expression conflicted. A few agonizing seconds go by before she says, "I got more information today about Leslie's death."

I hold my breath, afraid she's going to say that someone saw either me or Hudson going to Leslie's that night. It takes all my courage not to turn and run away. But I know if I do, I'll only look guilty. Besides, she may be bluffing. She might not know anything at all. So I hold my head steady and wait for her to talk.

"She was strangled just like Molly," she says.

It's a challenge to keep my poker face, but it's clear by the way Beth is looking at me that she's expecting some type of reaction. I won't give it to her. "That's terrible," I finally say. "But I still don't understand what that has to do with me."

Her face darkens. "Leslie was murdered right after she accused your son of killing Molly," she snarls.

Bile rises in my throat. *Hudson did have motive, after all.* I clear it and breathe in through my nostrils. "I think you have incorrect information. Last I heard, Leslie had changed her tune, thought someone else had done it." The look Beth gives me in response can only be described as one of pity, like she doesn't believe me, like *I'm* the one with the bad information. Then she clears her throat.

"The rest of us are worried, Valerie," she says hostilely.

"There is a killer on the loose. I don't know how you sleep at night knowing he's under your roof." She slams the door in my face. I flinch. Blink. Draw in a shaky breath. I've had enough. I storm across the street, more determined than ever to prove Hudson's innocence.

My entire body is buzzing with adrenaline and anger by the time I get inside my house.

"Wow, you're back early. Quick meeting?" Hudson's voice startles me.

I flinch, my muscles tightening.

He's on the couch, feet propped on the coffee table, *The Office* playing on the TV. I don't have the heart to tell him I wasn't welcomed into the meeting.

Instead I say, "I wasn't expecting you to be home. Figured you'd be out with friends."

"Nah. Got an early day tomorrow."

"They sure have you working a lot."

"Right?" He dips his hand into a bag of chips, and it crinkles.

"Hey, are you sure you overheard Leslie saying she suspected someone other than you?"

He drops the bag of chips onto the end table, snapping one between his teeth. Then he straightens, sitting taller, his feet falling from the coffee table. "Yeah, why?"

"Do you happen to remember who she was talking to?"

"Beth, and then that other lady she's always with—the one with the short hair."

"Shelly?"

"Yeah, I think so."

If she'd been talking to Beth about it, then the new lead had hardly changed Beth's mind.

I sigh, rolling out my shoulders. I'm ready for bed. "Where's Bowie?"

"Upstairs, I think." His eyebrows pinch. "You okay?"

"Just tired."

I find Bowie curled up at the foot of my bed. I perch next to him, resting my palm on his back, the mattress sloping beneath me. The laughter from the television travels up the stairs, slipping under my door. I hear the crack of a can. Hudson must be opening a beer or soda. I never used to have either in my house. Now it's common to open the fridge and find a shiny can or two on the shelf.

A lot has changed since he came back.

I stand and head to my dresser to change into pajamas. When I pass the window, my insides seize. I step closer to the glass, pressing my palm to the cool, slick surface. A man walks up to Beth's front door, and then raps on it. She opens almost immediately, wearing a large smile before ushering him inside.

Even though I don't see his face, I know who it is. I recognize his walk. His build. The shape of his head. I might not have, if it weren't for the fact that I saw him a week ago in front of Leslie's house.

James.

20

The next morning on my walk, I'm worrying over what it portends that James—no longer a neighbor here—was invited to a neighborhood watch meeting and I was not, when I spot Detective Daniels.

He's a few dozen feet ahead, talking to a couple I don't recognize. I glance at the home they are gathered in front of. Maybe they live there. This isn't my street, and although I walk it often, I don't know most of the people over here.

My muscles seize. I have no desire to talk to Detective Daniels right now. Bowie tugs on the leash as he trots forward along the sidewalk, blissfully unaware.

"Leslie was murdered right after she accused your son of killing Molly."

Backpedaling, I yank on Bowie's leash, swinging us both around. I can't let him see me. Head down, I walk swiftly back toward my house. It's not like he doesn't know where I live, but at least there I have some control, rather than him catching me unaware out here in front of everyone. As if last night at the neighborhood watch meeting wasn't embarrassing enough.

It isn't until I round the corner, with the house where I saw Detective Daniels obscured by trees and bushes, that I allow myself to breathe out.

"Valerie!"

My breath catches in my throat, mid-exhale, and my shoulders tighten.

"Valerie."

It's a woman's voice, not a man's, and I vaguely recognize it. Slowly, I turn.

"Hi." Tessa jogs toward me.

"Hi?" It comes out like a question. I don't correct it. Bowie's pulling wildly on the other end of the leash, confused as to why we're stopped. And honestly, so am I. Tessa has been my direct neighbor for years, but rarely speaks to me and almost never unprovoked. She and Leslie became fast friends shortly after Tessa moved in, and it was clear Leslie had poisoned her against me early on.

"I just wanted to say that I'm sorry about Beth." Her eyes are kind, and I find myself softening, but only a little bit. I've been stabbed in the back enough not to be too trusting. And Tessa has never given me any reason to trust her. "I was at the meeting last night, and I couldn't help but overhear your conversation with her."

I look back toward the corner I just rounded, keeping my eye out for Detective Daniels.

"And…um… I just wanted to tell you that you were right."

My gaze snaps back to Tessa. "Right about what?"

"The police were looking into someone besides your son."

"Really?"

She blinks. "Or, well…maybe in addition to, is a better way of saying it."

"What?"

"I just mean, I don't know…" She glances around, chomps down on her lower lip. "I shouldn't even be talking to you about this."

I hold my breath, afraid to urge her on. Afraid that my desperation will scare her off.

She leans in closer. "Leslie'd been talking to James. She contacted him after Molly was murdered, because she was scared." *Of Hudson.* She doesn't have to finish the sentence. I already know. "She wasn't supposed to tell us anything James told her, but you know Leslie." Again, her eyes shift anxiously back and forth. "Anyway, he told her to calm down, that the police had found some prints in Molly's house that don't match any in the system." I heave a sigh of relief at that. Then they're probably not Hudson's. I'm guessing that with the fights he was in and the restraining order, he's most likely, unfortunately, in a database somewhere. "And they found out Molly had a boyfriend."

"Do you know who he is?"

She shakes her head. "Leslie said she couldn't tell us that. Said James would kill her." Her eyes widen at her own poor choice of words. "You know what I mean."

Of course that's the one piece of information she withheld.

"But you think she knew?"

Tessa shrugs. "I kinda got the impression she did… I don't know what else she knew. I don't know if what she learned changed her mind…" About my son, she means.

At least now I know I was right about why James is back in the picture. Figures the only reason she'd reach out to him is because of her hatred toward Hudson. I can't speak to all the reasons James and Leslie broke up after Heather died—but I know that one was how angry she was with him for not condemning Hudson the way she had. The day before he moved out, James came over to tell me that he was sorry for the way Leslie was treating our family. "It isn't right," he said, and the hurt in his voice told me it wasn't just us that she'd unfairly attacked. He admitted that he was the one who'd had to break it to Leslie that all evidence pointed to Heather's death being accidental. She'd hated him for it, for giving up on their daughter.

There would be no way Leslie would ever reach out to James, unless she had an ulterior motive. He may not work for Sac County anymore, but I'm sure he has plenty of connections here.

"Is that why James was at the neighborhood watch meeting?" I ask.

"He was there at Beth's request. He helped us come up with an action plan for the neighborhood."

My chest tightens, wondering if part of their action plan involves watching Hudson and me.

"Okay, well, thanks, Tessa," I say, then turn around. Bowie, sensing that we're resuming our walk, lunges in front of me and takes off running. I almost lose my arm trying to keep up.

"Be careful, Valerie," she calls as I hurry away.

I need to find out who this boyfriend is. Right now it's clear that the entire neighborhood still thinks Hudson did it—I think of Beth's face, the certainty of her belief that Hudson was involved, her neighborhood watch homed in on our house. I have to come up with some information to prove he didn't before it's too late. If I can find out the boyfriend's name, maybe I can help the police. Dig up dirt on him. At least something to finally get Hudson off of everyone's radar.

When Leslie and I were friends, she was an incessant note taker. I used to tease her that she'd missed her calling. She should've been a reporter or gossip columnist. She'd laugh and say that she had been the editor of her school paper, and that before she dropped out of college, she'd been studying journalism. She had pads of paper throughout her house, to-do lists, reminders, but she talked often about keeping a diary. Said she had one for every school year growing up, and at that point the habit of writing was too engrained to stop. For a while—she laughed when she told me this—all she wrote was boring stuff about what she'd had for breakfast. But then she'd had an issue with some of our neighbors, Phillip and Diane, a couple who used to live behind her. Their dog was always getting out and tearing up Leslie's flowers, digging up her yard or crapping on the lawn. Every time she tried to talk to them about it, they got angry, shut her down. She started keeping a log of dates and times that the dog got out, so she could file a formal complaint.

That's when she got obsessed with chronicling things in the neighborhood. Once they left, bad dog in tow, she still kept diaries about her family's scheduling, about PTA and school board disputes, about people's comings and goings, new neighbors moving in, that sort of thing.

I'd bet that somewhere in her house there's a journal where she'd jotted down the name of this mysterious suspect. If I can get in there, I might be able to find it. No doubt the police have gone through her stuff, but they might not have noticed it—almost all little girls keep diaries, but among grown women it's much less common. I'm probably the only one who knows about them.

Or, maybe I'm not. Maybe the killer knows. Maybe he already found them. Or maybe he's planning to look.

My mouth dries out at the thought.

There's no time to waste. I can't bank on the police finding them in time, even if I call in with the tip. If they're still there, I have to find them now.

When I get home, I go straight to the junk drawer in the

kitchen. I don't bother with rifling through it. Instead, I pull it all the way out and dump the contents on the kitchen table. Somewhere in here is a key to Leslie's house. We used to watch it for them when they went on vacation, water Leslie's plants.

I sift through paper clips, receipts, old check logs, measuring tape, a gazillion pens—most with no caps—a package of pink birthday candles, a roll of stamps, and then voilà, I find them. Keys. About a dozen of them. I have no idea what they're all for, but one of them has to be to Leslie's house.

Two of them appear to be the wrong size for a house. Way too small. They might have been for the kids' school lockers or a mailbox of some sort—maybe a key Darren used for work. I'm not sure, but I shove them to the side.

That leaves ten.

I pick up the one bearing the colors of the American flag, instantly recognizing it as our spare. I set it aside with the small ones.

Nine.

The next one I pick up is elongated, a Honda symbol on the top.

Eight.

The rest are all a mystery. Any of them could be for Leslie's house. I just have to try them.

Palming all eight, I walk to the window and stare out. I'm anxious to race across the street and attempt to get in. But then I see Alex outside. He appears to be affixing something to his front door.

What is it?

I lean forward, straining to see.

He stands back to inspect his handiwork, and that's when it hits me. One of those doorbell security cameras.

I close my fist around the keys. Everyone is on high alert. There's no way I'll get over there and inside undetected. As if confirming my assessment, Beth appears in one of the front windows, peering out the way Leslie used to do. Skin crawling, I move out of sight.

It's probably not a good idea to try right now, anyway. Not in broad daylight with Detective Daniels poking around. I'll have to wait until tonight.

I only hope Leslie never had her locks changed. And that Alex's camera can't see too well in the dark.

21

Third time's the charm, I think as key number three seamlessly slides into the keyhole. Thank god, too. I didn't want to be out here on Leslie's front porch much longer. Not with everyone installing security cameras and special keypads in place of locks. Leslie seemed like the type to do something like that, or Leslie post-Heather, anyway. She suddenly, perhaps understandably, saw danger everywhere. It's odd to me that she hadn't changed her locks in ten years, especially knowing I had a key. Then again, neither have I, and I'm pretty sure she had a key to my house, too. I never even thought about it until now. Maybe she hadn't either.

I glance around, worried someone will spot me, even though I'm wearing all black, and the hood to my jacket is pulled all the way up over my head in an effort to camouflage myself into the dark night sky. And it *is* two in the morning. Who would be up at this hour?

I had to set an alarm to ensure I would be.

Before falling asleep tonight, I'd done some research online about the doorbell cameras to find out how wide their scope was. Then, using a pair of binoculars I found in a box of Hudson's old things, I stood in my front window, studying the positioning of Beth's. So far none of our other direct neighbors have installed one, so I only have to worry about avoiding hers. I'm assuming it's an initiative they discussed at the neighborhood watch, so soon they'll probably all have one.

From where Alex had installed the camera, it appears to be catching everything directly in front of their house, including their entire front lawn. So when I crept across the street, I did so to the left of Leslie's house to not be detected. I came up on the left side of the porch, crawling onto it through the board railings. I'm not as agile as I once was, so it was a struggle. I slipped a few times, but finally made it.

Thanks to trusty key number three, the knob turns easily, and I shove open the door and rush inside. When I firmly close the door behind me, I sigh with relief. It's dark, and I feel my way along the wall.

My eyes adjust slightly, but I can still barely see anything. I tug my phone out of my pocket to turn on my flashlight and pause. I need to be away from windows when I turn it on just in case a neighbor sees.

Fingertips skating along the wall, I walk further in. Once I'm in the family room, away from the entryway, I swipe up on my phone and click the flashlight. A beam of light sprays the carpet in front of me, illuminating my path.

It bounces along the wall as I turn down the hallway. To my right is the bedroom that used to belong to Heather. It looks like it was turned into a guest room; the four-poster twin bed that teenage Heather had been clamoring to upgrade is a neatly made double with a rattan headboard, a dream delivered far too late.

The next room had always been the office, and I'm grateful that seems to have remained the same. Holding the phone in front of me, I make a beeline for the blinds and tug the cord to close them. Then I head to Leslie's desk. Sure enough, the top drawer is filled with notepads, Leslie's handwriting scrawled all over the pages.

The first one I flip to is instructions on plant propagation, taking pothos cuttings, yada yada. I toss that one aside. The next is filled with to-do lists.

These aren't what I'm looking for. The ones she used to write in about neighborhood goings-on were more like diaries. Leather-bound books with pretty stationery-like pages. Not run-of-the-mill notebooks.

Leaving the office, I head into Leslie's room. The comforter is off-white with roses all over it. There is a mirror above the dresser, my reflection staring back at me in it. Her closet door is open. It's a spacious walk-in. She used to joke that it was the best feature in her house. As I step inside, I'm assaulted by Leslie's familiar scent. She'd worn the same floral perfume for years. I swallow hard, taking in her clothes hanging neatly from the racks. Below them are her shoes. I back out of the closet.

There is a decorative bookshelf in the corner. On the top two shelves are a collection of romance novels and some books on how to care for plants. But when I glance down at the bottom shelf, I find them. The leather-bound notebooks, little cutouts on the sides, dates written in Sharpie.

I drop to my knees and run my finger along their spines.

Reading the dates, I come across one from the year Heather died. Although it isn't what I'm looking for, I can't help myself from opening it.

The entry is dated a week before Heather's death. My palms moisten at the first line on the page.

Leslie had written, "Heather came home from Hudson's in tears. Said she doesn't want to go over there anymore. When asked why not, she told me she's scared to."

I stare at the words in disbelief. I never knew this. I mean, I do recall Leslie screaming at me one day that Heather had been afraid of Hudson generally—and that's how she knew her daughter's death was no accident. But she said a lot of things then. Anger-fueled, revenge-filled things. And much of it wasn't rooted in reality.

At least, I hadn't thought it was.

I hear a click. My scalp prickles. I don't dare move. When the heater clicks on, I feel silly. I'm kind of surprised no one thought to turn it off, then realize I don't know who that would be. Beth, maybe. Leslie doesn't really have any family left.

I am wasting time, though. I need to pick up the pace. I'm about to put the notebook down when I change my mind and tuck it into my sweatshirt. I want to see what else she wrote about Hudson and Heather at that time; I just can't right now.

She has a notebook for every year except this one. But there is a distinct gap between the last notebook and the end of the shelf. In fact, the last book is propped at an angle as if it fell that way when something had been removed next to it.

Had the police taken the last notebook? Surely a diary might be helpful evidence.

Or maybe I'm wrong and there never was a final notebook. Perhaps Leslie finally joined the twenty-first century and started taking notes digitally. Standing up, I hurry out of her room, return to the office and rush to the desk. I reach for the computer mouse to my right and shake it over the mouse pad, which is unsurprisingly a photo of a plant. Even in here, she has a few hanging from the ceiling. Odd that the computer is still here and had been left on. It almost deters me as I draw the conclusion that the police found nothing of significance on it. Then again, I might find something they wouldn't. The screen comes to life, blue light filling the room. When the lock screen comes up, I curse and try the most obvious passwords—Heather's name and then Heather's birthday, which I'll never forget because it's two days before Hudson's, a fact Leslie and I marveled about often. In fact, one year we took the kids to Six Flags for the day, a joint celebration. When that doesn't work, I try Leslie's birthday, which is also one I can't forget, the day after Christmas. She always complained about the fact that her birthday got caught up in the chaos of the holidays. When we were friends, I empathized. Afterward, I realized how childish and entitled she'd been.

I can't remember James's birthday, but I'd be shocked if she used that, anyway. Next, I try the day Heather died. Morbid, I know, but I wouldn't put it past Leslie. It was a date she obsessed over.

But that doesn't work either.

I'm out of ideas. The last thing I want is to get locked out. Then whoever goes on this computer next will know someone had been in here. Most likely that will be the police, and if they dust for prints…

Oh, god. I stare in horror at my hands. Gloves. There's a pair of black leather ones sitting on my nightstand. I'd gotten them out for tonight, but forgot to bring them. I'd made the same mistake at Molly's.

Ice spills down my spine.

I can't keep leaving my handprints all over crime scenes.

Panicked, I rush into the bathroom and tear a hand towel off the rack. Returning to the office, I wipe everything that I've touched. I have no idea if this will work, but I have to try. Sticking the towel in my sweater alongside the notebook, I walk back out to the family room.

I'm an idiot.

I did all of this and didn't even get any useful information.

I pause, take a breath. Where do I keep track of what *I* need to know? And then I think of one more place I can try. Aiming my phone at the carpet, I allow the beam to guide me to the kitchen. Underneath the calendar on the wall, a pad of paper sits on the counter. I snatch it up, read the first page.

Library books due 10/3.

I stare at the date. October. The month Heather died. It hadn't hit me until now how close Leslie's death date was to her daughter's.

Same season. Less than a month apart.

I shiver.

The rest of the pad is blank. I groan in frustration. This isn't helpful at all. The clock on the wall ticks. I need to get out of here.

After setting the pad down exactly where I found it, I back out of the room, careful to keep the light fixed on the ground. I don't want anyone seeing it through the window in the kitchen that overlooks the front yard. And while the family room seems safer, its main window faces Beth's side— even more dangerous.

As I get closer to the entryway, I'm about to turn the flashlight off when I spot something pale in the threads of the carpet. A fleck of gardener's perlite, or a tiny shell, perhaps? It's out of place, though, on Leslie's immaculate rug.

While I'm bending down to pick it up, my eyes catch something else. Something even more familiar just under Leslie's coral-themed coatrack. Is that...?

The notebook slides forward in my sweater and hits me under the chin. The towel is inching its way out as well. I shove them both back in. Then I pick up the shiny thing, hold it to the light, my mouth drying out.

It's one of my earrings. It's from a set Darren bought me years ago.

They were never my style, but I did force myself to wear them occasionally when he was alive. I never wear them anymore. Haven't since Darren passed away.

Surely it hasn't been hidden in her carpet all these years. That would be impossible.

So how did it get here now?

A shuffling sound catches my attention. It's probably the wind or an animal, but I swiftly shove the earring into my pocket and stand. I've already been here longer than I should.

Clicking off the flashlight, I'm blanketed in darkness. I stand in the shadows, the notebook poking me in the ribs, the earring nestled in my pocket and a nagging thought deep in the recesses of my brain, telling me that I've forgotten something even more important.

When I get home, I'm too amped up to fall asleep. It's like when I'd return from a gig, adrenaline pumping through my veins, highlight reel of the evening playing in my mind. Thankfully, Hudson is asleep. I hear his heavy breathing as I bolt past his door. In my room, I change out of my all-black attire and into a pair of cozy jammies.

Sliding under the covers into my bed, I open Leslie's notebook and fervently read through it. Much of it is what I already know: the start of the kids' school year in September, the stress of baking cookies for Fall Fest. She wrote something catty about a woman in book club that makes me laugh—I remember Ann Winston from my short stint in the club, and she *did* begin every opinion with, "Well, when I was at Stanford…" or, "Well, as my PhD professor used to say…" Leslie recounted a few of our conversations, and it's creepy how accurate they are. She took note of my haircut—the one and only time I got bangs—and apparently she was kind enough not to say to me what she was really thinking. And she mentions Hudson, too, mostly whether he'd come over, if he'd given Heather a ride somewhere.

Leslie's handwriting has always been distinctive: an odd combination of cursive and print, a method all her own. And I'm years out of practice on reading it, so every page takes me several painstaking minutes to decipher. My eyes are strained and blurry from the effort.

A few weeks before Heather's death, she writes,

Couldn't sleep. Got up to get a glass of water at around 4am. From kitchen window, I saw the light flick on in front of Val's house.

I sit up, remembering how Darren had installed a light with a sensor over the garage.

Val's front door popped open, and someone slipped inside and shut the door. Couldn't really make out who. I was worrying whether I should call Val to wake and warn her or the cops to get over right away or if I should rush over to help myself when I saw the light to Hudson's room turn on briefly before turning off again. Not a burglar, then. Was about to go to bed, but when I took one last look outside I noticed something all over the windshield of Heather's car and went outside to see.

The word SLUT written in shaving cream.

I've never been so angry.

Woke James in a fury. We cleaned it before Heather could see. Told James it had to be Hudson, but he said Hudson's a good kid and wouldn't do that. We didn't tell Heather—how could we? It would crush her!—but we

did ask her about how school was going? Friends? Hudson? She said everything was fine. But I know it's not.
I'm going to be watching.

Why hadn't Leslie ever told me about this?

Curious, I get out of bed, leave my room. Since Darren died, I've rarely gone into his old office. The air is stale and musty when I step inside. I flick on the switch, and dim light fills the space. The room is bare except for the desk in the corner with the old desktop computer sitting on top. It's outdated, and I never use it. In the corner is a file cabinet. The bottom drawer is filled with tax papers, birth certificates, the kids' vaccination records starting from birth on. The top one has all of the kids' school stuff—report cards, pictures and papers I'd saved. But in the very back, I've filed away my old planners and daily calendars.

My mom always kept stuff like that, saying that one day she might want to look back and remember. She wasn't the one who did. I was. Back when my mom's memory faded, I went through all of her old things, and reading through all that we'd done together—all the daily activities and events— kept the memories alive in me. I was glad then that, while so much of my life I've tried to be different from my mom, in this way I'd followed her example.

I pull the top drawer open and sift through the planners until I come across one for the year Heather died. Tiptoeing back upstairs with it and curling up in bed, I flip to the date in question. Hudson had a game that night and had ended up spending the night at Jared's. So there's no way he could've done it. Right?

Except... Jared used to live around the corner. Hudson technically could have walked here, done it, come home early.

I didn't make note, of course, of what time he returned. But why would he do that to Heather?

I keep reading.

After the SLUT incident, Leslie obsessively chronicled Hudson and Heather's relationship, writing down every time they went out and Heather's behavior afterward. How sometimes she came home with red eyes, mascara streaks on her cheeks as if she'd been crying.

A week and a half before Heather's death, Leslie had written,

> Bruise on Heather's arm. Asked her about it. Said a ball hit her in PE. But to me it looks like she was grabbed. Bruise is elongated and spread out like a handprint, not round like a ball.

If I'd read this back then, I'd have laughed. Since when did Leslie become an expert on bruising? But all I can see is that picture of Natalia. The bruise under her eye.

I shiver and flip the page, finally coming upon the one I'd read in Leslie's house.

I read past the initial sentence about Heather being scared, and find out that Heather had gone as far as to say she wanted to break up with Hudson.

Then, the night before the Halloween party, Leslie had scrawled,

> Heather has said all week she hadn't planned to go to the party. But today at dinner when I suggested we plan a family costume for the trick-or-treaters tomorrow, she said she changed her mind, that Hudson had talked her into it. Still doesn't seem like she wants to go. I don't want her to. But James is insisting she always goes out

with Hudson on Halloween and she'll regret it if she doesn't. I wish just for once, he'd back me on this. God, I swear he acts like Hudson is perfect. The son he never had. Why can't he see what I do?

I swallow hard. I'd had no idea Leslie felt this way about Hudson prior to Heather's death. Then again, I get why she didn't talk to me about it. Talking bad about someone's kid, accusing him of mistreating someone this badly, is a sure way to end a friendship.

It seems she talked to James about it a lot, though. As I read through the remainder of the diary, I see the crumbling of their marriage. How much he dismissed her feelings, from cleaning out Heather's room before she was ready to telling her to let her theories about Hudson go.

As I mull over what I've read, the word *SLUT* cements itself in my mind. It's a word I'd become well-acquainted with in the weeks after Mac's death—whispered about me by people I thought were my friends and anonymously sent to me online by disgruntled fans.

Kind of like that anonymous asshole commenting about Molly's death.

Reaching into my nightstand, I pull out the gold watch. As I run my fingertips over the inscription, I can't help but think there's an answer in here. If only I could find it.

Sticks and stones may break my bones,
But words will never hurt me...

Wind rushed past my ear, carrying a whistling sound. Behind me there was a crash as loud as a gunshot. I pressed my hands to my ears and ducked down, squeezing my eyes shut. When I heard my sister's laugh, I pried my eyelids open. She stood a few feet away, snickering.

My body was trembling as I glanced over my shoulder.

Then my stomach dropped the same way it does on a roller coaster. Mom's favorite vase lay in pieces all over the floor near the wall.

Had she thrown that at my head?

"What's going on?" Mom rushed into the room, eyes wide. When she saw the vase, she slapped her hand over her mouth. I could see the swell of her chest as it rose and fell swiftly. I backed away, outside of her reach. "Go to your room! We'll talk later. I'm too mad right now."

I looked to where my sister had been standing, but the spot was empty.

"But, Mom, I didn't—"

"Now!"

She stepped toward me, eyes flashing. I burst into action, racing into the hallway and up the stairs. When I passed my sister's room, I caught a glimpse of her inside, lying on her bed, reading a book. Angry, I stopped running. Peering over my shoulder, I didn't see Mom. I could hear her picking up the broken pieces of her vase downstairs.

There was time.

I stepped into my sister's room. "Andie." She opened her mouth to correct me, but I beat her to it. "Kendra."

It was a difficult habit to break. I'd been calling her Andie since I was old enough to speak—when I couldn't pronounce my *K*s and *R*s, and Kendra, softened to Endwee, morphed into Andie before anyone could convince me otherwise. Mom and Dad never got on board—they continued to call her Kendra— but that was okay. I liked that it was something between the two of us. It was really the only thing we had. Her letting me call her by a nickname was the only thing that made it feel like she might not hate me completely.

But Kendra had taken that away from me recently, insisting that I call her by her real name.

"We're not babies anymore," she'd said. "You can pronounce my name now. So say it right."

"You could've killed me," I said now.

She looked up from her book and rolled her eyes. "Oh, please."

"Mom thinks I did it."

"And that's my problem?"

I take another step. "I'm gonna tell her you did it."

Shaking her head, she laughs. "She'll never believe you. I was upstairs reading. You were next to the vase."

Anger rose up inside of me, hot and intense like that boiling water she'd poured on my hand. I was so sick of her games. Of being manipulated.

"I hate you!" I yelled, lunging toward her.

Tossing her book aside, she pushed with her feet to try to scoot away. But it was too late. I was faster.

I pushed her down on the bed, my knees sinking into her thighs. She cried out in pain, and a shiver of triumph ran through me.

"Get off me, you fuckin' loser." She writhed.

Reaching out, I clamped my hands around her neck.

"Mom!" she screamed.

With all my force, I pressed down. Her eyes became wider than I'd ever seen them, but at least she'd finally shut up. Her arms shot upward, her fingernails raking over the skin on my wrists and hands. But I kept squeezing. So hard I felt her pulse bounce against my fingertips.

For once I was in control.

The tiger.

The predator.

I had the power.

Not her.

"Oh, my god. Stop. Get off of her!" Mom flew into the room. She leaped onto the bed, yanking my arms away from my sister's neck.

My sister sat up, gulping in air. Her fingers ran along the skin of her neck, as if checking to make sure it was still there.

Staring at the red mark appearing on her pale skin, a slow smile crept over my face.

22

I roll over in bed and stare at my ringing phone in disbelief. Dr. Steiner's number.

It's 8:00 a.m. and I should be blurry with sleep deprivation, but the sight of the doctor's office on my caller ID wakes me right up. The turnaround is so fast, it's surely indicative of how dire the results are.

But I'm wrong.

"There's no sign of early-onset Alzheimer's or dementia in any of your tests," Dr. Steiner says so breezily it leaves me speechless.

"Valerie?"

I blink. Bowie pants near my feet. "Um...yes, I'm here. I just... I don't understand...there has to be some mistake."

"I'm emailing your results right now. Feel free to look them over and then, if you still have questions, you can call back. And if you'd like to make an appointment, I can transfer you to the receptionist, or refer you to a neurologist for further testing."

My head spins. It's too much. I don't know what to do. I can't even form a coherent thought.

"Okay…yeah… I'll look things over and get back to you." I hang up in a daze, haul myself out of bed and go straight to my laptop.

And there they are—the results from my lab work, my MRI, the cognitive testing. All normal.

It doesn't make any sense, and yet…

Still attempting to process, I pick up my phone and, with slick fingers, dial Kendra. She's in nursing school, so maybe she can make sense of this for me. Explain how this could happen. Surely, my forgetfulness and cotton-brain wasn't made up.

"Hey, Mom." She sounds tired.

"You okay?" I ask.

"Just didn't get a ton of sleep last night."

"Yeah," I say. "Theo told me Mason hasn't been sleeping that much at night."

"When did he tell you that?" she asked sharply.

"The other day when he dropped Mason off," I say. "He said you'd been driving him around at night to try to put him to sleep. I remember doing that with you, too."

"Really? With me?"

"Yeah. You liked the white noise and motion."

"And you took me? Or Dad did?"

I hate when she does this. Insists on pointing out the disparity between the time I spent with her and Darren spent with her. Sometimes, I wonder how long she'll punish me for the sins of her childhood. "We both did," I finally say.

"Yeah, well, I'm the only one who does it with Mason," she says, martyrdom thick in her tone.

"Theo did mention that the method mostly worked for you. Said Mason stayed wide-awake on his nights."

She snorts. "*His* nights."

"Everything okay with you two?"

"Fine. Why?"

"You guys just seem to be a little…" I try to think of the most gentle way to say this. "A little on edge around each other."

"I think we're just tired," she says dismissively. "Anyway, enough about all of that. I'm sure you didn't call to talk about my marriage or lack of sleep. What's going on with you?"

"A lot, actually. That's why I called."

"Really?" She sounds slightly more awake now. I recognize the tone, though. She thinks I'm going to spill the tea on her brother, even though I've never done that before. It's something she's been hoping for, though. I can tell.

"Yeah. I…um…saw Dr. Steiner earlier this week and had some tests done."

"You did? How come you didn't tell me?"

"I'm telling you now."

"No, I mean, before you went. I would've gone with you."

I'm a grown woman. I don't need an escort to the doctor. "I was fine. Anyway, I got the test results this morning, and they all came back normal."

Silence.

I wait. Clear my throat. Tap my nails on the table. One of them is chipped. I make a mental note to call my nail technician.

Did I lose her? "Kendra?"

"Yeah, I'm here. I just…what kind of tests were they?"

"I can send you the email, but it was some blood work, an MRI and a cognitive test."

"And you said they all came back normal?"

"Yeah, isn't it amazing?" Repeating it to Kendra has caused me to become less skeptical and more excited.

It's almost too good to be true.

"Yeah, it really is," she says, lacking the same enthusiasm I'm feeling.

"You don't sound too thrilled."

"I am, Mom. It's great news. The best. It's just..."

"What?"

"It just doesn't explain the memory lapses you've been having."

"That's true."

"But go ahead and email the test results," she says. "I'll look them over, and then maybe we can go to Dr. Steiner together, figure this out."

"Could the test results be wrong?"

"No, I'm sure they're right. There can be other reasons for cognitive issues. We just have to figure out what they are."

As I hang up, elation fills me. I don't have early-onset Alzheimer's. I'm not going to end up like my mom. It's the best news I could have gotten. I'm so happy that even Kendra's lukewarm reaction can't get me down. I should have expected it, anyway.

She's always so reserved. So logical. And oftentimes, skeptical. Hudson's called her Debbie Downer for years, inspired by a Rachel Dratch sketch.

But she said herself that the test results are correct. Whatever's going on with me, it's not showing up on these tests.

I call Hudson next, knowing he'll be happy about the results. He's the one who wanted me to see Dr. Steiner in the first place. He doesn't answer, which makes sense, since he's at work. But I leave a message: "Hey, just wanted to tell you I have some pretty great news. Dr. Steiner called with my results, and it seems I don't have Alzheimer's. Call me when you get this. Your sister's response was a bit lackluster. I need someone to celebrate with."

After hanging up, I rise from the kitchen table and go to the fridge for some water. I take in the Post-it Notes tacked to the fridge and flapping from the side of the calendar. Kendra's right about one thing, though. The test results don't explain the memory lapses. If I'm not losing my mind to dementia, then why have I been forgetting things?

Stepping closer to the calendar, I read my notes. The recent ones—MRI, Dr. Steiner, art class, Hudson working, Kendra coming over for dinner. Then I flip back to last month, scanning the days, the things I'd missed. My heart stops, my finger resting on one of the dates in question.

Mason, 5:30 p.m.

The handwriting.

It's different from the other days, the ones I'd recently scrawled down. *MRI, Dr. Steiner.* It's a subtle change. Barely noticeable, but there in the swirls of the lettering. In the deliberateness, as if someone had taken great pains to forge my handwriting, but that's ridiculous.

I tear the calendar off the wall, and my hand trembles as I study it, the paper crinkling beneath my fingertips.

Yes, I'm certain of it. I didn't write the note about watching Mason. On another date it says I have a dentist appointment at noon. I remember going to that, being told I was there a week early. I thought I'd made a mistake, but I see now that the handwriting is slightly off there as well.

If I didn't write it, who did?

Hudson lives here—he could access my calendar whenever he wants. But this was written before he came back.

Bowie runs into the room, shoots past me out the dog door. My limbs quiver as thoughts swirl through my mind, scary possibilities. But it's a ridiculous theory, right? I mean, who would write on my calendar, hide my keys, put things back in the wrong place? It's insane. Far-fetched. Like something from a movie. To calm my nerves, I pour water into the teakettle and set it on the stove.

I used to always drink tea before a gig. Everyone thought it was to open up my vocal cords, coat my throat. Mac was the only person who knew the truth—that I drank it to settle my anxiety. Chamomile always calms me.

As the tea steeps, I step out onto the back patio and watch Bowie run around the yard. I smile at his antics, barking and leaping at birds, and water the plants on the back porch. Some of them are looking a little droopy. Bowie and my succulents. Two things that calm me. Ground me.

When I head back inside, I toss the tea bag in the trash. As I pick up my mug, a noise upstairs catches my attention, almost like furniture being moved, the legs scraping against the hardwood floor. *Hello, Grace*, I think reflexively—then, remembering there were two women killed in my neighborhood, stand still and listen. This time I hear a creak like a gentle footfall. Someone trying not to be heard.

The hairs on the back of my neck prickle. I move slowly toward the stairs.

It's quiet now.

A car rumbles down the street. The breeze outside causes leaves to pounce on the glass, swift and tender like a kitten's paws.

I sigh.

My nerves are on edge. A little tea and a hot shower will clear my head, help me figure out what's happening. I do my best thinking in the shower. Always have. I used to take one when I struggled while writing a song. Under the hot spray of water, the lyrics would flow easily even after the worst writer's block. I need some of that clarity today.

In my room, I sip my tea and wait for the water to warm— a long wait in a house as old as mine. Once I see steam circling in the bathroom, I abandon my mug on the dresser and head into the shower. I close my eyes and breathe in deeply, allowing the pressure of the warm water to beat down on my achy muscles. I shudder as the heat takes over, drawing the chill from my bones.

I stay in the shower until my fingers are pruney, my skin red.

Then I step out, wrapping myself in a plush towel.

Before getting dressed, I sip the last few dregs of my tea. I pick out my favorite pair of sweats and a fuzzy sweater. As I step into one pants leg, I feel momentarily dizzy and have to grip the edge of the dresser to remain upright. I breathe in and out. Blink a few times. When I feel more steady, I try again, successfully getting both legs in my pants. But when I reach for my shirt, the room spins. Again, I hold on to the dresser. Squeezing my eyes shut to ward off the spinning, I gulp in the air.

It's a struggle to get the shirt over my head, my arms in the sleeves, as the dizziness threatens to take over. The walls bend and sway like a kite in the wind. I catch my reflection in the mirror above the dresser, pale and blurred. I clutch the dresser so hard my knuckles whiten.

What's wrong with me?

I was fine before the shower. My right hand bumps my teacup. *The tea.* Narrowing my eyes, I stare into the bottom of the cup.

When I glance back up at the mirror, I see someone standing over my shoulder.

Turning, I stare into eyes as familiar as my own.

"It was you," I breathe before I slump over, the darkness pulling me into its grasp.

23

I can't move.

I can't breathe.

My hands are stuck to my sides as if tethered, my eyelids so heavy I can't lift them. I fight to fill my lungs with air, panic seizing me with each shallow intake. Squirming like a rat in a trap, I use all the strength I can muster to pry my eyelids open. The room is out of focus as if I'm wearing the wrong lenses. I blink, and try unsuccessfully to sit up. My arms and legs are dead weight.

A shadow casts over me. I squirm more violently.

Someone's here.

"Mom, it's okay." A firm hand rests on my shoulder.

I open my eyes wide, focusing as best I can.

Hudson stands over me, his large hand pressing me back down into the bed. "Calm down. It's going to be okay."

I try to shake my head, but it won't move.

No, it's not okay. Let me out of this bed. I open my mouth, attempting to formulate the words, but they won't come. My lips feel weird—tingly and swollen—kind of like that time I tried that lip plumper, but way more intense. And my throat is raw.

"Trust me, you're gonna be all right."

He backs away from the bed, his hand leaving my shoulder.

I want to reach out and grab him, yank him back, but my limbs won't obey. I'm helpless, trapped in my own body.

My own home.

Help, I scream inside my head as Hudson reaches my bedroom door.

He hesitates a moment, his hand on the knob.

I wait with anticipation. *Yes, come back. Don't leave.* I need to warn him. The terrified voice in my own head hollers, the words rattling inside of my mind like the clanging of a cymbal. Bang. Bang. Bang.

He stares at me, weighty thoughts evident in his eyes. His lips press together, then pucker. Without another word, his hand turns the knob.

He swings the door open and steps into the hall. The door closes firmly. His footfalls carry him away.

I stare up at the ceiling, willing my body to move for several minutes. Then I hear the floor creak—and a horrifying sound. One I understand instantly, even as I feel sleep pulling me under.

Metal sliding softly against metal.

A hook and eye latch, like the one that used to hang in front of Grace's door.

Only now it must be hanging in front of mine.

24

The piano played high tinkling notes, a melody I recognized, but for some reason couldn't place. The music swelled around me, cocooning me in its familiarity, and then I knew what it was. "All I Ask of You" from *Phantom of the Opera*, the song I'd sung the day I met Darren. I felt the slick ivory beneath my fingertips, the faint buzz of the piano strings as I pressed down on the keys.

Around me the blurriness cleared, the room coming into focus. It was light and airy, the curtains open. I was sitting at an upright piano in front of a large window. Darren's and my first home—a duplex we rented in Carmichael. He'd snagged the piano at an estate sale. It was horribly out of tune. We didn't have the money to get it tuned. Yet I played, ignoring the off notes while I sang along.

Darren sat beside me, the piano bench rickety. It shifted beneath our weight, teetering every once in a while, so we'd have to press our feet down to steady it. My fingers flew over the keys, feeling the music. My protruding belly hit the edge of the keys, Hudson moved inside my stomach as if to the beat.

Kendra waddled into the room, her hair in two pigtails on either side of her head. She wore red overalls, a striped shirt. Her feet were bare, pudgy toes grabbing at the carpet as she stumbled toward us.

"Mama, up," she said, her arms thrusting upward, her little fingers wiggling in the air.

Giggling, I slid my fingers off the keys, scooted my butt back on the bench to make some space, and bent awkwardly to pick her up. After setting her in my lap, I reached around to place my hands on the keys once again. She babbled along with my singing. I felt Hudson's feet kicking my ribs. Darren leaned over, kissing my cheek.

I smiled, contentment filling me.

"No, here. Why don't we try this?" A male voice spoke. One that was out of place. One that shouldn't have been in this room with us. The song changed, notes being played on keys I wasn't touching.

Startled, I whipped my head to the right. It was no longer Darren beside me but Mac. He had a pencil in one hand, the other hand on the piano. He played a few notes and then jotted something down on a chord sheet propped up on the piano. We were no longer in my old duplex. We were at Mac's place. It was dim, nighttime. A lamp glowed in the corner.

He was so intent on scribbling down his idea, it was like he didn't even notice I was here. I loved him like this. Focused. Driven. Similar to me. It was a side of me Darren didn't appreciate. Mac did. We were the same.

I listened to the notes he played, adding a few of my own. His head swiveled in my direction as if just noticing me again.

Listening, he nodded. "I like that." Decisively, he jotted the notes down.

We played the parts together, and I added a line from our lyric sheet.

"Hidden in the shadows / darkness on our skin / where prying eyes can't see." I could feel the heat of his stare on my face, but didn't dare move a muscle. Yet when his hand came to rest on my leg, my name falling from his lips, I turned. Within seconds I was in his lap, our mouths fused.

Every time this happened, I told myself it would be the last. It never was.

Barking. *Bowie? Where are you, boy?*

I struggle to pull myself from the dreamlike memories and into the present. My eyelids flutter, my fingers grasping my comforter. In the distance, I hear the barking again. Bowie must be in the backyard. I try to yell his name, but it's a losing battle. Then the barking outside is joined by a shriek of laughter, sweet and light, and I realize Bowie must be playing ball with Grace. My vision is swimmy, as if everything in my room is in motion, rocking on the waves of the ocean. My skin is hot, my muscles loose like when I've had too much to drink.

I allow the waves to take over, my room vanishing behind my eyelids.

Clapping and cheering all around me. Lights shone brightly in my eyes. I glanced down at the mic in my hand. Squinted to see past the lights. People. Dozens of them, clapping and screaming. I caught movement out of the corner of my eye— the guys putting down the instruments, exiting the stage. Reluctantly, I slid the mic back into the stand. Show endings were always bittersweet for me. I longed to continue—I could have always sung all night—and yet it also felt good to hear the applause, to listen to the whistles and shouts for an encore, to celebrate, party, and eventually, rest.

But tonight was the last night of the tour, so it was even harder to get off the stage.

Tomorrow we'd head home. To reality. To our families.

After a couple of drinks, I returned to the bus. Mac was there waiting for me. The minute I stepped inside, his hands were on my face, on my skin, in my hair. Pressing me up against the wall, he kissed me hard. When his mouth moved down to my neck, his hands leaving my face and traveling down my chest, I drew away.

"What about the guys?" I asked, gulping in air.

"They met up with some girls. We have all night." Scooping me up, he carried me to the bed in the back of the bus and flung me down on it.

"I can't believe this is our last night." I buried my face in his neck.

"It doesn't have to be," he said and looked at me meaningfully before his head dipped lower on my body. It was something he'd been saying for a while now, something I'd fantasized about as well. But that's all it could be—a fantasy. Mac didn't get it. He didn't have a family. All he knew was the fun side of me. The version of me on the road. The me with no strings.

What would happen when we weren't on the road? When I showed up with half a house of belongings and two kids?

What would happen when things were hard? Or worse, boring?

"Mom," Kendra's voice breaks into my recollections, and the bus and Mac disappear.

Wait. I want to reach for him. *Come back.*

I feel a cool hand on my forehead. I'm burning up. An intense fever. Like I'm on fire. The coolness should be a relief. But it's not.

I remember the confusion of seeing her in the mirror behind

me. Our eyes locking. The way hers cut from mine down to the mug. *What did she do to me?*

I can't move. I can hardly breathe.

And whatever she did…why?

That's what I don't understand, and that's what scares me.

She seems so far away. It's dark and gray and warm. I can't make my lips work or my body move. The darkness is back. It's creeping in. I can't fight it. So I let go.

"Have you talked to Darren yet?" The back of Mac's hand grazed my cheek.

I lifted my head from his shoulder, peered up at his face, my fingertips playing along his bare chest. It's the question I'd been dreading. "I'm sorry, Mac, but I can't. Not right now."

His hand stilled. He sat up, causing my face to slip from his shoulder and abruptly fall to the pillow beneath us.

"When, then?"

I licked my lips, pushing myself up off the bed with my palms. His room smelled like sweat and sex. Like Mac.

"I don't know. Things are complicated now."

"Bullshit." Standing up, he raked his fingers through his hair.

"Excuse me?" I reached for my shirt and tugged it over my head.

Mac stood in front of me, unabashedly naked, despite the fact that his bedroom window was open, the blinds not all the way closed.

Hugging myself, I stayed put, drawing my legs in to my chest.

"You told me weeks ago you were gonna talk to him."

"And I was going to," I said, thinking of that night, of getting home to Darren passed out slumped in our bathroom, the kids asleep in their rooms, the remains of some scorched scrambled eggs congealing on the stovetop. Hudson, probably. At fourteen, he was a lackadaisical cook and a worse dishwasher. "But the timing's no good now."

"And I call bullshit."

I recoiled, surprised by his insensitivity. "How can you say that? You know things are bad right now. His drinking is out of control. It's affecting his health."

"But that has nothing to do with us."

"It has everything to do with us," I countered. "My family needs me right now."

"What about me?"

"Huh?"

"I need you."

I smiled. "And you have me."

"No, I don't. I want you, all of you, all the time. I love you. And you love me, too. You don't need to make excuses. If they all needed you so badly, you wouldn't be here."

His frustrated words nearly knock the wind out of me. I know I've been selfish, sneaking in these visits, trying to carve out time for what I love, for what—and who—I'm passionate about. But Hudson was beginning to act out at school. Heather sometimes seemed like she was avoiding our house; instead, he always went to hers. And, put-together as she was, Kendra's grades had slipped for the first time this semester.

Mac was right. I couldn't look away from the truth.

Too bad that truth wasn't what he wanted it to be.

My eyes pop open, a panicked breath escaping. I'm no longer in Mac's bedroom. I'm back in mine. I look around for Kendra or Hudson, but neither are in here. I'd heard Kendra's voice. Hadn't I? My door is closed. I listen but hear no noises. Did they leave?

My head pounds, my mouth dry.

I hope Hudson is getting me help.

As I stare up at the ceiling, praying for help to come, my mind replays all the fragmented dreams I'd been having. Darren. The kids. Mac.

If only I had been braver.

Maybe he'd still be here.

★ ★ ★

Less than a month after I'd broken things off with Mac for the last time, he'd called to ask about a notebook he'd been missing. One with some of the songs we'd worked on together. Later that night, I found it.

The next morning, I called but he didn't answer. So I drove to his house, intending to leave it on the front porch. It was an ordinary day. Blue skies. Bright sun.

I'd stopped at a Starbucks on the way over, and I took a sip of my mocha before stepping out of the car. It would no doubt be warm by afternoon, but that morning it was still cool. I tugged my jacket tighter around my body as I hurried up to Mac's front door, the notebook pressed to my chest. I wore a pair of jeans and knee-high boots, a low-cut black top, my favorite pendant necklace bouncing up and down on my breasts with each step. If he spotted me through the window or wanted to talk, I wanted my outfit to say that I was doing okay, that I was confident I'd made the right choice, even if my heart still felt shredded.

Memories of our relationship flew through my mind, all the familiar feelings flooding back as I bent down to set the notebook on the porch. I hated that this was the way things were ending. When I broke things off, I'd known it was the right thing to do, but I never took into consideration all I'd be giving up. Namely, the band.

Mac had said that it would be too painful to still tour and perform together. The other guys weren't returning my calls. And Suzanne had heard that they were searching for a new lead singer. I'd been shocked at how fast they were moving on.

The original plan was that I'd participate in one last gig, and we'd tell them about my exit together. But then, in the middle of our rehearsal—while we were working on one of the love songs we'd written together—Mac stormed out.

"What's going on?" I trailed after him, finding him out in the parking lot already lighting up a cigarette.

"I can't do this." He stuck the tip of the cigarette in his mouth, inhaled.

As he blew smoke up into the air, I said, "I know it's hard."

"Is it hard for you?" he snapped, flicking ash onto the ground. He bobbed his head toward me. "Look at you. At what you're wearing."

Stunned, I looked down at my tight jeans, low-cut leopard-print top and high-heeled boots. "I wear this all the time." I always liked to rehearse in something similar to what I might wear on stage, especially high heels. I found that it helped me get a feel for movement and space.

"Exactly. You're acting like nothing's changed."

I paused, bit my lip. "I don't know what you want from me, Mac."

"Clearly, you never did," he said. Angrily, he tossed his cigarette on the ground, stomped it with his foot. "Right now, I want you gone."

I recoiled as if slapped. "What?"

"I'll cancel the gig. Tell the guys. Don't worry about it."

"But that's not what we agreed on," I said.

"Shit, Val, I can't stand on a stage and sing love songs with you, okay? Not anymore." He ran a hand through his hair. "You wanna go play house with your little family, then go. Do that."

"Come on, Mac," I pled. "Just one more gig."

But he shook his head with a finality I could feel like a physical attack. "No, you made your choice. I'm done."

I have no idea what he told the guys about me. About us.

When I'd gone inside to retrieve my stuff, I wanted to say something to get ahead of what he would tell them. But I was too shattered to come up with anything. So I mumbled something about not feeling well and left before they could catch me crying.

Looking back, I wish I'd been stronger.

It seemed unfair that I was the one losing everything. The least he could do was hear me out, let me plead my case. It's not like the affair was one-sided. He was to blame as well. Surely, if I could deal with our breakup and be a professional, envision a future where we'd keep singing together, he could man up and deal with it, too.

With each thought, my anger mounted.

Scooping the notebook up, I stood and rapped on the front door a few times. Then I drew my hand back. Glanced around. Listened for the familiar sounds of Mac inside, stomping, singing, strumming. His house was small. Less than a thousand square feet. And usually, he had a couple of windows open. When a minute of silence passed, I knocked again.

His car sat idly in the driveway, so I knew he was home.

"Mac!" I called out. "It's me. I brought your notebook."

Still nothing.

"C'mon, Mac." The front curtain was still drawn. Annoyed, I made my way over to the side window. "We need to talk." I was getting more upset with each passing second.

But it was quiet. No movement or sound at all. I peeked in, since the window was open a hair, the blinds kinked on one side. His covers lay in a ball at the foot of the bed, his sheets wrinkled. A few clothes hung over a chair. Maybe he was in the shower or something. I listened for the sound of water running but didn't hear it.

"Mac!" I called again. "C'mon, I know you're in there."

Still, no response.

I returned to the front door, pounded on it again. At that point I was so irritated I almost tore his notebook into pieces and stormed off in a huff. But then I'd lose any chance of ever getting back into the band.

Mac had been our unofficial leader from the beginning. Not

because we'd appointed him or because he was the most talented musically. It was because the band had initially been his idea. He was the one who pulled it all together. The guys would never even consider letting me back in if Mac didn't sanction it.

But even with our history, I figured I might be able to talk him into letting me back in. Flight of Hearts was Mac's life, and together we were good. We'd come so far. I couldn't imagine him letting all that go.

I banged on his door a few more times. Harder than I probably should have, but I was mad. I knew what he was doing, and why he was doing it. And I wasn't amused.

"I get it." I finally dropped my arm and shouted through the closed door. "You're trying to punish me, and maybe I deserve it. But the guys don't. The band doesn't." Sighing, I stooped down, thinking I should just leave the notebook. Maybe that's why he wasn't answering. He wanted the notebook. Not me.

It's probably what I should've done. But I couldn't leave like that. I had to talk to him, force him to see reason. "Please. I just need a few minutes."

When minutes passed in silence, I let out a frustrated groan and took a step back. Maybe he wasn't home, after all. Maybe he went somewhere in someone else's car. One of the guys? Or…a girl?

My stomach soured at the idea, even though I knew I had no right to feel this way. I paced the length of the porch trying to shake off the thought, and that's when I noticed the slit in the curtain at the far right of the big window, the one overlooking his family room. I cupped my hand and peeked in.

It was a mess inside. Not that I was surprised. Mac's ability to focus singularly on the things he was passionate about left no room for things like tidying his house, and I'd watched him go through enough breakups before our own to know he tended to let things go when he was upset. There were beer cans and an open pizza box on the coffee table. On one of the end tables was an empty plate, smears over the white ceramic that resembled ketchup.

But glancing below the table, I saw it. The edge of Mac's bare foot. The rest of him was obscured by the table, but a funny feeling settled in my gut. Something wasn't right.

I knew the slider in the back didn't lock. I'd let myself in that way once when we were together—so he came home to find me naked in his shower, steam swirling. Dropping the notebook, I sprinted around the back of the house. Once inside, I hurried to the family room. If Mac was fine, passed out drunk or something, he'd be pissed that I had barged in. But it was a chance I was willing to take. Honestly, I was hoping for it.

"Mac," I breathed out, falling to my knees.

He lay on his back, staring up at the ceiling, eyes open wide. Too wide. Unblinking. I couldn't look at them. His right elbow was bent in an unnatural way. Near his hand was a pill container, an empty bottle of vodka. Blood pooled near his temple. It was smeared on the corner of the coffee table above him too as if he'd hit it on the way down.

With shaky fingers I felt his wrist for a pulse but found none. His skin was cold to the touch.

I couldn't bring myself to call the police at first. He was gone. There was no bringing him back. And these would be the last moments I had with him. Even though he couldn't hear me, I said all the things I wished I'd said during our last conversation. I told him he was the love of my life. I cried. I held his hand. I said I was sorry.

And then I called 911.

25

Darren hollered my name from downstairs, his booming voice echoing across the vaulted ceilings. Irritation rose inside of me. I was exhausted, having spent all day out with Mac trying to book gigs around town. We'd gotten more noes than yeses, and I was feeling slightly defeated. Sitting on the edge of my bed, I rubbed my tired feet. The stilettos I'd been wearing were discarded on the floor right below my toes. I made a mental note to wear flats next time, even though deep down I knew I wouldn't.

"Those heels make your legs look even sexier than usual," Mac said to me this afternoon while he trailed behind me into a club.

I smiled briefly at the memory and then shouted to Darren. "What?"

"Come down here."

I groaned. God, couldn't he read my mood? What I wanted

was a bath and some peace and quiet, not to be summoned downstairs for reasons unknown.

"In a minute," I hollered back. Rolling my neck, I blew out a breath. Then I reluctantly stood and shuffled out of my room on my sore, aching feet. I was desperate to change out of my skirt, but it looked like that would have to wait.

As I headed down the stairs I faintly heard soft jazz music playing. Rounding the corner, I found my family in the dining room. Candles glowed in the center of the table, four plates were set and in the middle were cartons from my favorite Thai restaurant. The scent of curry and coconut wafted under my nose.

Darren smiled. "We knew you'd had a long day, so…" He swept his arms out toward the table.

The kids stood on either side, grinning.

I instantly felt bad for my irritation upstairs. Stepping forward, I walked into Darren's waiting arms. "Thanks," I murmured into his shoulder.

"It was actually Hudson's idea," he said.

Of course. My sweet boy.

I turned to my son. Bending down, I wrapped Hudson in my arms. He melted into me, his sticky fingers on my neck.

When I stood, I glanced around. "This was so nice, you guys."

"I helped, too," Kendra interjected.

No doubt she did it reluctantly. Cresting on her preteen years, she'd been pretty moody and distant as of late.

"Thanks, honey." I touched her shoulder gently, unsure of what kind of affection she wanted. She'd never been an affectionate girl, even less so the last few months.

As Darren pulled out my chair and helped me into it, my smile deepened. But I felt a fresh wave of shame—over my affair with Mac, which meant not just infidelity, but also time stolen from my family. Dishing up my food, I glanced around the table and made a vow to myself that I'd break things off with Mac. That I'd be a better wife and mom.

"What is going on?" The desperate, hushed words coming from outside my bedroom door pull me from sleep. I'd been dreaming of when the kids were younger, and when Darren was still here.

I hadn't made good on that vow.

I try to sit up, but my body doesn't cooperate. My head feels like it weighs a hundred pounds, and my eyelids are so heavy I struggle to keep them open. The room is fuzzy like I'm looking at it through a glass of water.

"Mom is having an episode," comes the response. "I'm handling it. Don't worry."

Even muffled, I recognize the voices.

Kendra.

Hudson.

"What does that mean? And why is she locked in?"

"It's for her own good. It's happened before. You shouldn't worry too much."

"I *am* worried about it. She's not herself, Kendra," Hudson says. "What did you do to her?"

I listen intently, grateful that Hudson doesn't seem to be buying any of this. If he sees the truth, then surely he'll get me out of here.

I picture the odd expression on Kendra's face when she appeared in the mirror. I'd been clinging to the dresser, trying to stay upright. At first I was relieved, thinking she could help, but that relief only lasted a second. She was staring at me with a hatred I'd never seen before. Sure, she'd been mad at me lots of times, but this felt different. It was like she was relishing in my discomfort. Like she wanted to watch me squirm.

It chilled me to my very bones.

And now I had no idea what she was capable of.

"You don't know what you're talking about, Hudson," Kendra says in her usual condescending tone. "I know Mom's not herself right now, but this is part of the disease."

No, she's lying.

"She's been fine with me," Hudson says firmly, to my relief.

"Yeah, for the last month, maybe. But this has been going on for a while. You don't know because you weren't around. You haven't seen the progression of the disease. Sometimes she seems lucid and healthy. And perhaps she'll be like that for days or even weeks, but then she'll have an episode, like the one she had today. It's the reason I tried to get her to stay with me." Kendra's tone softens a bit. "I know you're worried, and this is all new to you, but you don't need to be. I'm here, and I know how to care for her. Don't you have work to get to? It will be all right. Go. I've got this handled."

I shudder at what that might mean.

"I'm not leaving Mom."

"That's a first," Kendra says bitterly.

"How long are you going to throw my past in my face?" Hudson asks, and it is a valid question. One I've often thought of over the years in regards to my own relationship with Kendra. "I'm here now, aren't I?"

"I'm *talking* about now. Even since you've been back, you're not really back, are you? Mom says you've been out pretty much every night."

Inwardly, I cringe. I never should have told her that. It was an offhanded comment I made the last time she picked Mason up. She'd asked how it was having Hudson around all the time, and her tone was biting, as if she thought that the only thing he did was lie around being waited on hand and foot.

"He's actually not around much," I'd responded, thinking I was defending him. "He's either working or out with friends."

AMBER GARZA

How was I to know she'd use it against him this way?

"I'm actually surprised you're here now," she continued. "I assumed you'd be gone tonight."

"Is that what you were banking on when you drugged her?" Hudson asks.

"Oh, my god. You've always been so dramatic. I've hardly drugged her."

"She's clearly on something."

"She was agitated, Hudson. When I found her, she was huddled and wet in the shower, talking nonsense to Grace, and she got combative when I tried to get her into bed. So yes, I had to sedate her, but it was for her own protection."

I want to scream. There is movement, a shuffling of sorts. Then Kendra speaks again. "Look, Hudson, I know this is hard. But trust me. I'm a nurse. I know what I'm doing. It's best if you just leave everything up to me."

For a few seconds it's silent. Then I hear footsteps—two sets—on the stairs.

No, please don't leave me.

The footsteps get quieter and quieter until they disappear altogether.

I don't know why she swallowed the fly...
I guess she'll die...

Heather was afraid of me.

At least, that's how she was acting lately. For the past week, she'd been avoiding me. I worried that maybe it wasn't fear at all. Maybe she'd found out that I cheated on her. But who would've told her? When I finally pressed her about it, she admitted she was scared of Kendra, not me.

I was relieved she hadn't found out I cheated. It was just a stupid kiss, anyway. A mistake.

But I was also pissed at my sister. She was always messing up everything for me.

Most people believed that out of the two of us, my sister was the responsible one. The smart one. The good one. At school, she was quiet, studious. At home, she went over and above with chores, and constantly dredged up my mistakes in front of our parents. As if to remind them of who was the better child.

But I knew who she really was.

I'd seen a side of her no one else had.

Until now.

The last time Heather had ever come over to our house, we were in the kitchen minding our own business and eating a snack when my sister waltzed in, a devious smile on her face.

It was clear to me that she had an agenda. That it wasn't a casual trip to the kitchen to grab a water. She had that funny sparkle in her eyes. The one she had the day she poured scalding water on my hand or threw that vase at my head.

She was fully in the kitchen now, standing almost directly next to where we sat on the bar stools against the counter. It was too late to escape, so instead I ignored her, chomping down on a tortilla chip.

"Whatcha guys doin'?" she asked in a weird singsong way that was too friendly to be real.

"Eating chips and dip," Heather said, pushing the bag in my sister's direction. "Want some?" I knew Kendra made her uncomfortable. She'd told me for years times that she thought my sister didn't like her. But still, she always tried so hard. She was one of those people that wanted to be liked by everyone.

Often to her own detriment.

Kendra wrinkled up her nose and shook her head as if Heather had offered her a bag of cow shit. It annoyed me, and I wished we'd left the kitchen when we had the chance. Mom didn't like when we hung out in my room, but she wasn't home right now.

"No, thanks. I'm watching my girlish figure," my sister said in a baby-like voice, running her hands down her sides.

I cringed.

What the hell was she up to?

She grabbed an apple out of the glass bowl on the counter. Palming it, she tossed it up and then caught it. Then she grabbed a knife from the knife block.

"Wanna see a cool trick?" she asked, setting the apple on the counter.

"Sure," Heather said at the same time I said, "Not really." She ignored me.

"Spread your fingers out like this," she said to Heather,

pressing her palm into the counter and stretching her fingers out so her hand looked webbed.

My stomach knotted, knowing what she planned to do.

"No. She doesn't want to do this," I said, but it was too late.

Heather was spreading out her fingers while saying, "It's fine."

But I knew it wouldn't be.

My sister brought the knife down, slamming the tip into the counter between my girlfriend's index and middle finger. Then she did it again between her ring and pinky finger. I held my breath as she started to speed up, striking between her fingers faster and faster.

"Ouch!" Heather suddenly cried, and my sister drew the knife back.

Blood dribbled from Heather's thumb.

"Goddammit," I snapped, reaching for a rag.

Heather's eyes were wide as she held her hand tight to her body. I wrapped the rag around it, pressing it to the cut. My sister watched on as if fascinated.

"You're crazy, you know that?" I said to her.

"No, I'm not." She stuck out her lower lip in a pout like a petulant child.

"Then what the hell do you call this?" I asked.

Thankfully, the cut wasn't too bad. I put a Band-Aid on it, and Heather was as good as new. How was I to know a week later she'd suffer a fate that would leave her too broken to ever be put back together again?

26

I'm woken by the sound of metal raking against metal.

My pulse jumpstarts. *The hook and latch.*

A second later, the door pops open, Hudson bursting through it. His eyes are wild, repeatedly darting over his shoulder as he sprints to my bedside. Leaning down, he grabs my hand, his fingers like ice.

"Mom," he says urgently, shaking my hand.

For the first time in what I'm assuming has been hours, I'm able to lift my arm slightly. I squeeze his hand, grateful my muscles are responding now. Working my jaw, my lips feel more normal. They tingle like a limb after it's been asleep, tiny pinpricks on the skin.

"Hudson," the word finally comes, albeit scratchy and hoarse, but at least it's audible. "Kendra's lying. There's… nothing…wrong with me…no Alzheimer's."

"I know," he says, lowering slowly to his knees beside the bed while still gripping my hand. Leaning in closer, he glances fleetingly at the door and then whispers, "I think she poisoned you. I called the police. They're on their way. We just have to hang tight for a few minutes."

"What's going on?" Kendra storms into the room, immediately fixing Hudson with a glare.

"Mom isn't sick." Hudson releases his grip on my hand and stands up, creating a barricade between me and Kendra. I'm grateful for his protection.

"You don't know what you're talking about," she says.

"I do. I saw the test results on Mom's computer."

"You can barely read, Hudson," she says acidly, "let alone read complex medical diagnoses. Why don't you leave that to me?" Smiling, Kendra moves toward the side of the bed Hudson isn't guarding.

I scoot back into the pillows, closer to Hudson.

"It's true, Kendra." I swallow hard in an attempt to lubricate my itchy, dry throat. "And you know it. I told you." My voice is getting incrementally stronger, but my body still feels limp, my bones like jelly. I'm certain I couldn't walk right now. Hell, I probably couldn't even get out of this bed.

"I know you did," she says gently, wearing a condescending smile. "I looked over your test results, too. You emailed them to me, remember?" I remember no such thing, but I want to believe that it's not my brain missing the memory— it's a lie she's trying to spin. "The ones he ran on you were blanket tests. There are many other markers for dementia that Dr. Steiner didn't check for."

Any other day I'd believe her.

But that was before she poisoned me.

"Look at you, Mom. You're not healthy," Kendra continues, her hand covering mine. Hers is cold and clammy.

"You did this to me," I say, attempting to pull my hand back. But she holds it in place, her grip hurting me, her eyes narrowing. "The only thing I've done is help you. You're actually lucky I showed up when I did today. You were delusional and could barely stand up straight. I got you into bed."

"It was…the tea." I painfully rotate toward my dresser where I'd left my teacup, but it's not there.

Kendra follows my gaze. "What tea?"

"The tea I drank earlier." A headache pricks between my eyes, my mind fuzzy.

"I didn't see any teacups, Mom," Kendra insists.

"But… I'm sure I had some…" I blink. "I mean, I think I had some…" I did, didn't I? I feel a flash of panic, a moment of doubt that maybe Kendra's right about all of this—but then I remember the face in the mirror moments before the world went dark.

"Cut the shit, Kendra," Hudson says. "We all know you did something to her."

"You don't know anything." Her face hardens. "He's just trying to pit you against me, Mom."

"Look at her, Kendra." Hudson angrily throws his arm out to point at me. "I've never seen her like this before."

She huffs. "I gave her a sedative, that's all."

I reach a shaky hand up to touch my hair. It's damp in the back. The shower. Yes, I took a shower. I clearly remember drinking tea before getting in the shower.

I look over at the deflated pink ball in the corner. Kendra knew about my visions. The ones involving Grace. I'd confessed to her about hearing tapping noises over the years, and that I'd always pictured Grace bouncing a ball. Had she planted it?

Theo had said Mason wasn't sleeping well. He told me Kendra had been driving him around in the middle of the night. They live less than a ten-minute drive away. She could have easily stopped here, little Mason snoozing in the back. But would she do that?

And if so, why?

It can't be a coincidence that she drugged me today—the day I called about the test results. What is the reason for wanting me to think I have Alzheimer's? It doesn't make any sense. She's been trying to help me, encouraging me to see the doctor, bringing me vitamins and probiotics.

Oh, my god. The vitamins.

"You've been drugging me all along," I say aloud.

Kendra's head snaps toward Hudson, her eyes bugging out. "See, I told you. Delusional."

But I wasn't. She'd been bringing me vitamins for the better part of a year, ever since she'd taken a class on nutrition. Once in a while, she changed the brand—"Oh, these were on sale this week"—and a month or two ago, she'd arrived with new ones: "My professor says these are the best. Prescription-strength." I remember a few days later thinking what perfect timing—I was really starting to forget things, wasn't I?

Then I remember how right after Hudson moved in there had been a few days where I'd forgotten to take the vitamins. Those days I felt lucid, more normal. Well, except for that night at the Tavern, but I'd had too many sangrias then.

"This whole time it's been you," I wheeze.

Kendra offers me a condescending smile and pats me as if I'm a five-year-old. "Yes, Mom, this whole time it's been me taking care of you," she says, twisting my words. Before I can respond, though, her eyes widen. She reaches for the gold watch that sits on my nightstand.

"What's Theo's watch doing in here?"

27

"It's Theo's?" I ask. "You're sure?"

Kendra turns it over. "Yes. That's the inscription I got. I bought it for him on our first anniversary."

"What does the inscription mean?" I have to know.

"When we met, Theo used to joke that he'd hit the jackpot when he met me. He wrote it into his vows, even—guess that's something else you don't remember?"

Jackpot. Not angels or numerology.

Luck. Lucky number sevens.

She tosses it back down on the nightstand so hard it almost clatters off the surface. "You didn't answer my question. What are you doing with it?"

"I found it at Molly's," I say.

Kendra's face blanches. Hudson's eyebrows jump up.

"What the hell were you doing in her house?" Kendra says.

"I think the more important question is, why did I find Theo's watch there?" I ask.

Kendra's expression hardens, her eyes mere slits on her face, her lips a tight line. It's the same expression she wore when Theo introduced us to Molly in the front yard. "Probably because he was fucking her," she says bitterly.

Theo.

And Molly.

I should've known—surely one former adulterer could spot another. But it hadn't even crossed my mind. I chalked that look up to run-of-the-mill jealousy. Kendra had been so insecure lately. I thought it was wrapped up in all of that postpartum angst. I never once believed that Theo had given her a reason to feel that way.

"Now I get it." Hudson shakes his head. "Theo. That was her type. Must be why she shot me down, then."

"Shot you down? When?" I ask.

"That night at Midtown Saloon. I asked her out. She said she wasn't interested. Now I know why." His eyes meet Kendra's. "She already had a man. Kendra's." He waggles his eyebrows, clearly enjoying this.

"Fuck you, Hudson," Kendra says.

"Maybe I was wrong about Theo's arms being too scrawny to strangle anyone. Maybe he did kill Molly," Hudson says.

Oh, god, could that be true? My head slowly rolls over toward Kendra. I'm still finding it hard to get my body to obey my brain.

She narrows her eyes. "No," she says flatly. "Theo wouldn't hurt her. He was planning to leave Mason and me for that whore." Her tone is laced with disgust. "He was gonna choose a slob who eats junk food, drinks like a fish, wears trashy lingerie and fucks married men over me. Can you believe that?" She looks at me. "Well, I guess *you* can believe it."

She knew. She knows.

I was always afraid she might. That both of them would

learn about the affair. The rumor mill was going at warp speed at the time. Fans were speculating about the breakup and Mac's death—what could have caused it—and I suspected that eventually Kendra and Hudson would hear about it online, if not from some cruel classmate. But neither of them had ever mentioned it, so I'd allowed myself to believe that they were the only two people that didn't know.

"You know, I caught you once," Kendra says, her attention fixed on me. "It was before a show. One that Dad took us to, actually." I lick my dry lips, wishing I could hide under the covers. "I wanted to see you before you went out, wish you luck. Usually, Dad didn't let me, but this time he did. I think because we were so close to the back. I didn't have to walk far to get to you." She pauses, and even Hudson appears uncomfortable, his lips pursed, his eyes squinty. "I was thirteen, but I remember feeling so grown-up walking through the bar alone, heading back to the dressing rooms reserved for the band. When I got to yours, I saw the sign with your name and I felt so proud—my mom, the rock star."

Oh, god.

"I didn't want to bother you," she continues. "I opened the door a little just to poke my head in and say hi. I didn't want to barge in. But with the door open just a crack…that's when I saw you and Mac all over each other."

My cheeks burn. Hudson's frown has deepened.

"I'm so sorry, Kendra." It's the only thing I can think to say.

"Are you really sorry, Mom?" She's pacing now, the way she does when agitated.

Hudson's watching her as if planning a move. I catch his eye and shake my head. Kendra's obviously hurting. The only way of surviving this is to placate her.

"Yes," I say honestly.

"Liar." She laughs bitterly. "You never cared about Dad."

"That's not true," I say.

"It is," she says firmly.

"C'mon, Kendra," Hudson starts, but Kendra cuts him off.

"He fucking worshipped her, and she neglected him. Treated him like shit." Her words are loud, venomous. I recoil. "She's the reason he's gone. He drank himself to death because he was depressed and lonely."

She's wrong, of course. Her dad didn't start drinking because of my affair with Mac. He didn't know about it until after Mac died. He suspected it earlier than that, but I'd never admitted it. In my grief, the truth had become obvious to Darren. And then when the band shunned me and everyone found out, his suspicions were confirmed.

But his drinking problems had started years before that.

A tear falls from Kendra's eye, and she angrily brushes it off. "I tried to be enough for him, but I wasn't. It was her he wanted." She says *her* like it's a dirty word.

I'm struck with the memory of Kendra as a child, the way she'd follow her dad around.

"My little shadow," he'd tease in a singsong way, touching the tip of her nose with his finger. She'd giggle, wriggling her nose and nestling into him.

When she got older, it was him she went to with her problems. Him she'd call when she was in trouble. It may have been part of the reason it meant so much when Hudson reached out to me. At least one child wanted me, so I couldn't have been a total failure, right?

"I've always hated you for the way you treated him," she says quietly, her shoulders dipping as if she's just released the weight of a lifetime of loathing.

"That's why you did this to me? Just because of your dad?" I ask. Drugging me slowly, making me question my sanity—

it's such an elaborate scheme, and so many years after Darren's death.

She snorts. "You still don't get it. You never have."

"I'm trying," I say desperately.

Her smile transforms to more of a grimace. "You always choose him. The only person in this family you ever cared about was Hudson. You even turned to him when your memory started to go. Not me, the nurse, the one with actual training. The responsible one. The one who could take care of you. No, you still wanted Hudson."

Is that why she did this? So I would choose her? Need her? Was my reliance on her the end goal, or the means to something else?

She sniffs, shakes her head. "God, it doesn't even matter what he does. Even after Heather's death, you sided with him. And you're still doing it today."

"I can't listen to this anymore." Hudson groans. "I've been covering for you our entire lives, but I'm done with this shit. Where are the damn cops?" His hand grazes my shoulder. He shoots daggers at his sister with his eyes.

Kendra's brows furrow. "The cops? I haven't done anything wrong."

"Call me crazy, but I think murdering two women and poisoning your own mom constitutes doing something wrong."

A flicker of something—fear, I think—passes over her face. "I didn't kill anyone."

"You're not fooling us, Kendra, so you can ditch the act," Hudson says.

She lifts her head, her lips twitching. "You're the one who has motive to kill Leslie, not me."

I think about what Tessa said. How the police had found out that Molly had been seeing someone. Had they found out about Theo and Molly? Had they started to suspect Kendra? Had Leslie?

Had Kendra known?

The earring. The one I found on Leslie's carpet.

Darren had bought Kendra and me identical pairs that Christmas. While they weren't my style, they *were* Kendra's. Plus, they were from her dad, so she wore them all the time. They were one of her go-to pairs before Mason was born and she'd stopped wearing earrings to protect her ears from reaching, grabbing baby hands. But she'd been wearing them when she came over for dinner that first week Hudson had been here.

It wasn't my earring at Leslie's.

It was Kendra's.

Kendra had been sneaking around my house for months. What would have stopped her from taking Leslie's key out of my junk drawer?

And once she was inside her home, did she slip something into Leslie's tea the same way she had mine?

"Leslie had found out about Theo's affair," I say hoarsely. That had to have been the name she refused to tell Tessa and Beth.

"That woman knew every fucking thing about this neighborhood," Kendra says. "She was the worst."

"And the police knew, too. They'd found fingerprints. Were they Theo's? Or yours?" I speak slowly, piecing it together.

"God, Mom, shut up!" Kendra shouts, holding her head in her hands. "You think you're so damn smart. Going behind my back and calling Dr. Steiner. Finding out about Theo's affair. But you don't know everything, okay? So just stop."

"That's why you did this," Hudson says. "Once Mom had the test results from Dr. Steiner, it was only a matter of time before she found out you'd been poisoning her. You tried to silence her the same way you silenced Leslie."

"I didn't want to do any of it," she snaps. "It's your fault. You're the one who came here and stirred everything up. I had everything under control. This is your doing!"

She darts for the door, and Hudson leaps after her, tries to stop her. They crash to the floor together in the hall just outside, and for a moment, she's on top of him, her hands clawing at his throat—a reversal of years ago. But Hudson bucks, catches hold of her arms and rolls, grappling with her as she shrieks, and the shrieks give way to sobs. I realize that I am crying, too.

Just then sirens ring out, coming closer and closer.

28

I was questioned by police the night of Heather's death.

I'd done exactly as I promised. Hid a few miles away in my car and waited for Hudson to call me after the police arrived. When I returned, I found Hudson talking to a police officer. It was cold. Dark. His teeth were chattering, his face pale.

In my panic, I'd forgotten about Kendra being there. It wasn't until I'd stood by Hudson's side, offering him support with my presence, that I noticed her across the field, talking with a different police officer. Her gaze found mine, and she raised her brows. Looking back, she might have been silently asking for my help, but I didn't interpret it that way at the time. Normally, Kendra was in control. She'd rarely needed my assistance. Why would that night be any different?

Besides, Hudson was the one who needed me. It was his girlfriend who had died. It was clear from the moment I arrived that the police were suspicious of him. He looked scared and tired, like the weight of the world was on his shoulders.

I was worried that all of these things would be interpreted by the police as guilty. I knew exactly what that was like.

Mac's death had been a mere eight months earlier. It's the reason I instructed Hudson to make sure he wasn't the one who found Heather. Finding Mac had been my undoing.

News of our affair broke, no doubt leaked by my former bandmates. Everyone blamed me for his suicide—fans of Flight of Hearts, as well as Mac's friends and family. I had strung him along and crushed his heart. And what was I doing at his house, wearing that low-cut top? Trying to weasel my way back into his band, careless about his pain, as he died in the name of love on the other side of the door.

It's why I pulled back from performing. Nobody wanted to hear me sing, to hear my side. They'd already written it for me.

Ironic that I'd broken things off with Mac in hopes of healing my marriage, but it ended up destroying it. Sure, Darren and I stayed together, but not out of love. At first it was for the kids. Then it was because of Darren's illness. But we were never the same. We never came back from the damage I'd done.

That's why the night of Heather's death, I lied for my son. I didn't want him enduring what I had in the months after Mac's death. The horror of being publicly declared a suspect. The endless interrogations. The accusatory whispers and stares around town.

I told the police our fabricated story. That he'd called me after one of Heather's friends said they hadn't seen her in over an hour, and the last place she'd been seen was near the edge of the cliff. He'd told me he was with buddies when he heard a scream after one of her friends had flashed a light down the cliff, spotting her body. He hadn't seen Heather for hours, and never imagined the scream had to do with her. Not until the news spread through the party.

As far as I knew, Hudson and Heather had been getting along great. No problems. They'd been very much in love.

The police had believed our story. I'd thought it was all going to be over after that night.

I had no idea that Hudson would be tried and convicted in the court of public opinion, just as I had been, but with my best friend, Leslie, as the judge and jury. I didn't know where she could have gotten the idea that he might have done something wrong—how she could have even known to suspect him. But Heather was Leslie's only child. She and James had never had a great marriage. So, really, Heather had been the most important thing in her life. I knew Leslie would be devastated. But I never thought she'd blame Hudson.

I never thought she'd end up hating us the way she did.

These are the thoughts going through my head as I sit on the edge of a hospital bed, answering the questions lobbed at me from a potbellied policeman with a bushy mustache, Officer Angelo.

I had to have my stomach pumped when I arrived. But I'm feeling moderately better now.

"Ma'am?" he says, grabbing my attention.

I blink. How long have I been silent? "Yes?"

"You were saying how you had made some tea and then went outside. Is that when you believe the sedative might have been deposited into the tea?"

It would be so easy to come to Kendra's defense. To diffuse the situation. I could make this all go away with one simple lie.

Actually, I'd been having trouble sleeping, so I took the sedative. But I'd forgotten I'd already taken some earlier. I've been so forgetful lately.

I could do for Kendra what I'd done all those years ago for Hudson.

"You always choose him."

Was she right? Do I always choose Hudson over her? I never thought so. They've always been so different. Kendra so put-together. So independent. At least, that's what I'd been led to believe.

Maybe this is my chance to prove her wrong. To be the kind of mother she wants me to be. I picture the look of pure hatred on her face when she talked about how much I'd hurt Darren. She was justified in feeling that way. I had hurt her dad. Is this my penance?

My chance to find redemption?

"Mom?" Hudson comes to my bedside, rests a hand on my arm, effectively yanking me back to reality. "She almost killed you. You need to tell him what happened."

I nod, remembering how my limbs felt like jelly, how I couldn't speak or move. My belly quivers at the recollection of the hook and latch locking into place.

I've clearly done my daughter a disservice. For years, she'd been making digs at me for my absent parenting, for putting my career first. I'd always gotten defensive, worrying more about protecting myself rather than taking responsibility. It's time to put Kendra's needs above my own. Do the right thing. Get her the help she needs. Keep her in a place where she can't hurt anyone else.

What happened with Hudson doesn't compare. Giving testimony now isn't choosing one child over another. It's choosing between right and wrong. Accident and intentionality.

Nodding at Hudson, I turn to Officer Angelo and tell him the entire story.

29

When we return to the house, it's the middle of the night, or technically early morning. I don't know that I've ever felt so tired in my life, although I'm not sure it has anything to do with the time. I'm mentally exhausted. Emotionally spent.

"I still can't believe Kendra would do this. It seems so out of character. Do I really just not know her at all?" I ask as Hudson helps me into bed, pulling the covers up to my chest the way I did for him when he was a child. The tables have officially turned.

Hudson presses his lips together, his face crinkling into a look of pity.

"Oh, god." I groan. "You knew she was capable of this?"

"I've seen this side of her before," he says sadly. But there's something besides sadness in his eyes. Fear, maybe. I've seen it on his face before. But when?

My pulse quickens.

The album's release party.

He was so scared to be left alone with Kendra.

Chills overtake me. I'm terrified of the answer, but I have to ask. "The night of my release party—tell me about the break-in."

His entire face droops, all of his features seeming to sink like a rock after being thrown into a creek.

"I'm not sure there was one."

Flames lick up my spine.

"I mean, I can't be sure. Kendra rushed into my room, told me someone was in the house. We closed my door, hid behind it. I thought I heard sounds, creaks, someone murmuring—but it could have been my heart racing. Eventually Kendra took one of my bats and said she would check things out, call the police. I begged her not to go, not to leave me. She locked me in my closet—" he shudders "—and told me I'd be safe there. The next thing I know, I hear crashing. Men's voices, muffled. I heard Kendra scream, which was terrible, but the silence that followed was worse. There were big, heavy foot-steps right up to the closet door. I thought they'd found me." Hudson swallows hard. "When she let me out right before the police came, she said she'd gotten away and hid in the basement. But I found a pair of Dad's shoes in her room, like she'd been clomping around in them. Years later, I watched this heist movie with Browning, and I swear the dialogue was just like what I'd heard from downstairs. It sucked me right back to that night—I nearly had a panic attack. And when I thought about it…the only noises I'd really heard were when she was out of the room. But things like that always happened when I was left alone with her."

I cock my head to the side, confused. It was the only time I'd ever been aware of something bad happening. "What do you mean?"

"She would just always play these sick games. She used to

steal things from me, school assignments I'd been working on, lunch money you'd given me. Tore pages from my library books. I could never catch her—but I did see her spitting in my drink sometimes. I always volunteered to set the table so she wouldn't have the opportunity. One night when we needed to cook dinner..." He glances at me, aware that he's calling Darren out for being too drunk to do it, and me for not being there to help. I nod, dread filling my gut. He needs to say it. "Well, I put the colander in the sink like she asked, and she poured the pasta water right onto my hand." I remember that burn, the way he whimpered at the pain in his sleep. Darren had said it was a clumsy accident and left it at that. He'd had no idea, had he? "And it was her who tore all the heads off her dolls. But she blamed it on me, and you were so angry... I couldn't sleep, knowing you were mad at me. That's why I tried to tape the heads back on."

Hudson was quiet a moment, staring at the lines in his palms. "The break-in wasn't the first time she'd locked me in the closet. She used to lock me in there for hours and hours when she babysat me. I'd scream and claw at the door, but it didn't matter. She'd leave me there, sometimes the whole time you and Dad were gone."

I shiver, thinking about the scratch marks. Those were Hudson's? I feel sick. Reaching out, I touch his hand. Maybe if I'd been home and present more, I would've noticed. Surely his hands were bruised or bloody. Then again, his hands often were. He played rough. Most likely, if I did notice, I chalked it up to him being a playful child. I'd never have guessed the truth. Who would? "I wish you'd have told me back then."

"I couldn't." He shakes his head firmly. "It was when I'd threaten to tell on her that she'd lock me in. She promised that things would be worse for me if I did tell." His gaze meets mine. "I believed her."

I don't blame him. I stare out my bedroom door and see a hint of metal, the hook and latch hanging from the door frame.

"I did tell Dad once. Not everything, just that Kendra picked on me. He didn't take me very seriously. Just told me that sometimes older siblings did that, and I should just try to get along with my sister. He must have said something to her, though, because a week later, Chompers was dead."

Oh, god.

Chompers.

Once again, I'd had it wrong. All my memories were backwards. The hamster. The headless dolls. Even him strangling Kendra looked different in light of this new information. I'd want to strangle someone, too, if they'd tortured and bullied me all those years.

I think about the nights recently when I'd found him curled up on the couch. Had he been afraid of being in his room? Maybe the memories were too much for him.

"I'm so sorry that your dad didn't take you seriously," I say, suddenly furious with Darren, even though I have no right to be. I might have reacted the same way. Lord knows that Darren was more attentive than I was.

Silently, he nods.

"I know he meant well, though. He probably just didn't understand the scope of it," I say.

"No one did," he says. "Sometimes even I underestimated her." Swallowing hard, he lowers his gaze to the floor. His eyes are sad. "If I hadn't, then Heather would still be alive."

"What?" I sit up straighter, my heart pounding in my chest.

He sighs, picking at a tear in his jeans. "Heather had been over at our house one afternoon. We were doing homework and shit, and when she left, there was this note folded up neatly on my bed, right under where her backpack had been. Curiosity got the better of me, and I read it. It was a note between Heather and some guy, and it was, like, really dirty. A lot dirtier than she ever got with me. And I was pissed."

He blows out a breath, stares at his hands. "I should've talked to her about it, but instead I decided to get even. This chick at school, Bri, had always been into me, so I went for it." He pauses a moment before continuing. "But then one day, I think it was like a week or so before the Halloween party, I was in Kendra's room looking for my favorite A's hat. She used to take it from me and hide it just to fuck with me, I guess. Anyway, I didn't find it that day. But I did find the same note that Heather had left in my room." He squints. "Only not exactly the same note. Like variations of it. As if someone was practicing forging Heather's handwriting. And practicing writing like a guy. That's when I knew that Kendra had planted that note."

I think about the story in Leslie's journal about the morning she found the word *SLUT* written in shaving cream on Heather's car. If Hudson had been at Jared's that night, it could've been Kendra who used Hudson's shaving cream to write on her car. It would be in line with all she'd done to mess with Heather and Hudson's relationship.

"Did you confront her?"

"Yeah. Even took the notes as evidence, but she did what she always does. Got angry with me for going into her room. Then she promised to get revenge."

Humpty Dumpty sat on a wall.
Humpty Dumpty had a great fall…

I made so many mistakes the night Heather died.

The first was not telling her my sister would be at the party.

Truth is, I didn't know until a few hours before we left. And by then, I didn't have the courage to tell Heather. It had been so hard to convince her to go with me. She'd been acting strange. Distant. I knew there was more to it than just her fear of Kendra.

I was starting to think she did know about the kiss with Bri. And I worried she wanted to break up.

I'd had a crush on Heather since we were ten years old. Back then, she saw me as her best friend. The neighbor boy who climbed trees and rode bikes with her. I didn't make my move until sophomore year.

"I like you," I'd said tentatively one night while we watched TV. The lights were out. That's what gave me the courage. Not having to see her face when I said the words.

"'Bout time," she'd said.

"What?" I turned to her then, and the TV cast a bluish hue on her face, giving the illusion she had frostbite.

Giggling, she threw me a wink. It made my insides feel

funny. Fluttery, but in a good way. "I've known this for a while."

My face warmed, my mouth drying out. "You have?"

Nodding, she scooted closer to me, placing a soft hand over mine. "It's okay, I like you, too."

After that, we were always together.

Attached at the hip. Two peas in a pod.

That was the way our parents described us, anyway.

The party was in a field on the outskirts of town. Big, open space, trees and bushes the only thing separating all of our cliques and groups. I'd driven a windy road up a hill and parked in the dirt.

I had hoped we wouldn't even run into Kendra at the party. She had her own friend group, and most of the time I didn't even think she liked me. But the minute we arrived, Kendra smiled and waved, calling out our names as if we were BFFs.

"Your sister's here?" Heather's body moved closer to mine, her fingertips brushing mine.

I latched on. "I didn't know she would be," I lied. Squeezing, I offered a smile. "But she's got her own friends. Just ignore her."

Kendra sat in a circle with her friends, holding a can of beer in her hand. It was weird to me, since I never knew my sister to drink. But she was sitting near a boy I'd never seen before, and I thought maybe she was trying to impress him.

I offered Kendra a perfunctory wave and then hurried in the opposite direction. But not before noticing the scowl that passed over her face at my dismissal.

Heather and I went in search of my friends. We found them huddled around a makeshift bonfire, ash and smoke lingering in the air. Browning hooted and came at me with a fist bump. The next couple of hours were a blur of beers, making out with Heather and then joking with the guys. At one point, Heather went off with her girlfriends. She was out of my sight, but I didn't think much of it.

I was in that warm place after a few beers where my bones were jelly, my head fuzzy, my veins buzzing. Besides, we were at a party with friends. What's the worst that could happen?

30

"Eventually, I realized that I hadn't seen Heather in a while, and I went looking for her." He frowns. "You know where she was found."

I squeeze his hand. Had Kendra been responsible for Heather's death, too? "She was already dead?"

He looks back down to the hands he plays with in his lap. Thick fingers lacing and unlacing. "No, she was still alive. She was standing by a tree near the edge of the cliff, crying. When I asked her what was going on, she said that she'd been looking for a place to pee when Kendra found her, asked her why she wasn't with me. Heather told her I was with my friends, and I guess Kendra said something like, 'Oh, I thought maybe he was off making out with Bri again.'" His hands fist at his sides, his jaw clenching and popping. "Kendra'd put the whole thing in motion, and now she was turning Heather against me. I was so mad, I kinda lost it for a minute."

My chest flutters as I wait for him to explain what he means by that. My fingertips skate over the skin on my neck, lighting on the fabric of my shirt.

Finally, he swallows and continues, "I started to go off about Kendra, but then Heather told me to shut up. Said that I had no right to be mad at Kendra. Can you believe that? I had no right to be mad at Kendra?" Redness spills across his cheeks and down his neck. "She said that at least Kendra had the decency to tell her the truth. I told her that Kendra was only trying to mess with me. And then she was like, 'So it's not true?' I hate to admit this, but I was going to lie about it. But Heather knew me too well. So I nodded. I did tell her the thing about the fake note that Kendra planted, but she was like, 'Why didn't you come to me?' and I didn't have an answer to that. She was so mad then, and she tried to walk away, but I grabbed her arm. Pled with her to talk to me. Only..." He bites his lip, his eyes watering. "She tugged her arm out of my grasp and stepped back. And then she…she lost her balance. She was too close to the edge, and she started to fall. I tried to grab on to her, but it all happened so fast."

His voice wavers, the tears in his eyes falling now. I'm horrified by all of it, just like I was that night. Such an awful, tragic end for a sweet girl with her whole life ahead of her. My heart aches as it has for years. For Heather. For Hudson. For the senselessness of it. "I just wanted to make things right, Mom. I never meant for her to fall. You know how much I loved her. If only she hadn't gotten so mad. If she'd just stayed calm and listened to me, she'd still be here."

"I know." Lifting my hand, I rub his back with my palm.

The sobs are coming hard and fast now. I sit with him, mourn with him and for him.

"I'm sorry," he says suddenly as if embarrassed by the display of emotion. Sniffing, he runs a hand down his face. His skin is red and damp, his eyes sad and watery.

"I'm sorry, too. Sorry for everything you went through," I say. "Sorry that I never helped you with Kendra."

"How could you if you didn't know?"

"A better mother would have known," I say. "The signs were there. I should have picked up on them." I always thought Kendra was responsible. Good. It's what Darren thought, too.

"No." Hudson shakes his head. "She was a master manipulator. Look at what she did to you. And to Molly and Leslie." Exhaling, he stands. "If it weren't for her, Heather would be here today. If only she'd kept her big mouth shut."

I'm thrown for a moment, confused. Is he really blaming Kendra for telling Heather, when he's the one who chose to kiss the other girl in the first place? But then, Kendra's meddling was clearly ill-intentioned. She seems to have spent much of her life causing chaos and enjoying it.

How have I been so blind to it all?

Hudson is right. She's a master manipulator, and she'd had us all fooled.

Kendra was right about one thing, though: I wasn't around like I should have been. I'll never apologize for pursuing my dream. That was something I needed to do. But as much as I loved Mac, my affair with him had hurt my children. I wish I'd done it differently. Put my family first. Then maybe I would have seen what was happening in my own home.

I look at my son, thinking of the horrors he's endured.

"I wish I'd been a better mom," I say to him now, a lump in my throat.

It was similar to what I'd said to Darren, holding his hand in the hospital while he was dying. Tubes were everywhere, machines beeping and humming. His mind was gone, and I doubt he heard anything I said. Still, I had to say it.

"I'm sorry I wasn't a better wife. That I took you for granted. That I didn't put you first."

I'd thought I made amends then, but apparently there were still amends that needed to be made.

Hudson returns to my bed, taking one of my hands in his. "Mom, you are the only woman that's ever been good to me. You're the only woman who will never hurt me."

It's a nice sentiment, and I'm grateful for his kind words. It feels like a mercy I don't deserve.

"I really should let you get some sleep." He bends down, kissing my forehead. "We can talk more tomorrow."

When he closes the door, I flinch, panic surfacing for one second. But then I hear his footsteps on the stairs. No hook and latch. No lock. I don't know why that had even crossed my mind. Of course he's not going to lock me in. It might take a while for me to get over what happened today.

It isn't until Hudson is downstairs that I realize I never told him to send Bowie up. When we'd gotten home, Bowie was asleep in his bed in the corner of the family room, and I didn't have the heart to wake him. I imagine getting out of my bed, peeking my head out into the hallway and calling Bowie's name. But I'm much too tired to actually make my body do that. Instead, I nestle down into my pillow, tugging the covers higher up my body.

As I roll over, the events of the day play out in gory detail. I hear Kendra's voice in my head, screaming as the police drag her away.

"I didn't do anything wrong."

I worry about where she is now. What she's going through. She may have done horrible things, but she's still my daughter. I never want her to feel pain. And what will happen to Mason? Panic grabs me by the throat. *Oh, god, Mason.*

I worry for a moment that I've made a mistake. A boy needs his mother—more than I'd even realized, I think guiltily. But then I think of all the pain Kendra's caused, the terror she's secretly inflicted. The Kendra I've seen is a responsible mom, but who knows what she might do to Mason if she doesn't get help. No, I've done the right thing for Kendra and for Mason.

My blinds are open, and I stare out at the early-morning sky, knowing that below my window is Leslie's house.

When I left her house after our last conversation, I'd felt so defeated, thinking I'd failed to convince her of Hudson's innocence, but looking back, I realize she'd never actually admitted to pointing the finger at Hudson.

It was two days later when I saw them wheel her body into the ambulance. If only I'd said something different. Something more. I'm not sure what that would've been, but something that would have given us both closure.

Now that she's gone, I'd always have that regret. Of a friendship gone stale. Of all the years we hated each other.

I'd been right all along. Hudson hadn't killed Heather. It was an accident, just like I had insisted. I know that now. I hadn't needed to be afraid of letting him tell the truth. But still, I understand her need to avenge Heather's death. To hold on to it. I know it in the same way I know I still love Kendra fiercely, even after all she's done. The way we feel for our children defies logic. They are a part of us. Leslie blaming Hudson was probably her way of keeping Heather alive.

How had I missed all the signs?

It will take me a while to process all that's happened today. I'll have to retrain my brain, rewrite the narrative I've believed for years. All the memories I've attributed to Hudson that were actually Kendra.

The doll heads, the hamster, the break-in, even Heather's death.

All these years, I'd thought our house was haunted by Grace, but really it had been haunted by Kendra.

I hear Bowie downstairs, and I sit up. Even though I'm exhausted, I know I won't be able to sleep until Bowie's up here with me. I need his comfort tonight more than ever. Sliding my legs out from under the covers, I feel them drop over the edge of the bed, my feet hitting the cool floor. I test my movement, flexing my toes, then push my weary body up off the bed. Force myself to stand.

I shuffle gingerly across my bedroom floor, press my door open, and step into the hallway. From this vantage point, I don't see Bowie or Hudson. Based on the noises, I'm guessing they're in the family room. I feel too weak to call him, but I'll be able to see if I walk to the edge of the stairs.

As I pass Hudson's room, its open door, my toe snags over something sharp and small. Crouching down, I spot a tiny clump of white clay on the ground. There is a trail of it leading into Hudson's room. Most of it is a mere dusting, almost invisible.

My heart seizes.

That's what's been bugging me. The nagging thought in the back of my mind. The thing I saw in both Molly's and Leslie's homes. Clumps of clay nestled in the fibers of the carpet. It didn't register until this moment. Maybe because of all the medicine I'd been on, Kendra's cocktail of antianxiety medications and sleeping pills.

But the clay—it had been there in Molly's bedroom and Leslie's hallway. The speck of perlite, I thought, reaching for the earring.

My eyes follow the chain of them into his room. From my crouch down low, I can see into the mess under Hudson's bed—and I suck in a ragged breath. I crawl forward, my back aching with the effort. Tucked above a bin of sweaters is a leather-bound book. I squint into the shadows, taking in the date on the side. Written in Sharpie.

It's Leslie's missing notebook.

The one from this year.

"Turns out, there are worse things than being cheated on."

"Hudson was scary jealous."

My conversation with Natalia plays in my mind. I see her face in a new light, how fearful she looked when she spoke of Hudson—her mouth curled downward, the terror in her eyes. That wasn't made up. I hadn't wanted to admit it, but her emotion was real.

"If it weren't for her," Hudson had said earlier tonight, *"Heather would be here today. If only she'd kept her big mouth shut."*

He'd blamed Kendra for his fight with Heather that night, truly believing it was her fault they'd gotten into it. Not that his actions were the catalyst. And I think about the dates and words in Leslie's journals. Why had Leslie thought Heather was scared of Hudson, not Kendra? No matter how Hudson tried to swing it, wouldn't Heather have told her mom if she'd been afraid of Kendra instead?

In my memories, I always see Hudson and Heather so happy together. But that wasn't always the case, was it? I'd overheard them fighting. Yelling. Multiple times over the years. And there were weeks where they barely spoke. A period of time when Heather barely came around. Is it possible that I'm only allowing myself to remember the good?

I think about Kendra's desperate words as the police carted her out of here, protesting her innocence.

But what if she hadn't been lying?

"Bro, stop hitting me up or I'm gonna block you."

Maybe…maybe Blondie *was* Molly. Theo had said he'd hook him up, and he did so in front of Kendra. I'm sure he thought if he didn't, it would look bad—especially if she already suspected him of having an affair. Perhaps he did give Hudson Molly's number.

Hudson had seen Molly the night she died. He himself had

admitted that she rejected him. If Natalia was telling the truth, Hudson doesn't like being rejected, especially not by women. But that wouldn't be enough reason to kill her, would it?

"You're the only woman who will never hurt me."

The TV clicks on downstairs, startling me. I flinch, suppressing a gasp. Then I quickly snatch up the journal and press it to my chest.

Journal in hand, I make my way back to my room, staring with dread at the hook and latch hanging from the door frame, wishing it were on the inside of my door instead. I slip into my room and firmly close the door behind me.

Ashes, ashes,
We all fall down…

I prop my feet up on the coffee table, thinking about how finally Kendra is getting what she deserves. Just like she'd so cavalierly said about that mouse, she had done this to herself.

This time she'd gone too far, and she would pay for it.

She'd underestimated me.

Leaning back on the couch cushions, I click through the channels, trying to find something to watch. I marvel at how relaxed I feel—the most comfortable I've ever felt in this house.

Mom thought it was her fault that I'd taken off years ago and never came back, but that was never the case. I'd stayed away to avoid Kendra. To finally be safe from her torment. It's why I never stressed about my phone being shut off or jumping from couch to couch and place to place. Harder to locate that way. Far off of Kendra's radar. Just the way I liked it.

I wouldn't have come back this time, except that I'd been worried about Mom. She'd always been so confident, self-assured, independent. Hearing her sound scared and needy really messed with my mind. I had to see for myself if she was okay.

But after I'd moved in, she seemed like herself. Sure, she was much more of a homebody than I'd ever remembered, but other than that, she appeared to be okay. She had little bouts with forgetfulness, but who doesn't? I felt like maybe she was just overthinking things. Grandma's illness had taken a toll on her.

It was clear Kendra was uncomfortable with me being here, though, and that was part of the reason I wanted to stay. I liked watching her squirm. I wasn't a little kid she could control anymore—and from that first Friday night, I had the strange feeling she was up to something. It's why I asked Theo to go out. I knew it would piss my sister off. Well, that and I wanted to find out more about the hot blonde he worked with.

After Natalia, I wasn't looking for anything serious. I wanted uncomplicated. Fun. A casual hookup.

Molly seemed like she might be up for that. I felt it in her flirty smile when Theo introduced us. The way her eyes narrowed in that seductive way, and how strategically she licked her lips, brushing a stray hair from her face.

Natalia had been a frigid bitch the last few months of our relationship, twisting my love for her into something ugly and mean. But I wasn't a monster. I just needed a girl who could see that. Even if it was only for a little while.

The night I went out with my brother-in-law, I let him pick the place.

"Midtown Saloon?" I had asked, eyebrows raised when Theo pulled his Honda Pilot into the parking lot.

"What's wrong with it?"

"Nothing, man. I just pegged you as a swanky restaurant bar guy."

Theo turned to me. "I am. But I thought you wanted me to hook you up with Molly."

I smiled. "She's here?"

Theo shrugged. "Maybe. I know she comes here a lot."

To my dismay, Theo's hunch had been wrong. Molly was nowhere to be seen.

"Well, better luck next time," Theo said, but I didn't think he sounded too bummed that Molly wasn't there.

When we sat down at the bar, I ordered a beer, while Theo ordered some fancy whiskey drink, reminding me of my dad. Whiskey had always been his drink of choice, too. I briefly wondered if that was one of the things Kendra liked about Theo.

But then Theo said, "Don't tell your sister I'm having a drink. She'd kill me."

"Yeah, what's with that? Is it like a religious thing?"

Theo laughed. "No, it's a Kendra thing."

"How are things with you two?" I asked as the bartender slid a beer in front of me. "She seemed kinda bitchy with you last night."

Theo picked up his fancy cocktail, the one large ice cube clinking against the side of the glass. "Yeah, she's always been a little uptight." He paused, took a long sip. I wondered if he'd speak again. I knew I was pushing it, calling my sister bitchy to her husband. But then Theo put the glass down on the counter, still staring into it. "She was on these meds for a while. Antianxiety meds and sleeping pills. And they worked. She was actually pretty chill when she took them."

"Kendra, chill?"

"Right?" Theo laughed. "But she stopped taking them when she found out she was pregnant. She told me she went back on them after Mason was born. It's why she didn't breastfeed. I've picked up the prescription for her a few times, and even seen the empty containers in the wastebasket." He took another sip. "But I know she's not taking them."

"You sure?"

Theo nodded soberly. "I know what she's like on the drugs and off the drugs, and trust me, she's not on them."

I was about to ask Theo what he thought Kendra was doing with the drugs, but just then, Molly swaggered over to us, wearing a low-cut top, tight jeans and strappy high heels.

She was even hotter than the first time I met her.

My palms moistened.

"Theo?"

"Oh, hey, Molly." I noticed my brother-in-law's cheeks go red. I assumed it was from the alcohol. "You remember my brother-in-law, Hudson?"

"Sure." She smiled. "Good to see you again."

"You, too." I touched the empty bar stool to the left of me— Theo was to my right. "Join us."

She glanced at Theo momentarily, almost as if asking permission. I sort of understood. They did work together. Maybe she was afraid drinking at a bar with a colleague would make her seem unprofessional. But Theo nodded subtly. She smiled and said, "Okay," and walked toward me, her tits bouncing with every step.

We talked for a little bit, and I was delighted to find out that Molly was legitimately cool, but then some of her friends showed up. I reached out and grabbed her hand before she could leave, and I asked for her phone number.

She hesitated, and I couldn't help but notice her glancing over at Theo again. It was odd, but I thought maybe she was more cautious about meeting new guys than I'd thought. Maybe she wanted some kind of assurance that I was a good guy—and I could understand that. I'd been burned before, too. So I just smiled at her, and after a few uncomfortable seconds, she finally shrugged and rattled off her number.

I typed it into my contacts, dubbing her BLONDIE.

The next day, I came home to find Mom passed out on the couch, an open container of vitamins in front of her.

"I've seen the empty containers in the wastebasket. But I know she's not taking them."

I thought back to all the times Kendra mentioned my mom's condition. The way she'd reminded Mom to take her vitamins a dozen times when she was over on Friday night.

I hid the vitamins from Mom, and the next day she seemed fine. Normal.

I'd been texting Molly, asking her out, but I got no response. I worried that I'd put her number in wrong, so I called and got her voice mail. When her voice came on the line, I smiled. Definitely her.

Later that night, I finally got a response: *Sorry, bro, but I'm sorta seeing someone.*

She hadn't acted liked someone in a relationship at Midtown Saloon. She'd been more than friendly. She'd been flirty.

I tried again: *Don't worry. I won't tell him. lmao.*

I texted Theo about it, but all Theo said was that maybe I should leave her alone, then.

But I just couldn't figure out what had happened between when we'd flirted at Midtown Saloon and now.

I knew where Molly lived, so I went over there, hoping we could talk about it. But she wouldn't open the damn door. I just wanted to know what her deal was. I swore she was home. Lights shone through the windows and everything, but she still never answered.

I was sick of being ignored and villainized by women. I needed her to at least talk to me, but clearly she was too uptight to have a simple conversation.

I had Mom's "vitamins" stashed under my bathroom sink. Curious, I popped a few. Within an hour, it was clear this was no vitamin. It didn't hit me as hard as it clearly had Mom. I was laid out flat for a few hours, but then I recovered. Mom had been sick for an entire day. It made sense, though, the more I thought about it. I recalled seeing Mom take more than one of the vitamins the day before she got sick. I chalked it up to her forgetfulness, or possibly the fact that she drank a little more wine than usual that night (evidenced by the empty bottle she'd left out).

At first, I planned to tell Mom, rat Kendra out.

But the next day, when I was getting ready to go out with Browning, a different plan emerged in my mind. I thought of how loose and fun Natalia would be when she was drunk or high. I definitely preferred her that way. Toward the end of our relationship, it was the only time I could get close to her.

What if I used Mom's pills to loosen Molly up a bit? What would be the harm in that? I'd only use enough to get her to talk to me, to admit she had been flirting with me that night, and then I'd tell Mom about the pills. No harm, no foul.

That night when I was out with Browning, I slipped one to a girl I was chatting up at the bar, but it seemed to have almost no effect on her. When I went home, I studied the pills. They were clear capsules, ground up medicine inside. Some were fuller than others. If Kendra had made these herself, maybe some were stronger than others. I'd have to keep that in mind.

By Saturday night, Molly's responses were getting volatile. Uncalled for.

Bro, stop hitting me up or I'm gonna block you.

That's when it hit me. Her flirtiness—maybe it hadn't been directed at me at all. Both times I saw Molly, I'd been with Theo. And she did keep looking at Theo as if asking for direction...or permission. Also, how had Theo known where Molly liked to hang out if they just worked together?

Was Molly into Theo?

Maybe she was one of those destructive girls who went for married guys or unattainable guys. If only Molly could see how much happier she'd be with me. Theo would end up hurting her.

Armed with a fractured ego and a pocketful of whatever the hell Kendra had been slipping Mom, I Ubered to Midtown Saloon with Browning on Saturday night. To my delight, Molly was there.

She wasn't pleased to see me. I ended up getting into it with some stranger who told me to leave Molly alone. But the guy was too late. I'd already opened two capsules into her drink. I couldn't risk giving her a weak one like I'd done with that chick the other night. This time it had to work.

They hit her hard. She started slurring her words and had trouble standing. Browning got so drunk he had to get an Uber home. After he left, I offered to walk Molly to her car. She was in no condition to drive, so I took her keys, placed her in the passenger seat and took off.

Once at her house, I'd taken her inside and laid her in her bed. I'd wanted to talk sense into her, but that clearly wasn't going to be an option. The least I could do was put her to bed.

I'd undressed her slowly, pleased by her matching lilac bra and panties. She might have been self-sabotaging when it came to dating, but she clearly took care of herself in other ways. I was about to tuck her in when she woke up.

Her eyes frantically ran down her naked body, her clothes discarded on the floor.

"What the hell?" she screamed, the words sloshing together. "How did you get in here?"

I'd tried to calm her down. "It's okay. You invited me."

She grabbed her head, shook it. "No. No, I didn't. Oh, my god. You drugged me, you sick fuck."

"No, I just wanted to talk, but then you passed out," I'd insisted.

But she wasn't listening. She was fumbling around, looking for her phone. If she found it, I was done for. She would call the police, and I knew exactly how that would look. I couldn't afford to get in trouble with the law again.

"Stop." I grabbed her by the arms, pinning her to the bed. "I didn't do anything to you. You drank a little too much. That's it."

"No," she slurred. "You're lying. Get the hell away from me."

"Shut up," I said, frustration burning to the surface.

"Get off me!" She was writhing now. Kicking with her legs and thrashing her head around. I had to make her stop.

"Calm down." I grabbed her around the neck, held her tight. "Just calm the fuck down." I couldn't stand the look on her face, so I screwed my eyes shut. I should have known this wouldn't go well. I thought of Natalia and her restraining order; of Kendra pouring boiling water over my hand; of Mom leaving me night after night to Dad's drunken neglect and my sister's whispered threats. Finally she stopped fighting. Stopped moving altogether. When I released my hands, I heaved a sigh of relief. Until I realized she was too still.

Oh, god.

Her eyes stared vacantly up at me.

Shit. Shit. Shit.

Panic threatened to overtake me, but I couldn't let it. My life would be over if anyone found out. And there would be no one to take care of Mom—no one to tell her what Kendra had been doing. I had to think.

This was Theo's fucking fault. Which meant it was really Kendra's damn fault. She was the one poisoning our mother with "vitamins." She was the one freezing out her own husband to the point he'd started sleeping around and then introducing his mistress to his brother-in-law. How sick was that?

And that's when I came up with a plan.

I could kill two birds with one stone. I could get myself out of this mess and finally make my sister pay for all of the horrible things she'd done to me over the years.

I could become the tiger.

They were her pills, after all.

I left a couple of the pills behind, but cleaned up all traces of myself, wiping down doorknobs and places I'd touched.

Sneaking in late that night, I realized I couldn't tell Mom what I knew about Kendra's vitamins, so I put them back. But I encouraged her to make an appointment with her doctor, so she would find out the truth that way.

Everything would've been perfect, too, if that fucking bitch Leslie hadn't seen me come home from Molly's that morning. I'd had to walk back since I'd driven Molly's car. And when I got to the driveway, there was Leslie standing in her goddam front window. She never could mind her own business. She started watching me all hours of the day and night like some stalker. It's not like I was doing anything shady, but clearly she knew something. Why else would she be following me around? I couldn't chance that. I had no choice but to silence the old bitch once and for all. I knew it would be easy. Mom had a key to her house, for god's sake. Planting one of Kendra's favorite earrings was icing on the cake. It was so easy to get it. Kendra had practically presented it to me. On that Friday night when she and Theo had come to dinner, it had fallen out of her ear. I didn't notice it until the next day. A shiny little pendant on the floor. I tossed it on my dresser, planning to tell her the next time I saw her. But then I kept forgetting, and eventually I found a better use for it.

It had all gone perfectly. The police were taking longer

than I'd hoped getting to Kendra as a suspect, but then, her downward spiral earlier today—completely unexpected, but absolutely perfect—had wrapped the whole thing up with a giant bow.

Now I flip through the channels on Mom's ancient TV before deciding on *The Office*. Then I open a beer and take a long swallow. Bowie curls up in the corner. There is a creaking noise coming from the top of the stairs. I turn and look up, but no one's there. I think about Grace Newton and her infamous fall. Picture her small body tumbling down the steps until she stills at the bottom. Over the years, I've often wondered if it was really an accident or if she'd been pushed. It would've been so easy for someone to do. I should know. It had only taken one swift thrust of my arm to shove Heather off that cliff. She hadn't even seen it coming.

The creaking returns. Must be Mom moving around in her room. I feel confident that she won't ever let me down. I've always been her favorite. She's always had my back.

And if she doesn't, well—I think of the pill bottle in my room—I have a contingency plan.

I smile. Isn't it lucky that I came home?

31

I stand at the window, looking down at the quiet street below. Yellow light glows from my neighbors' windows, behind drawn curtains. All the other families are in their homes, not a care in the world, watching TV or slurping up bowls of ice cream. I once had that.

My heart slams against my rib cage when I see them approaching. Red and blue lights flashing in the sky. I glance down at the cell phone on my nightstand, hating that I was forced to make that call. To be the one to turn my son in. How much sadness can one heart take?

I hear movement downstairs.

Bowie barks.

My hand flutters up to my neck. In the window I see my own reflection staring back. Eyes wide and scared, cheeks sallow, lips trembling.

The police cars park in my driveway. Men hop out wearing blue uniforms, guns holstered to their hips. I turn away from the window and breathe deeply. Tears fill my eyes. My cheeks are hot.

I hear raps on the front door, Bowie barking, footsteps inside, men's voices downstairs.

My heart rate spikes. I stare at my bedroom door, praying no one comes up here. I can't take any more questions tonight. Deep down, I want to run down the stairs, to hug my son once more, but I don't dare.

He'll know I did this, and he won't forgive me.

I've done so many things wrong when it comes to my children. This time, I have to do what's right.

If only I hadn't covered up Hudson's part in Heather's death all those years ago, things would've turned out better for all of us. Maybe he would've gotten the help he needed. Maybe we all would have.

I turn back to the window, pressing my palm to the glass. Leslie's house peers up at me, dark and empty.

Leslie materializes, standing in the middle of the lawn, holding a pot of purple irises. She's young again, wearing jeans and a T-shirt, bright green gardening gloves covering her hands. Heather runs around beside her, squealing, an unabashed smile on her face. Leslie smiles, waves in my direction. I wave back.

And then she's gone.

Other neighbors have come out, though. They stand in their doorways, pepper their front lawns, all gawking, staring, pointing. It's what they've been waiting for. Oh, the triumph they must feel at being right, as I stand in the window, high above them all, silhouetted by the light behind my back. But I won't cower. I won't hide. I will see this through.

My son is in the driveway now, hands fastened behind him. A cop holds his arm as he leads him to a police car. Hudson glances up. I know he sees me, but I can't look away. A tear streams down my face.

It's the second time I've watched the police take away one of my children today.

My heart is shattered.

I watch until he's in the car. Until they drive off. Until I can no longer see them.

Then I walk slowly to my bedroom door, and open it.

I call for Bowie, who comes running immediately. The sound of his paws on the stairs brings me comfort. I sink to my knees and press my face into his fur. I cry for my children. For my mistakes. For what they've been through. For what they've done.

Then I gather myself up off the floor and make my way to my bed, Bowie trailing after me. I slip between the sheets, pulling the covers up to my chin, and rest my hand on Bowie's fur. I hear the clock tick, the house creak, the familiar tapping I've always associated with Grace.

I'm alone again—an old woman living in this house with her dog and a ghost—exactly like I was before he came back.

★ ★ ★ ★ ★

Acknowledgments

The last couple of years have been tough, collectively, for all of us. This book was partly written during the lockdown, with my family just feet away and my mind swirling with anxiety and grief. But in Valerie's big Victorian home, I found refuge. An escape. I will forever be grateful for that.

I will also forever be grateful to the following people:

My agent, Ellen Coughtrey, who spent countless hours brainstorming on the phone and on the page. Ellen, I don't know what I would do without your magical editorial touch and your fierce support of my books and career. To Will Roberts, Anna Worrall, Rebecca Gardner and the entire team at The Gernert Company, I appreciate your constant support so much. To my film agent, Dana Spector, your tireless work on my behalf does not go unnoticed. An email from you always has the capacity to make my day.

To my editor, April Osborn, I am so grateful to you for believing in me and my books, and for your keen editorial eye.

Thanks also to Lia Ferrone and the entire MIRA team for all your hard work and support.

Booktokers and bookstagrammers are marketing rock stars, and I'm so grateful to all of you, particularly Abby, @crimebythebook; Sonica, @the_reading_beauty; Sydney, @sydneyyybean_; Jessica, @the_towering_tbr; and Dany, @danythebookworm_.

A big thank you to my bestie, Megan Squires, for always being a sounding board, a shoulder, a safe place and my favorite writing partner and beta reader.

It's never easy asking authors to read and review your work—Ashley Winstead and Eliza Jane Brazier, your blurbs for this book made me cry. I appreciate you taking the time to read and blurb for me.

And to Samantha Downing, Samantha Bailey, Mindy Mejia, J.T. Ellison, Sandie Jones and Christina McDonald for blurbing in the past, and continuing to share and cheer me on. The writing community really is the best.

To two of my best friends—Angela Lee, who designed my beautiful website, and Sarah Belda for social media expertise and graphics for my socials. You both enrich my life so much.

To the rest of my friends and family—there are too many of you to name—but your support and encouragement mean the world.

Andrew, thanks for sharing your life with fictional characters and being cool with it. I couldn't do any of this without your support, and I love you for it.

Eli and Kayleen, you are my whole heart, a legacy more important than any word I'll ever write.

God, thank You for giving me this talent for writing and this big imagination I can escape into. You knew it was what I would need to survive, and I'll always be grateful.